Looking
for
Laura

Ellen Shapiro

INDIES UNITED PUBLISHING HOUSE, LLC

ISBN13: 978-1-64456-095-2
Library of Congress Control Number:2019956971

INDIES UNITED PUBLISHING HOUSE, LLC
P.O. BOX 3071
QUINCY, IL 62305-3071
www.indiesunited.net

Ellen, a real-life PI, kept me Looking for Laura deep into the night.
- *Debby Caruso, Author of Merry Hanukkah Series*

Bursting into the mystery genre, this PI/New Author has started an intriguing series with an independent female PI.
- *JennieReads.com*

To my daughter Carrie, who I love dearly and brings joy into my life every day

To my dear friend Susan, who has always been there for me

CHAPTER 1

The morning skies were bright but by 3:00 dark clouds rolled in. My mood was as dark as the clouds. Business was really slow, and with all my bills to pay I didn't know if I could get through the next month. My office rent was due in two weeks, and unless I could come up with the money, my landlord might not be inclined to renew my lease. I contacted a client that owed me five hundred dollars and tried to keep desperation out of my voice.

I started my PI business ten years ago and it's been a struggle building a clientele. Most of my cases are fairly routine, background checks, locating witnesses to testify at a trial, deadbeat dads, or people being sued. Every once in a while someone will hire me to conduct surveillance on their spouse to see if they're cheating, but those I farm out to investigators who do it all the time. Unfortunately TV makes it look easy, but it's tedious and there are many ways you can lose the subject.

I was shutting down my computer when I heard the doorknob turn. In walked a man trying to look as dignified as he could with water dripping down his face, and his umbrella forming puddles on my carpet. He was about 6'2", dark hair that curled up in the back of his neck, fair complexion with a body that was most likely sculpted at the gym. He appeared to be around my age, in his mid-thirties. He must have thought I was an idiot since I was just staring at him without saying a word.

I shoved my bills under my computer, stood up and stuck out my hand, "Tracey Marks."

"Sam Matthews. I'm sorry to barge in on you. You look like you're ready to leave."

"No, no, I was just finishing up some paperwork. Sorry I don't have a towel to offer you." I grabbed a roll of paper towels from the cabinet and handed it to him.

We both sat down and Mr. Matthews blurted out, "my wife never came home Friday night and I'm really worried. I know she would have called unless something happened to her. Can you please help me?"

"Have you reported her missing?"

"Yes, Saturday morning, but from the questions I was asked by a Detective Harris I got the impression he didn't believe me and probably thought I was being paranoid."

I couldn't believe my luck. Finally a case I could sink my teeth in. My first missing person case, but I had no intention of letting the cat out of the bag.

"Can I get you coffee or tea?" I said, trying to keep my enthusiasm to a minimum.

"No, thank you."

"Before I decide to take your case, I need to ask you some questions," knowing that unless this guy was a psycho, I couldn't afford to turn him away.

"First, what's your wife's name?"

"Laura."

"When was the last time you saw Laura?'

"Friday morning. She had the day off from work. She mentioned she was meeting a friend and said she might be home a little late. We made plans to have dinner out when she got back. I waited till 8:00 and then called her cell phone but it went straight to voice mail. By 9:00 I was getting pretty worried and called her friend Melanie. She had no idea where Laura was but said she would call me if she hears from her."

"Do you know who she was meeting?"

"No, I didn't think to ask," looking annoyed at himself.

"Were there any problems in your marriage?"

"Not that I'm aware of. We were happy. Laura and I have only been married a year, and we're making plans for our first vacation.

"Was she acting different lately, or do you think she may have been depressed?"

Mr. Matthews told me that he hadn't noticed any changes in his wife's behavior. He was adamant that she was not having an affair and that he would never cheat on her.

"Mr. Matthews, do you have any enemies that might want to take out their anger on you or your wife?"

"I don't know anyone who'd want to hurt Laura or me," shaking his head.

"Is there any place you can think of that your wife might have gone?"

"No. I'm sorry I'm not being more helpful."

"One last question, is this the first time Laura hasn't come home?"

"Yes, that's why I am so concerned."

I didn't know if I believed him. It could be as simple as she left him, but it's also possible something did happen to her. I know he might not be telling me everything. People seldom do.

"Mr. Matthews I'll take your case, but I can't promise you anything except that I'll do my best to find out what happened to your wife." Though the words came out of my mouth, my doubts of whether I could handle the case were weighing on me.

"My hourly rate is $100. I'll e-mail you my one page retainer agreement for your signature, and in the meantime I want you to make a list of her friends, habits and anything else you can think of that might be important."

"Thank you very much," he said, sounding relieved.

When Sam Matthews left I just stared at the check he gave me for $5,000. I was so relieved I could pay my rent on time I gave out a shout of joy.

I thought about my interaction with Mr. Matthews. Something was off. It seemed a little strange that he would hire me without asking about my experience.

After he left, I took out my PI manual and went to the chapter on missing persons. I wanted to read as much as I could to get some pointers so as not to make a complete fool of myself.

CHAPTER 2

About an hour later I shut everything down and walked out of my office into a monsoon. I stood by the front doorway waiting for my Uber. I live on the Upper Westside in the 70's. Ten years ago I was living in Brooklyn working for a private investigator in Manhattan. When he married, he subleased his apartment to me and I was eventually able to lease it under my own name.

I made a mad dash to the car but was completely soaked before I even opened the door. On my way into my apartment building, Wally greeted me with a big smile. Wally is my doorman, who I probably have the longest male relationship with.

"Hello Miss Tracey. You better get out of those clothes before you catch a nasty cold."

"Thanks, I'll do that." Wally has been the doorman in our building for more than thirty years. He's a big guy carrying some extra pounds around the middle. He's probably close to seventy but looks younger. His skin is a velvety shade of brown and he has dark piercing eyes.

As I put the key into the lock of my apartment door, my cell phone buzzed. I fumbled for my phone while trying to open the door.

"Hey it's me, how about meeting at Anton's for dinner around 7:00? Hopefully the rain will let up."

I hung up from my best friend Susie. As I entered

my apartment I placed my keys on my mahogany antique table in the entrance hallway. Though I am not normally scattered, keys are my nemesis, so I thought having them in the same place all the time would solve the problem.

My one bedroom apartment is sprinkled with antiques my mother had collected which include an oriental rug that I have in my living room between two small light blue sofas. In my bedroom I have light gray walls with white trim and a white and gray duvet cover that sits on my sleigh bed. I have to admit that I have a television in the bedroom to keep me company at night.

I dumped my wet clothes on the bathroom floor and ran a hot shower. I looked at myself in the mirror, not always a wise thing to do. I'm 5'8", have straight light brown hair that is cut at the end of my jawline and light green eyes. I would like to say I look like Taylor Swift, but that would probably be a lie.

While I was getting dressed I replayed my conversation with Sam. Was he in denial about his wife or did he really believe she was missing? Sometimes people aren't willing to admit their spouse would walk out on them. They would rather believe it's foul play.

I pulled on my jeans, slipped on a white cotton tee-shirt, and zipped up my short black leather boots. It's my standard outfit, though in the winter I usually go with a pullover sweater. Having to contend with limited attire makes my life less complicated.

It was the middle of September in New York and the nights were still seasonally warm. When I got downstairs the rain had let up and was now a fine mist. I had my umbrella so I walked the ten blocks to the restaurant. Anton's was one of those neighborhood restaurants that has great home cooking, and where you can actually hear the person across the table from you. Some of the trendier restaurants are so noisy; I feel like I am in a shouting match.

Susie waved to me from the bar. We have been best friends since high school where we met in Algebra class. Our desks were next to each other and we spent more time fooling around rather than listening to the teacher. It turned out that Susie was a wiz in math and I had no aptitude for it. A match made in heaven.

Susie's adorable. She's about 5'2", probably weighs only 100 lbs., with a boyish figure, curly red hair, big dark brown eyes and a great smile.

"What are you drinking?" I asked her.

"Vodka and cranberry."

We were called to our table as the bartender handed me my glass of Merlot. The waiter came over right away. Since we both knew what we wanted, I ordered linguini with clams and a beet salad for me. Susie had the lasagna.

"How's work?" Susie is head of the matrimonial department of a law firm in Manhattan. Her office is ten blocks south of mine.

"Terrible, George is breathing down my neck again complaining we need more billable hours. He wants me to hustle and bring new business into the firm but he's not willing to give me a percentage of what I take in. He's driving me crazy."

"Why don't you look for another job?"

"It's not so easy. The market is flooded with attorneys. Remember how long it took me to land this job. Enough about my woes. What's happening in the

PI world?"

"Well, I was just about out the door when this man walks in my office and tells me that his wife never came home Friday night. He's sure something happened to her."

"Seriously? Maybe she left him."

"That's what I was thinking, but he swears everything was great between them."

"Do you believe him?"

"I don't know. The jury is still out. I just hope I'm not in over my head."

"I wonder why he would hire you when you've never worked a missing person case."

"I asked myself that same question, I just didn't want to pose the question to him."

"You'll be fine, don't worry. And you can always run things by me.

"How is Mark doing?" I asked.

"He's good, but he wants me to move in with him. I love Mark but I'm not ready to take that step. Does that make me a terrible person?"

"Of course not! But Mark's a great guy, so what's the problem?"

"I like living on my own, and if I was living with Mark I would have to take his feelings into account. Now I do what I please, and don't have to run it by anyone. Besides, how many people do you know that have really good marriages? Before my parents divorced, there was constant arguing, and I hated listening to it. I swore that would never be me."

"You're just scared. You're afraid if Mark sees you at your worst, he'll run the other way."

"Look who I'm talking to. It's easy to give advice when you're not the one involved. Your track record sucks."

"Well, you got me there," I said. "But you know that living with someone has never been a top priority for me. Maybe being an only child has something to do with it. All those hours I spent amusing myself never seemed to bother me. I actually liked not having to share my toys with anyone."

Every so often I entertain the idea of seeing a shrink to find out if there is something I'm harboring from my childhood, but it quickly passes.

"My treat," Susie said, as the waiter dropped off the check. "In honor of your first missing person case."

We left after dessert and I promised to keep Susie updated on my new case.

The following morning the alarm went off at 6:00. I dragged myself out of bed, put on my sweats, grabbed my gym bag and went out into the cool morning air jogging eight blocks to the gym.

I usually go to the gym early. It gets my day started and I'm so happy when it's over. Besides the fact that I have a neurotic fear that I would fall apart otherwise. After finishing my workout routine consisting of pushups, sit-ups, and weight training, I ran on the treadmill for twenty minutes, working up a sweat.

I showered and changed at the gym. As I was walking the fifteen blocks to my office I stopped at my favorite café. Anna was behind the counter and she greeted me with a big smile.

"Hi Anna. I'll have my usual," a large coffee and a granola muffin. I'm a creature of habit but I sometimes throw Anna a curveball and order the cranberry nut muffin. I love living on the edge.

My office is in a brownstone on 65th Street. The floor is subdivided into three offices. The two other offices are occupied by a tax attorney, Max Goldstein, and a small insurance company owned by my cousin Alan. The top floor is an apartment rented to Mr. and Mrs. Alvarez, a young professional couple who have lived in the building for two years. Max has helped me with my taxes, but thank heavens I've never needed him for any problems with the IRS. I was lucky to get the space. Fortunately Alan knew I was looking for an office to rent, and when he found out that the prior tenant was leaving he contacted the building owner right away.

As I opened my office door, my cell phone buzzed.

"Good morning. It's Sam Matthews. Did you get my e-mail?"

"It's right in front of me. I need to look it over and if I have any questions I'll call you. Also, I would like to stop by your place tomorrow morning and take a look around. Let's say 8:00?"

"Okay, but what do you expect to find?" he said with hesitation in his voice.

"I don't know, but I like to be thorough." I wondered if there was something he didn't want me to find.

We hung up and I glanced over the information Sam gave me. There wasn't much there that I didn't already know from our meeting. I conducted a preliminary background check on him just to make sure he wasn't a serial killer. After some cursory database searches, nothing of consequence showed up except for a divorce filed in 2012. That may be of interest. There were no criminal records or driving violations. The only real estate Sam owned was his co-op with Laura.

At this point I made a short term plan to talk with Laura's friend Melanie and Laura's boss. In the meantime, I ran a background check on Laura under her maiden name Tyler. The report had very little information, prior addresses, vehicle information, and the names of her parents with their dates of birth and death. I was hoping something would catch my attention but no such luck.

CHAPTER 3

The next day I took the bus crosstown to Sam's apartment on East 72nd Street. I was nervous since this was the first time I had been in this situation. Where do I start and what am I looking for? I had no idea, though Sam was probably clueless also.

When I arrived, Sam led me into the living room. The décor surprised me. It was a mixture of antiques and country furniture. It was similar to my taste, though somehow I thought Sam's place would be very modern. Maybe his wife was in charge of decorating.

Sam said, "I'm going out of my mind. I've left several messages on Laura's cell phone."

"I know you're upset but let's not get ahead of ourselves. There is still a possibility she left on her own accord."

The living room was in perfect order and it didn't appear there was any struggle that took place.

"Was there anything in the room that was out of place or felt different that day?"

"Nothing that caught my eye. Unless it was something pretty obvious, I probably wouldn't have noticed."

I followed Sam into the bedroom. It was tastefully done in light blue tones with white trim. The floor had a large needlepoint rug that looked really expensive. I checked her nightstand and rummaged through her closet looking through shoes, pocketbooks and anything my hand would fit into. I searched through boxes that were on the top shelf.

"Do you mind if I take a look in your bathroom?"

I opened the cabinet over the sink. There was aspirin, cotton swabs, a razor and other stuff people usually have. There were no prescription drugs.

"Can you tell me if you noticed anything missing?"

"I just don't know," he said, nodding.

"What about a laptop, did she have one?"

"Yes, it's gone, but that's not unusual since she normally takes it with her."

I'm no Sherlock Holmes, but if something happened to Laura it didn't happen here, I thought.

"Can you tell me how you and Laura met?"

"How will that help?" he said, sounding annoyed.

"Anything I learn about Laura can be important."

"It was at a restaurant in the City. I was sitting at the bar waiting for a business acquaintance and Laura was waiting for a friend. We struck up a conversation and I asked for her number. I fell in love with her almost right away. She was charming and beautiful. We dated for about three months before we married. I know it sounds quick but I knew my ex-wife for more than two years and our marriage lasted only a short time, so I thought why wait?"

"Can you tell me why your marriage ended?"

"Is that really necessary?"

"It may be." Was he trying to hide something?

"From the beginning, it was a mistake. Peggy was a homebody and would rather stay in at night watching a Netflix movie while I was just the opposite. I liked going out, meeting friends for dinner or a drink. A few months into the marriage she decided she wanted to start a family, while I wanted to wait so it could be just us for a while, to have time together before we had children."

"If you give me your wife's cell number I can try and access her phone records to see who she's been in contact with lately. That might give me something to go on. Also can I have a recent photo of Laura?" Sam handed me a photo of Laura. She was very pretty with beautiful large blue eyes and wavy blonde hair that rested on her shoulders. Sam told me she was 5'8" and weighed about 120 lbs.

As I was leaving, I remembered I had asked Sam for a list of Laura's friends.

"To tell you the truth, the only friend that I know of is Melanie. If Laura had any other friends she didn't mention them to me," he said, shrugging his shoulders.

I left Sam's place and went back to my office. On my way I stopped for a large latte and a blueberry muffin. Now that I had Laura's cell number, I called Joe, a friend who has his own company that specializes in getting information I don't have access to.

"Joe, it's Tracey. How are you?"

"It's been a while, what can I do for you?" he said brusquely.

"What, no foreplay," I said. My cheeks flushed. "Look, I need a favor and I'll owe you."

"How many times have I heard that line from you?"

"Well, how about lunch at the restaurant of your choice?'

"Make it dinner and you have a deal."

"You're on. I need cell phone records going back two months."

"Okay, give me a day or two."

I gave him Laura's cell phone number and we hung up.

Joe and I had some history. Two years ago we had a brief fling, but that was all it was for me. Joe wanted more, so I ended it.

I looked up the number for Boston College where Laura had attended and spoke to someone in the records department. I went with the standard reason; I was checking references for a job she was applying for. After providing the woman with Laura's social security number and date of birth, I was informed that she had, in fact, graduated from Boston College. Well, at least there was one thing we knew about her for sure.

Next I went to the jewelry store where Laura worked. From my little knowledge of jewelry, this place looked very expensive. There was a gentleman behind the counter, about fifty-five years old, with graying hair and wire rimmed glasses, neatly dressed in a grey pinned striped suit and a pink shirt.

"Mr. Nichols, my name is Tracey Marks. I was hired by Laura's husband to look into her disappearance."

"I can't believe she is missing. I don't understand what could have happened to her. A few days ago when she was here, she seemed fine. Maybe she'll show up in a day or two. I'm sorry to babble on. It's just that I'm very fond of her."

"What can you tell me about Laura?"

"Well, she's an asset to the store, excellent with the customers and always on time. I do hope she's all right."

"Did Laura seem different lately, maybe distracted or anxious?"

"No, I don't think so, but I have to say I'm not that good about reading people. My wife would be the first to tell you that."

"Did she talk about her past at all?"

"Not that I can recall. She did fill out an employment application, though I believe her husband is listed as her contact person."

"Did she list her last employer?"

"Yes, of course, I'll make you a copy. I'll be right back."

Mr. Nichols came back a few minutes later. On the application it listed a company in Boston called Berg Consulting.

"Did you call them for a reference?" I asked.

"To tell you the truth, I didn't. Laura said she'd only been there a year, and when she left she was not on good terms with her boss."

"Did she give you any explanation why?"

"She said the job changed. She thought she was hired to oversee the everyday functions of the business and to make sure things ran smoothly, but he wanted her to drum up sales which wasn't what she wanted to do."

I was curious why she listed him as a reference, though maybe she had no choice if she wasn't gainfully employed for any period of time.

"So you hired Laura on her say so?"

"I did. I know that wasn't wise of me but I believed she was honest and I liked her instantly. She seemed very friendly and well spoken. As it turned out, I was right since she is an excellent employee."

"I see she didn't list any other employers. Laura is thirty-two and has been out of college for several years. How did she explain that period?"

"She told me that she had taken a couple of years off from college when her parents died. She worked a few different jobs in the interim. Unfortunately the job in Boston didn't work out but now that she was married she was looking forward to settling down."

"Do you have any employees who Laura might have been friendly with?"

"Yes, Jane. I know sometimes they went out to dinner. Jane's off today, but I can give you her address and telephone number."

I thanked him and left. With Laura's employment record, would I have been so trusting? Maybe Mr. Nichols did see something in Laura that made him hire her. The more I learn about her the more puzzling it gets.

CHAPTER 4

I grabbed a salad at the neighborhood deli near my office and ate at my desk. My mind was swirling. Did she really have a problem with her prior boss, and even if she did, why leave Boston, why not try to get another job there? Hopefully the cell phone records will reveal something.

I called the telephone number Mr. Nichols gave me for Jane Stevens. It rang several times before I left a message on her voice mail. A few minutes later, as I was doing some paperwork, my cell phone buzzed.

"Ms. Stevens, thank you for getting back to me so quickly. I was wondering if we can meet sometime this afternoon. Laura's husband Sam has hired me to find out what happened to her."

"Yes, I would be happy to. There's a coffee shop a few blocks from my apartment building. I could meet you there at 5:00."

It was still light out when I left. I recognized Jane from the description she gave me, dark brown hair pulled back in a ponytail and round red glasses. I waved as I walked toward her table and sat down across from her. The waitress came over and I ordered coffee.

"Thank you for meeting me. Your boss said that you and Laura met outside of work. What can you tell me about her?"

"I'm not sure how helpful I can be. Though we

went out occasionally, I didn't know much about her. I can't believe she's missing."

"What did you two talk about?"

"The jewelry business, books, movies, stuff like that. I'm single so I was more than happy to talk about my love life and Laura was more than happy to listen while I droned on and on. Come to think of it; I did most of the talking."

"Did she tell you anything about her past or her relationship with her husband?"

"I don't usually pry or ask a lot of personal questions. Laura did mention there was some sort of problem she had while she was living in Boston, but she never told me what it was, and I never asked."

"Is there anything else you can think of that might assist me in finding her?"

"Well now that you mention it, I don't know if this has anything to do with her disappearance, but one time we were having dinner and she looked at me and said, 'did you ever do something and regret it but didn't know how to fix it?' What was odd about it was that I got the impression she was talking to herself and not to me. Does that make any sense?"

"Yes, it does."

"I'm sorry I couldn't be of any more help."

"Thank you. If you think of anything else, please contact me."

I made a mental note to contact Laura's prior employer.

It was past 6:00 and since I didn't feel like going home, I called Susie and asked her if she was up for dinner. We met at Marco's, one of our favorite Italian restaurants.

Susie greeted me with a big smile.

"You look really chipper," I said. "Did you win the lottery?"

"No, I finally got a new divorce case. My client told me his wife has been having an affair for the past three years. Isn't that great? I mean I feel bad for the guy, but a gal's got to eat, so I guess not that bad. Maybe that will get George off my back for a while."

"Wow, and I thought I was cold blooded," I said laughing

"Are you ready to order?" the waiter asked.

"Sure, I'll have the eggplant with a small house salad and a glass of Chianti."

"And you?" looking at Susie.

"I'll have the shrimp scampi, the house salad, and a glass of Cabernet Sauvignon."

"How's the missing person case going?"

"Slow. I hope I'm up for it. It appears no one seems to know Laura all that well, including her own husband. I still don't know if he's lying to me."

"There could be a few different scenarios. One, she left because she was scared of him, two, maybe someone was threatening her, possibly an abusive boyfriend from her past, three, she may have gotten caught up in something that caused her to run, or four, she's dead. I think you should try to rule out the husband if you can."

"You said he has an ex-wife, so talk to her. See what she's willing to tell you. At this point you only know what your client disclosed to you and you can't trust what he says is true. I'm curious why he would hire a private investigator when the police could handle it."

"I asked him that very question. He said that after the police questioned him, he didn't get the feeling that they would take him seriously unless she wound up dead."

"Well, that's a fair point. I know you haven't had much experience with this type of case but you're smart and inquisitive, which makes for a great investigator."

"Yeah, but I'm worried. What if Sam thinks I'm not getting any results? He might fire me, and I really need the money. Not only that, I'm really excited about working the case. You know I love what I do but I always hoped I would get a more challenging case. I just pray I don't live to regret those words."

"I know but you can't let fear drive you, and I'm here if you need to brainstorm. Now how about if I set you up on a date, hasn't it been a while?"

"Absolutely not, the last time you fixed me up, it was a complete disaster. The guy was all over me before I even finished my appetizer."

"I think you're exaggerating."

"Look, I appreciate your concern, but I really can take care of my own love life. If I get stuck, you'll be the first person I call."

The next morning as I unlocked my office door, my cell phone beeped.

"Tracey, it's Joe. I have the printout of Laura's cell phone records."

"Great, can you e-mail them over?"

"Sure, but first how about dinner tonight?"

Joe wasn't going to go away so easily. "Okay, I'll see you at 7:00 at Giovanni's."

I checked my e-mail and saw the attachment. As I looked through it I noticed two numbers that were called frequently in the past two months. They both were Connecticut numbers.

I called Sam and asked him if he recognized either of them. He said he thought one could be her friend Melanie but the other one he did not recognize at all.

I did a reverse check of the other number and it came up to a Seth Green. I decided not to call him yet since it was always better to try to get the element of surprise. I thought I would drive up to Connecticut first thing in the morning and stop by Melanie's place first.

For the next two hours, I wrote up everything I knew about both Laura and Sam for my file, which wasn't very much.

At my apartment I changed into my running clothes and headed out. When I got back, I took a quick shower. Since I didn't want Joe to think this was a date I dressed pretty casually, black jeans, a light gray long sleeve cotton top and black boots.

Giovanni's was a trendy Italian restaurant with white table cloths and walls covered with paintings of places in Italy. One day I hope to take a trip there while I'm still able to walk. Joe was already seated at a corner table. The best thing about Joe was his boyish good looks and a great body.

After some small talk, we ordered dinner and a bottle of wine. I had my usual linguini and clams and Joe had the spaghetti Bolognese. We each had a salad. I have to admit I'm not the dainty type who shyly eats just because I'm with a guy. I dig into my food and usually have dessert, which I never share. After two glasses of wine my mind was a blank and my fingers and toes were tingling. When we left the restaurant we both knew where we were headed.

LOOKING FOR LAURA

As soon as his apartment door closed we were ripping each other's clothes off. It had been a while and I forgot how good it felt. After we finished, there was a part of me that wanted to stay since I was so cozy under the sheets but I didn't want Joe getting the wrong idea. As he was nodding off I slipped quietly into my clothes and headed home.

CHAPTER 5

The next morning before picking up my car, I stopped at my neighborhood Starbucks for a coffee to take with me on my drive to Norwalk, Connecticut, where Laura's friend Melanie Ross lives.

The address was a center hall white colonial with green shutters. The grass looked recently mowed. I knocked and a tall, full figured woman about 35 years of age opened the door. She was wearing black sweats and a tee-shirt. Her long blonde hair was tucked behind her ears. I explained who I was and asked if I could talk with her. Melanie led me into the living room. It was a lovely sunny room with a soft gray couch and a beautiful oriental rug on a polished hardwood floor. There was lovely artwork on the walls, a beach scene that could have been painted in the South of France or maybe even Brooklyn at Brighton Beach.

We sat down on the couch. "Ms. Ross, I'm looking into the disappearance of Laura Matthews."

"I didn't know she was missing, though her husband had called me worried and wanted to know if I knew where she was."

"Have you spoken to her on the phone recently?" I didn't tell her that I knew she had.

"It has been a little while."

"And why is that? Her husband said you were good friends."

"Ever since she moved to New York we haven't seen as much of each other."

"What can you tell me about her?"

"Laura grew up in Connecticut. When she was in college, both her parents were killed in a car accident. As you can imagine, Laura was extremely upset over their deaths and took a leave of absence. She eventually went back to school and finished a few years later. When she married Sam, she moved to New York."

"Someone had mentioned she was working and living in Boston for a while."

"Yes, she did take a job there, but it didn't work out, so she came back about a year later."

"Do you know what happened?"

"Not really, just that the job was not what she thought it would be," she said fidgeting with her hands.

"What about boyfriends?"

"As far as I know she was in a few relationships but nothing serious."

"Do you know of any reason why Laura would just leave her husband?"

"No, I don't. Last time I spoke with her everything seemed fine," she said, averting her eyes.

"Did you get the feeling that she was afraid of something or someone?"

"As I said we haven't seen much of each other lately, and when we spoke I didn't get the impression anything was wrong."

"Melanie, I need you to be completely honest with me. Is there anything else you can tell me?"

"Look you're putting me in an awkward position. I'd rather not talk to you about Laura," she said, looking nervously at her watch.

"If Laura is in trouble, I need to know so I can help her."

"Leave me your card and I'll think about it."

"Please call. I promise I'll be discreet with any information you share with me. Laura could be in danger."

As I headed to Seth Green's place in Stamford, I wondered if Melanie was hiding something and if Laura put her up to it.

I drove up to a beautiful stone house on a tree lined street. I parked in front and rang the bell. A petite woman about thirty with straight dark brown shoulder length hair, wearing a white tee-shirt and tight jeans answered the door.

"Hi, my name is Tracey Marks and I'm looking for Seth Green?"

"Yes, I'm his wife, can I help you?" she asked curiously.

"Do you know a Laura Matthews?"

"No, should I?" she said hesitantly.

"Maybe you know her under the last name of Tyler? She has been missing for a few days and I was told that your husband and Laura knew each other."

From the expression on her face it was apparent this was not a welcome surprise to her.

"Her husband hired me to find out what happened to her."

"If you have a card, I can let him know that you stopped by." Her curt tone suggested this is a lady ticked off that her husband had kept a secret from her.

I handed her my card and asked her to have him call me as soon as possible. I thought I would wait a day or two to see if he contacted me before I try again.

As I got into my car, my phone buzzed.

"Tracey, it's Sam. Just want to know if you found anything out yet."

"No Sam, but I've been talking to people she knew and I have some leads." I realized I was biting my lower lip. "I just talked to Melanie and she was not very forthcoming. I don't think she is telling me everything she knows and I am not sure why the secrecy."

"Where do we go from here?"

I didn't want to tell him I had no idea, so I just said I had some avenues to pursue and we hung up. I was still not sure that Sam was telling me all he knew.

The week had flown by and I spent the weekend cleaning my apartment, catching up on errands and a Netflix series I binged on.

On Monday morning before going to the office, I stopped for coffee and a cranberry muffin. Taking another look at Laura's cell phone records, I noticed one number that showed up several times throughout the two months; the calls only lasted a minute or so. I tried finding out whom it belonged to but no luck.

When I called the mysterious telephone number it was disconnected.

At this point it was 10:30. I decided to go back to my garage for my car and drive to Scarsdale, where Sam's ex-wife Peggy lives. I came up to a Cape Cod style house with a high oak tree on the front lawn and a small tricycle by the front steps. I rang the bell but there was no answer. Since I was in no rush to get back I waited in my car. I dug out my bottle of water from my backpack and chewed on a health bar that tasted more like sawdust. Why do I bother trying to eat healthy? About forty-five minutes later a blue Honda pulled up into the driveway. A slender woman with short brown hair exited the car. I quickly reached her before she went inside.

"Ms. Landau, my name is Tracey Marks."

"Yes, how can I help you?" with a surprised look on her face.

"I'm sorry, I didn't mean to startle you. I know your ex-husband Sam and I was wondering if we could talk?" I handed her my card. "Sam has hired me to find his wife, who is missing. Can I speak to you for just a moment?"

"I don't have much time. My daughter will be getting out of pre-school in a little while."

"This won't take long." I followed her into a sitting room off the kitchen.

"Unfortunately, because of a confidential issue, I'm not able to go into details. I just have a few questions. Sam mentioned there were some differences in your marriage that caused your break up."

"Before we go any further if Sam hired you, why would you need to ask me about our relationship? Why don't you ask him?"

"I did, but I would like to hear your version. There's always two sides to a story."

"Does he know you're here?"

"Actually no, I was hoping to keep this between us. Sam said that you married young and wanted a family but that he wanted to wait a while."

"Yes, that's true," she said with a faraway look on her face.

"Is there something else? Was he abusive?"

"Let's just say he was very controlling. He liked to get his way, and after a while I didn't want to put up with it anymore. He became verbally abusive, but not violent if that's what you're implying."

"Who initiated the divorce?"

"I think we both wanted it."

"Is there anything else you can think of that might be helpful?"

"No, and I really have to get going."

"Thank you for your honesty. Please call me if something else comes to mind."

On the way back to the city I was thinking about what Peggy had just told me. It didn't mean Sam had anything to do with Laura's disappearance, but I couldn't overlook it either. Instead of dropping my car back at my apartment building, I took a chance that there was a parking spot near my office. I found one two blocks away.

Walking to my office I noticed there was a missed call from Sam demanding I call him back. I figured his ex-wife had contacted him the minute I left, and I was not looking forward to our conversation. My choices were to put it off or confront him now. I decided on the latter.

"Sam, it's Tracey."

"Why the hell did you go behind my back and talk to my ex-wife about me?" he yelled.

"Calm down Sam. I was just being diligent. It's important that I have all the facts."

"And are you satisfied?'

"Yes." I wasn't, but I kept that to myself.

Sitting at my computer I searched for a telephone number for the place out in Boston where Laura worked. I couldn't find a listing, which was odd. It's possible they were no longer in business.

The next morning I got up at 5:00 a.m. and drove to Stamford to stake out Seth Green's house. I had not heard back from him and needed some answers. I parked on the opposite side of the street a few doors down where I had a view of his house. At 7:30 a gray BMW came out of his garage. I couldn't see who was in it, but I took the chance it was Seth. I started following, praying he wasn't going to the train station since I didn't think that I could leave my car there without getting a ticket or towed. Fortunately, after about fifteen minutes he stopped in front of an office building. I hurried to find a spot and caught up to him just before he got on the elevator.

"Mr. Green, my name is Tracey Marks. I left a message with your wife the other day."

"Oh yes, I just hadn't had a chance to get back to you. How can I help you?"

"Do you mind if we sit somewhere?"

We took the elevator up to the fifth floor where Seth led me down a long hallway into an office with floor to ceiling windows. He offered me a seat and sat opposite me behind his desk.

Seth was a tall, good looking man around 35 years old. He had very dark brown hair and piercing dark brown eyes with an olive complexion. He reminded me of Rafael Nadal, a tennis player I have a crush on.

"Why are you interested in Laura?"

"Her husband hired me to find her. Apparently she is missing and of course you can imagine how worried he must be."

"Why aren't the police handling it?"

"Mr. Matthews wanted someone working full time to find her. How do you know her?"

"Laura and I met in high school and have been friends ever since. We talk every once in a while to keep in touch. I can't believe she's missing. I just spoke to her about two weeks ago and she seemed okay."

"Did she confide in you about her relationship with her husband?"

"She told me she wasn't sure if she made a mistake. When she first met Sam, Laura was very vulnerable and he was very charming. Before meeting him she had come back from Boston disillusioned. She thought going there would give her a fresh start but apparently it didn't work out as she planned. I'm not exactly sure what happened in Boston and Laura didn't want to talk about it. I couldn't get her to open up. Laura had taken the deaths of her parents very hard and I'm not sure she ever got over it."

"Did she say anything specific to you about Sam?"

"No, not that I can recall," he said, staring out his office window.

"Did she mention that she was thinking of leaving him?"

"If she was, she didn't tell me."

I noticed a hint of anger in his voice.

"Did you talk to her friend Melanie?" he said.

"Yes, but she wasn't very forthcoming. Do you have any idea why?"

"Melanie and Laura were very close. If Laura was in trouble, she might want to protect her."

"Oh, by the way, I'm just curious. Your wife didn't seem to know about your relationship with Laura. Any reason why?"

"Laura and I dated back in college for a while. Nothing serious but I just thought it would be best if she didn't know. Like I said, we just spoke on the phone every once in a while."

"Nothing else?"

"Nothing."

I thanked Seth and asked him to contact me if something else came to mind. Another person who I thought had something to hide.

CHAPTER 6

When I got back to the office I googled Berg Consulting. I needed to find out what happened in Boston. I found that they worked with companies to plan marketing strategies. There was a link to their website. The chief executive officer was a man named Raymond Berg. There was no telephone number, but there was an e-mail address.

I e-mailed Mr. Berg sending him a very generic message that I needed to speak with him.

I did a search of businesses located near Berg Consulting. There were two close by. The first one I called was The Tri State Agency and I left a message on their answering machine. The next one was Melissa Thomas Advertising and I left another message.

About an hour later I received a call from Alex at Tri State. He told me that Berg was no longer in business. I asked him where I might be able to find him. He had no idea. I called Melissa Thomas Advertising again and Melissa answered right away. I introduced myself and asked her about Berg Consulting. She also said that they were no longer in business but thought Mr. Berg lived on the outskirts of Boston.

I searched a website that listed addresses and telephone numbers. There were two Raymond Berg's listed around the Boston area. I called both numbers and left messages. A few hours later I received a call from Mr. Berg, who said he had been the CEO of Berg Consulting.

"I'm calling about a Laura Tyler who listed your firm as a reference on an employment application. What can you tell me about Ms. Tyler?"

"I can tell you she was employed with me for about a year but it didn't work out."

"Why is that?"

"She wasn't suited for sales, which is what the job required."

"I was informed that Laura had left Boston abruptly. Have you any idea why?"

"Sorry, I don't, but I remember she came in one day and I could tell she'd been crying. I asked her what was wrong and she kind of laughed and said something like, man problems."

"Was she friendly with anyone that might know why she left?"

"There was one person, Amy Brent, but I don't know how friendly they were, and I have no idea where she lives. If you're just checking references why are you asking such personal questions?"

"She's applying for a job where she'll be handling finances and we just want to be thorough." I didn't want to tell him the truth if there was any possibility he may be involved in some way.

"Oh, by the way, what happened to your firm?"

"I decided I no longer wanted to run the company, too many headaches."

"Thank you for your time." After giving him my number, we hung up. I had the feeling there was something that he was lying about, I just didn't know what.

I located an address and telephone number for Amy Brent. When I called it was disconnected. I couldn't seem to catch a break. I searched for relatives associated with her name and there were two possibilities, a Jason Brent and a Michelle Brent. I found a telephone number for Michelle and called her. She answered on the first ring. Ms. Brent told me she was Amy's mother and that Amy moved but she didn't have her new address or telephone number.

"Ms. Brent it's really important that I talk with her. A friend of your daughter, Laura Tyler, is missing and I was hoping Amy might have some information that could help me."

"If I hear from Amy, I'll give her your number," she said, sounding nervous.

I didn't believe Ms. Brent for a second.

"Please tell her it's important. If Laura's in trouble it's possible, so is your daughter." I hung up. Maybe that will scare her into relaying my message to Amy.

I decided I needed a break. I went next door to my cousin Alan who runs the insurance agency. Alan is actually a distant cousin on my mother's side of the family.

"Hi Tracey." Alan's receptionist Margaret greeted me with a big smile.

"How are those rug rats of yours?"

"Good, Tommy is fully into soccer and Jaden has decided to take up the violin. I'm now seriously thinking of getting earplugs. Work saves my sanity," she laughed.

"Is Alan busy?"

"He always has time for you. I'll let him know you're here."

"Hey there," I said to Alan.

"I haven't seen you in ages, why so scarce?" he said.

"Just been busy. What are you up to?"

"Patty and I are in the middle of redecorating. Why don't you come for dinner tomorrow? I know she would love to see you."

"You talked me into it. I'll bring the wine."

Alan and Patty are two of my favorite people. Though we are cousins, growing up, Alan and I never hung out together since he was a few years older. I remember when I was around twelve, I was walking through a park that was near my house, and three boys, maybe fifteen or sixteen years old ganged up on me. One of the boys pushed me hard and I fell to the ground, my hand hitting something sharp. Blood was seeping all over the ground. I was trying very hard not to cry but tears were slowly leaking down my cheeks. Luckily, Alan happened to be in the area and came to my rescue. Seeing the blood Alan rushed them but with three against one, he took a beating. I felt awful but he was my hero and I have always thought of him as my big brother.

I called it quits for the day. Though it was chilly outside, I walked the fifteen blocks to my apartment.

"Hi Wally. How you doing?"

"Real good, you're home early."

"Yes, and I'm looking forward to a nice relaxing evening curled up with a book after I go for a run."

On my way to the office the next day I stopped in at my local coffee place for my shot of caffeine and a lemon poppy muffin. Anna was nowhere to be seen. I wondered where she was.

My mailman Steven popped his head into my office. "Tracey, my lady, what goes?"

"Did you bring me any checks today?"

"I hope so. By the way, I picked up this manila envelope that was on the floor in front of your door. Have a lovely day."

"You to," I said without looking up.

The manila envelope had no return address. I opened it up carefully and pulled out a single typewritten page that said, 'THIS IS A WARNING – BACK OFF!'

CHAPTER 7

My stomach did a flip flop. What did I get myself into? I started pacing back and forth, my heart pounding against my chest. I looked out the window to see if there was anyone suspicious hanging around though whoever left the envelope would probably be long gone.

My first thought after I attempted to calm myself down was who the hell did I tick off. It could have been anyone I recently spoke to about Laura. Well, the good news is I may be on the right track but which track is that? Another thought came to me; it could be Laura if she's alive and doesn't want to be found. I'm not sure how alarmed I should be but I decided I should bone up on my shooting skills. My gun was neatly tucked away in my office safe where it has been since the last time I went to the range about two years ago.

I opened up the safe and my gun was still there. My hand was shaking as I took it out. Before going to the range, I cleaned my gun, thankfully, without shooting myself in the foot or other parts I still needed. I looked up the nearest shooting range in the area and found a listing for the Westside Rifle & Pistol Range on 20th Street. I hopped on the subway with my gun safely tucked in my ankle holster.

When I arrived, the man behind the counter greeted me with a jovial hello. "You're a new face," he said.

"It's Tracey, nice to meet you."

"Bill. Glad to make your acquaintance. Is this your first time?"

"No, I have a Glock 19 and would like to brush up."

"Great, here's some ammo and you can go to stall number 7. If you need any help, just give a holler."

"Thanks Bill." The shooting area was crowded and noisy. I put on my earplugs and goggles and loaded my gun. While I was on my second round, the corner of my eye caught the guy in the next stall staring at me.

"You need any help?" he asked.

He probably thought I was a damsel in distress that needed rescuing. I just shook my head, not in the mood for chit chat.

After about twenty minutes I was getting used to the recoil of the gun and was able to keep my hand steadier. It's definitely not as easy as it looks. The target was about 20 feet out. The first round barely hit the target paper. The next round was a little better. By the third round I was hitting pretty far outside of the bullseye but at least I was on the paper.

As I was leaving the guy who was in the next stall came up beside me.

"I didn't mean to stare before but it's not often I see a woman here, especially one so pretty."

I couldn't figure out if he was just a complete jerk or was trying to make a move on me. I was ignoring him but he was having none of it. He was now following me outside.

"Why the hell are you following me?" I asked in an annoyed tone.

"I'm just trying to be friendly. My name's Daniel but you can call me Danny," he said with a teasing smile.

"Well, Daniel or Danny you sure don't take a hint."

"So what's your name since you already know mine?"

"If I tell you, will you get lost?"

"I may, but you might have just missed the one chance to meet your Prince Charming, and you may never get another one. The ball is in your court," he said with a grin.

"It's Tracey, now if you'll excuse me, I'm in a hurry."

"Look Tracey, I really am a nice guy though of course I would say that. I don't normally pick up women, but as I was watching you practice the expression on your face was filled with such intent and purpose, I couldn't help thinking I'd like to meet you. Before you walk away just listen. I live in the city, have my own business helping companies set up their computer software, I am not, nor have I ever been married, no children that I know of. I can go on if you like?"

"No that's quite alright," I said, trying to suppress a laugh. "Look Danny why don't you give me your card and I'll think about it."

"Well at least you're being honest. Most women would say they'll call just to get rid of you."

"To show good faith, here's my card."

"Tracey Marks, Private Investigator. Should I be worried?"

"Only if you're guilty of something," I said with a twinkle in my eye and left him standing there.

I couldn't believe this guy, though I have to say there was something appealing about him. Danny had a great smile that showed dimples on both his cheeks. He was about 6 feet tall with sandy brown hair. He wasn't quite handsome since his nose was a little crooked but he was kind of sexy looking. It surprised me that I even gave him a second glance. It's not that I don't like men because I do, but I certainly don't waste much time ruminating over my love life. As I mentioned, I like living alone.

On my train ride back I was thinking how much I love the city, even with the noise, the litter, and the crowds. I wouldn't want to be anywhere else, though the subway can be a challenge at times. I grew up in Queens so being in the city is not a far stretch. The summers can get hot and sticky, but I don't mind. No different than a lot of other places in the universe.

I cleaned my gun before tucking it back in the safe. I called Detective Harris hoping he would be able to tell me something.

"Detective Harris, this is Tracey Marks, I'm calling about Laura Matthews. I'm a private investigator and her husband has asked me to look into her disappearance. Are there any developments?"

"Ms. Marks, you know I can't give out any information. All I can tell you is we have no suspicions at this time that she didn't leave on her own free will, but we're checking into it."

"I was wondering if you spoke to any of her friends?" I asked, trying to play nice but I was gritting my teeth.

"I can't get into any details. I have your number and if there is anything I can share with you, I'll get in touch."

We hung up. I knew it would be a while before they started investigating, and I didn't expect to hear back from Detective Harris.

It was after five. I wanted to get home, take a quick run, shower and be at Alan's by 7:00. I also needed to stop at my local liquor store and pick up a bottle of wine. Thinking about all I had to do was making me a little dizzy, so I skipped the run.

Alan and Patty live in a beautiful brownstone on the east side in the 60's that Alan inherited from his grandfather who once had a seat on the stock exchange. I am not by nature a jealous person but this was as close to it as I come.

The living room, dining area and sun/sitting room were on the first floor and the bedrooms were upstairs. Since they had no children and were not planning on having any, they broke down one wall that was adjacent to the master bedroom and designed an area with space for a computer desk and chair. It also had a comfortable love seat with a TV hung on the wall. The second bedroom was reserved for guests.

Patty, besides being a lawyer advocating for children's rights, was an amazing cook.

"I am so happy to see you," Patty said, greeting me with a big hug. "I wish you would come over more often."

I knew Patty meant it. They were the closest people in my life. My father died when I was twelve and my mother died when I was twenty-four of breast cancer. Since I had no other relatives in New York, it was nice to know they were nearby. I have a few other cousins out there in the world but none that I am in contact with.

If you could say a couple looked alike, that was

Alan and Patty. They both were on the short side and slender. Each wore glasses. His were wire rimmed and hers were tortoiseshell. They both dressed very preppy.

"What can I get you to drink?" Patty asked.

"Any wine you have open."

We sat in the sitting room that was lined with built-in bookcases. There was a pale blue love seat and two cream colored upholstered chairs with blue and green stripes opposite the sofa. On the wood floor was a round beige rug.

"How is business?" Alan asked me.

"It had been really slow. I was going out of my mind, and then I got a case involving a missing person. This guy tells me his wife never came home and he wants me to find out what happened to her. There is no evidence that she was taken, at least from the house. He swears everything is great between them. No money issues."

"Is this your first missing person's case?" Patty asked.

"It is, which is exciting and a little scary."

"What are you going to do?" Patty asked.

"I've interviewed several people so far and it seems like everyone has something to hide."

I filled them in on the case, including the threatening note.

"Are you sure you want to continue. I don't want to discourage you but you know I worry," Alan said.

"I know but I think taking this case will be good for me. It's time I got involved in something more challenging than the mundane cases I usually work on, and it's good money."

I didn't want to mention to Alan how strapped I

really was since I knew he would want to help me out.

Patty chimed in, "I for one think it's great. I have full faith in you. Do you have any idea what you are going to do next?"

"Not at this very moment but I'll think of something."

"If you run into any problems or you need our help, we're here for you."

"Thanks. You never know when I'll take you up on your offer."

Patty had made a French stew that was out of this world. I could hardly come up for air.

"The place looks fantastic, guys."

"I give all the credit to Patty. She designed the new changes; I just had to live with the mess during the renovations. The good thing is it's almost finished," said Alan.

"Nosey me wants to know if anything interesting is going on in your love life?" Patty asked.

"I did meet someone who may be of interest but we haven't even gone on a date yet. And you know me and relationships, but I promise you one thing if it ever gets serious, you guys will be the first to know."

"I have some news," Patty said. "I'm taking in a partner. The practice is growing and I need someone to share the load. At first I thought I would hire an attorney to assist me with the overflow but I realized I don't want to supervise anyone; I want someone who is very experienced and can share the cases that come in the door."

"That's exciting. Having a partner will give you someone to bounce ideas off of. I'm happy for you."

"And a partner will lighten your load," Alan said. "You work too hard."

"I'll drink to that," I said.

"Do you want to tell her, or should I?" Alan said looking at Patty.

"What, what's going on?"

"I'm pregnant."

"Oh my god, how did it happen, I mean I know how it happened so help me out here."

"Since I'm in my forties I guess I thought I couldn't get pregnant. I had stopped taking birth control pills about a year ago. Obviously this was not planned, and we had no intention of having children, but now that it's happened we're thrilled."

"I'm shocked, but so happy for both of you."

"We have to do some additional renovations since we'll need a nursery but that's minor. The good news is we won't have to move and now that I have a partner it will make things easier."

"If you need babysitting duty I'll be glad to help out but I'm going to need a crash course on baby stuff."

"You and me both," Patty laughed.

After a scrumptious dessert of homemade apple pie and a scoop of vanilla Haagen-Dazs ice cream, I said my goodbyes and left.

Though it was after 10:00, I walked back to my apartment thinking about my relationships with men and why I shy away from getting close. As soon as I begin to feel that the person is getting too close, my antennas go up and I want to bolt.

Memories of the day my father died came swirling into my head. It was as if it just happened. I was doing my homework at the kitchen table and my father was making my favorite dish for dinner, macaroni and cheese. My mother was somewhere in the house. The next thing I heard was a really loud thud. I looked up and I saw my father on the floor. I screamed at the top of my lungs and my mother came rushing into the kitchen. I wanted to rush to my father but I was frozen in my seat. After that, it was kind of a blur. People came and took my father away and I never saw him again. I still can't believe someone you love can be taken from you that quickly. A chill went through my body.

CHAPTER 8

The next morning I slept till 8:00, which was a luxury for me. I decided to work at home for a change. I put on the coffee maker and slipped on a pair of sweats and a tee-shirt.

I placed a giant corkboard on a chair in the living room and took out some three by five blank cards filling each one with the name of every person I had talked to regarding the case and thumbtacked them on the board. It made it easier to see exactly what had transpired so far.

First, I don't know if something happened to Laura or she left on her own. Let's go on the assumption something happened to her.

I thought I could rule out Melanie Ross. She may be hiding something but I don't think she had anything to do with Laura's disappearance.

Seth Green claims he and Laura were just friends but I have only his say so on that, and there is the fact that he never told his wife about their relationship. I guess his version is plausible. I can see that the wife might get a little jealous so why tell her. The problem with that is the wife usually finds out. Another thought, maybe Mrs. Green already knew about Seth's relationship with Laura but she never said anything to him.

Raymond Berg, Laura's former boss, might be interesting. He claims Laura wasn't suited for the job.

I should check with her friend Melanie again to see if Laura felt the same way. Maybe something happened in Boston that had Laura abruptly leave. Is Mr. Berg hiding something?

What happened to Amy Brent? She's the one person who could probably tell me why Laura left but where is she? Her mother sounded reluctant to speak with me. What mother doesn't have her daughter's cell number even if she moved? Why wouldn't she give it to me is the question?

I was determined to see if I could obtain Amy's number on my own. I went into my databases and looked under the name Amy Brent in the Boston area. There was one that probably fit her age. The other Amy Brent was in her seventies, way too old. I clicked on the Amy that was thirty-four. It listed a Verizon cell number but no current address.

I called and left a message on her voice mail. I stressed the urgency and hoped she would call me back.

I then left a message for Melanie, Laura's friend. As I hung up, my phone rang.

"Tracey, it's Danny, the stalker from yesterday."

I couldn't help but smile. "Well you don't waste any time, do you?"

"A woman as fabulous as you could get scooped up pretty quickly."

"Okay I get the point. You could stop with all the flattery. What can I do for you?"

"How about dinner tonight if you're not busy? We can meet any place you want, or I can pick you up."

I agreed to meet Danny for dinner at a little French restaurant on 92nd and Madison at 7:00

though I wondered why I relented. He was a little goofy but he made me laugh, which is not an easy accomplishment.

As soon as I hung up, Melanie called. "Thanks for getting back to me," I said.

"I was going to call you. When we first spoke I was hesitant about talking with you. I thought Laura might have just gone off for a few days because of her husband, and I didn't want to say anything since you're working for him, but now I'm getting worried. I tried calling her a few times but it just goes directly to voice mail. All my texts go unanswered."

"Can we meet? I'd like to ask you a few more questions if you don't mind," I said.

We hung up after agreeing to meet at my office the following day at 1:00.

I stared at the corkboard trying to get some inspiration. Something happened in Boston but what? I'm having a hard time buying Berg's explanation of why they parted. Is Laura's leaving connected to Boston or something here? Why would Sam want to harm her?

The phone rang and it was Sam. "Any news, Tracey?"

"Nothing to report though I did receive a threatening note to back off or else."

"Now I'm really worried. I was hoping that Laura needed some space and went off for a while but this doesn't feel right. I have a call into Detective Harris and I'm hoping he'll have something to report."

After hanging up I went for a run to clear my head. The weather was cool but the sun was shining. Since the note spooked me a little I changed the route I normally take. On the way back I stopped for a cappuccino and meandered into a neighborhood bookstore. I browsed for a while and picked up a Michael Connelly book, The Crossing, which has one of my favorite characters, Harry Bosch, a Detective in Los Angeles.

When I got back I showered and dressed for my date with Danny. I decided on a pair of black slacks, a white silk blouse and black flats. I put on some eye makeup and rose colored lipstick. I grabbed a light sweater on the way out and took an Uber to the restaurant.

Danny was waiting outside dressed in khaki's, a button down blue shirt and a V neck white sweater. Pascalou was a small, cozy French Restaurant. The hostess led us upstairs to a corner table.

"Can I get you something to drink?" the waiter asked.

We both ordered red wine. "This is a really cute place," I said.

"I found it by accident. I was walking on Madison Avenue on a beautiful sunny day and out of nowhere, it started pouring. I was on my way to lunch at another place but the gods had a different plan. I was standing right in front of this restaurant when the rains came down."

"I have a few neighborhood restaurants where I meet friends, mostly Italian. So what got you into guns?" I asked.

"I have a friend from high school that was brought up around guns and he took me to my first target practice. I'm not really a gun person, but every once in a while I'll go to the range. What about you?"

"That was my first time in two years. Being a private investigator I can own a gun but I'm not a gun advocate. I just figured if I have it, I should be able to shoot it with some sort of accuracy."

Danny was easy to talk to. He had an openness about him that made me feel comfortable; maybe it's the way he focuses his attention on me when I talk.

The waiter came over with our drinks and asked if we were ready to order. Danny asked him to come back in a few minutes.

"So what have you had here? It all looks good," I said.

"It is. Usually I have fish, since I try to stay away from meat. What do you like?"

"I eat almost anything, though there are three important things you should know about me and food."

"Okay, now you are officially scaring me."

"Not to worry, just that I hate cilantro, I'm not bashful about eating a lot in one sitting and I never share my dessert."

"Wow, I would never have guessed that about you," he grinned. "But as long as we are confessing, I am also a flawed person. People love Greek yogurt but I can't stand it. I hate raw onions and cream cheese. I guess we make quite a pair."

"Are you ready to order?" the waiter asked when he returned.

"Yes," Danny said. "I'll have the Skate and the house salad and another glass of wine."

"I'll have the Salmon with the house salad. I'm still working on my wine."

I found out that Danny was a talker, which was good since I wasn't. Small talk did not come easy to me. He told me about his brother Josh who is a career officer in the Army which at times frightens Danny.

Right now he is safe with his wife and nine year old son in Belgium or as safe as anyone can be in this world. His parents are retired and live in Florida. Danny was raised in Ardsley, New York but always wanted to live in the City.

"So the sixty-four thousand dollar question which I'm sure you have been asked at least that many times is why did you become a private investigator?"

"I grew up watching cop shows and reading mystery books where the main character was a PI. Actually the question I'm asked the most is, do I carry a gun? The answer is no, but I'm working my first missing persons case, so it's new territory for me."

"Can you tell me about it?"

Our food came and I dug in. "Maybe another time since it's involved and may take a while." I didn't feel comfortable telling Danny about the case since I just met him.

After dinner we had Crème Brûlée for dessert with vanilla ice cream. So good. We left the restaurant and shared a taxi stopping first at my place. Danny asked the driver to wait while he walked me to the front of my building. He said goodnight and kissed me lightly on the lips.

On the way up in the elevator I thought about the fact that Danny didn't ask to come up. Though I'm glad he didn't, I think my vanity was slightly injured. I needed to be careful since my history with men did not bode well. I have a tendency to rush into a relationship and then bolt.

When I turned my phone back on, I had missed a call from Susie. It was late so I decided to call her in the morning.

The next day I went to the gym, did my usual

routine and also took a spin class. On the way to the office I picked up some yogurt with fruit and a granola muffin.

The mail was waiting for me with no ominous looking envelopes. I was looking forward to my conversation with Melanie, hoping she had some information that might be helpful.

Before I had a chance to call Susie, my phone rang.

"What are you up to?" I said to Susie.

"Mark is meeting some buddies for dinner tomorrow evening. Are you interested in getting together, maybe a movie or a museum and some dinner?"

"Sure, I'll call you later and we'll figure it out." We hung up. Besides talking to Melanie I had no plan going forward and I needed one. I was hoping that Amy Brent would call. I really wanted to talk with her.

By the time I went through the mail and paid some office bills, the door opened and it was Melanie.

"I know I'm a little early, is that okay?"

"Sure, have a seat. Would you like some coffee? I just made some."

"Okay, black, no sugar is perfect."

Melanie seemed a little anxious. She kept crossing her legs back and forth. I handed her a cup of the freshly brewed hazelnut coffee and got down to business.

"So you mentioned on the phone that you were worried about Laura, can you explain?"

"Ever since Laura came back from Boston, she seemed different."

"In what way?"

"It's hard to put into words. She was a bit more

edgy than usual. I asked her if anything was wrong but she said no. I got the impression she was hiding something but maybe I was just imagining it. We talked less. At first I thought it was about her relationship with Sam. I asked how things were between them and she said they were fine. They weren't married that long so I thought it was a bit odd that she didn't seem happier."

Though I had a lot of questions I kept silent since Melanie seemed like she wanted to talk and I didn't want to interrupt her.

"I think she was disappointed that the job in Boston didn't work out. When she met Sam she seemed happy at first but I sensed something had changed. I just don't know what was troubling her."

"I spoke to Raymond Berg, her ex-boss and asked him why she left. He told me that Laura was not suited for the position and it was a mutual parting of the ways. What did she tell you?"

"She said the job wasn't what she thought it would be and wasn't happy there. I didn't think much about it because that happens with jobs. The only thing is she didn't seem that disappointed, which I thought was odd since she moved to Boston for the position."

"What was her relationship with Seth Green?"

"What do you mean?"

"Well, Seth mentioned to me that he and Laura dated in college for a short time but it wasn't serious and they remained friends."

"That's news to me. I knew they had dated but I didn't know they were still in contact. Maybe she didn't mention it because it was insignificant to her."

"It's possible. Did she mention anyone by the name of Amy Brent?"

"Not that I can recall."

"What about anyone she could have been dating in Boston?"

"She did mention a guy she dated a few times but I have no idea what his name was. Sorry I can't be of any more help."

"Did she mention anything about Mr. Berg? Did she have a problem with him?"

"If she did, Laura didn't say anything to me."

"Keep calling and texting her, maybe she'll answer," I said.

"I hope so. It's not like her to ignore my calls. By the way this might not be anything, but Laura mentioned Sam was having trouble with someone at his company, though I can't imagine what that would have to do with Laura."

"It probably doesn't," though I made a mental note to ask Sam about it.

Melanie left promising to let me know if she hears from Laura. I was actually getting a bad feeling about this. If she was in trouble, who would she turn to? At this point there were only two scenarios I could think of, one she was hiding somewhere because she was afraid or two, she was dead. I hated the thought of the latter. Even though Melanie called me and genuinely seemed worried about Laura she still might be covering for her.

CHAPTER 9

I decided to go to the well one more time and contact Joe to see if he could get me the address listed for Amy Brent's cell phone.

"Hey Joe, I need to ask you for one more favor," I said sheepishly.

"Tracey, I won't make you go through hoops but this is the last one."

"I promise." That was probably a lie and he knew it too. "I need you to get an address from a cell phone number."

Okay, give me the number."

After thanking him profusely, we hung up. I thought if I could get Amy's address I'd take a ride to Boston on Monday and pay her an unexpected visit since she wasn't returning my calls.

Before I left the office I called Susie and we agreed to meet tomorrow at the Metropolitan Museum of Art.

As I was heading home I got a text from Joe with Amy's address in Massachusetts. Maybe I'll send him a gift card for Starbucks. That's the least I could do.

I stopped along the way to pick up some groceries and then to my favorite place on earth, with no exaggeration, the Corner Sweet Shoppe. I usually stop in at least twice a week either for their homemade ice cream or homemade chocolates. The owner, Mr. Hayes, is a dead ringer for Mr. Rogers from the TV series, and his trademark is a white apron that he always wears, but after making the chocolates and the ice cream for the day, it looks more like a painter's palate.

"Hi Tracey. How are you?"

"Good. What's the flavor of the day?"

"Toasted Coconut. Would you like to try it?"

"Why not. Delicious, but I think today I'll have a pint of pistachio." Though I always ask what the flavor of the day is, I rarely buy it. I stick to pistachio or dark chocolate, my favorite flavors I loved as a kid. Sometimes I buy the dark chocolate covered rum balls.

I spent part of Saturday cleaning my apartment which is a ritual of mine. I'm kind of a neat freak. Since my mind is always cluttered I like my surroundings in order.

I met Susie at three o'clock at the Metropolitan Museum of Art where we saw the Chagall Exhibit. Afterward we took the train downtown and went to an Indian Restaurant Susie had read about.

As we were gorging ourselves on chicken tandoori, curried fish biryani, curried chickpeas and flatbread, I filled Susie in since we last spoke, including the threatening note I received.

"Well the good news is you spooked someone, that's progress," Susie said.

"I think I need to go to Boston and try to find out what happened there."

"I agree. Something isn't kosher though it may or may not have anything to do with her disappearance. What about the husband, what kind of vibe do you get from him?"

"Not sure, and I am certainly not eliminating him. For all we know he hired me to throw suspicion off of himself. Unless a body shows up the police will probably treat it as nothing more than a wife who ran out on her husband. The thing is I still don't know much about her."

"Even though her parents are dead there may be a relative or a childhood friend that could shed some light on Laura. Maybe she mentioned an aunt or an uncle to someone. I would ask her friend or her husband," Susie said.

"Good idea."

On Sunday I lazed around watching the morning news shows and finished reading my Agatha Christie book. As I closed the book, my eyes started getting droopy. I was nodding off as my thoughts drifted to Danny. I put him out of my mind and must have fallen asleep because I awoke to a buzzing noise. I wasn't sure where it was coming from since I was still half asleep until I realized it was my cell phone.

"Hello," sounding groggy.

"Hi Tracey."

"Who is this?"

"It's Danny. Did I wake you? It's three o'clock on my side of town."

"Very funny. Yeah, I fell asleep but that's all right since I probably would have had a hard time sleeping tonight if you hadn't called. How are you?"

"Good, I thought I could entice you with dinner later though I know it's last minute."

"Can I take a rain check? I'm going to Boston tomorrow on the case I'm working on and I need to prepare. I may have to stay over for a day or two, so can I call you when I get back?"

"That would be great though I'm deeply disappointed," he said amusingly.

I could picture the grin on his face. "You're a big boy; you'll get over it."

"I'm jumping into a cold shower as we speak. Be careful tomorrow."

He hung up and I wondered why I begged off. I liked Danny. I hope I wasn't getting scared since I really wanted to give this a shot and see what happens.

I needed some fresh air to wake me up. I went for a short run, and on the way back I picked up some Chinese food for dinner and stopped at my neighborhood bakery for a chocolate cupcake.

After a quick shower, I gobbled up my dinner and tried to figure out my plan for tomorrow. I probably wouldn't get up to Boston until 11:00 a.m., and since I didn't have a clue where or if Amy was working, I might have to sit around for hours until she got back to her place. I thought I would also pay a visit to Raymond Berg, Laura's ex-boss. I might get a better read on him in person.

As I was thinking about all this, I realized how much I liked working on this case. It was certainly more challenging and interesting than my other cases, even though I still had no concrete results. I had no clue whether I was spinning my wheels or making any progress.

I got up at 5:30 the next morning and packed a few things just in case I needed to stay over. Before I headed to my car, I stopped for a large coffee and a granola muffin. I put on my GPS and headed out of the city. I called Sam and filled him in on what I was doing. He hadn't heard from Laura and sounded genuinely worried. I wanted to believe he had no connection to Laura's disappearance but that would be naïve to rule him out yet. I decided not to ask him about the person he had an altercation with at his company until I returned from Boston.

I arrived at Amy Brent's apartment complex a little after 11:00. What did people do before GPS and Google? I would be lost before I got out of Manhattan.

Amy lived in a huge brick complex with apartments both on the ground level and on a second level a few stairs up. It was kind of seedy looking from the outside. There were a few trees but mostly concrete.

I parked in the visitor area and walked around looking for Amy's apartment number. When I found it, I knocked on her door several times to no avail. An elderly lady walking with a cane came out of the apartment next to Amy's. She gave me a big smile and I returned the favor.

"Hi," I said. "I was looking for Amy Brent but she doesn't appear to be home."

"Of course not, she's at work. Are you a friend of hers?" she said curtly.

"Yes mam. She didn't know I was coming. I thought I would surprise her."

"Well isn't that thoughtful of you. Such a nice friend."

I was cringing on the inside. "Do you happen to know where she works or what time she would be home?"

"Oh I believe she works at the Walmart about two miles down the road. She usually gets home around five or six."

Thank heavens for nosey neighbors. "Thank you so much. Can I help you down the steps?"

"No, I can manage. I may be old, but I'm not dead

yet," she said in a huff.

I watched as she hobbled down the three steps and walked slowly to an old beat up Chrysler. I was grateful that I wasn't a passenger in her car.

Though I knew where Amy worked I thought it was better to wait till she got home. Ambushing her at work might turn her off completely.

Since I had time on my hands, I thought I would drive around and find a place for lunch and then see if I could talk with Raymond Berg. From Google maps it looked like his place was about a half hour away.

I found a diner about three miles from Amy's apartment complex. From the outside it looked like an old fashioned diner. The inside was very 50's with red counter stools and red vinyl booths. The walls were filled with black and white photos of old movie stars and baseball players. My father was a Dodgers fan so I was glad to see a photo of Jackie Robinson on the wall. Since there did not appear to be a host or hostess, I slid into one of the booths. At the far end of the booth there was a small jukebox that had songs from the 70's and 80's. A very friendly looking waitress came over. She looked to be in her sixties with dyed blond hair that was teased in a style that fit the same decade of the diner.

"Hi there hon, is it just you?"

"Yes, and I am starved," I said.

"Well honey you are in New England and I recommend the clam chowder. You won't be disappointed."

"Well then, how about a grilled Swiss cheese and tomato sandwich and a bowl of your clam chowder. I'll live dangerously."

"Honey if that's your idea of living dangerously,

you're in trouble," she laughed. "Anything to drink?"

"Coffee please."

"You're not from Boston are you?"

"No, a New Yorker born and raised."

"I keep telling myself that I have to get down there one day but it doesn't seem to happen. I'd love to see one of those Broadway shows."

"Well if it makes you feel better, I live in the city and I never get to see any plays."

Her name tag said Charlotte. She walked over to the counter and yelled in my order. She came back with my food about ten minutes later.

"If you want any coffee refills, just give a holler."

As I devoured my lunch I wrote down some questions I wanted to ask Berg. I had to be somewhat honest with him but in case he was the reason Laura was missing, I didn't want him to know I may suspect him.

"More coffee?"

I lifted my head up. Before I had a chance to say anything, Charlotte was pouring coffee into my empty cup. "Thanks Charlotte, by the way can you suggest a motel around here, some place clean, nothing fancy?"

"Well about a mile south is Echo Lodge. It fits the bill, clean and the rates are good. I think during the week they should have rooms available."

"That sounds great. The clam chowder was delicious; maybe I'll be back for dinner."

I paid the check, left a big tip for Charlotte and used the bathroom before I left. I arrived at Berg's house, which was located on a street where all the homes looked like they were cookie-cut and void of charm. They looked more like bungalows. There was a big black SUV parked in his driveway. A straggly looking tree was planted on his front lawn. The grass appeared to be recently mowed.

I parked across the street and knocked on his door. When it opened, I was staring at a tall, lanky man who was naked from the waist up. He looked to be about fifty, sporting a thick mustache.

"Mr. Berg, my name is Tracey Marks. We spoke on the phone about a week ago, can we speak for a moment?" I handed him my card.

He moved aside, and I entered into a small foyer that led into a fairly large and very neat living room with a dark brown leather couch in the middle of the room facing a fireplace. There was a beautiful photograph above the mantel of a lake with mountains covered in snow in the background. The wood floors were dark stained. I was surprised at how lovely the room looked.

"I'll be right back," he said.

When I realized I was inside Berg's house not knowing if he could be the reason Laura was missing, my hands started to sweat. I wanted to bolt but if I did that, it would mean I wasn't up for the job. I crossed my fingers praying he wasn't coming back with a gun.

CHAPTER 10

I breathed a sigh of relief when he came back wearing a black tee-shirt and the same jeans and no sign of a gun.

"Look, I want to be upfront with you Mr. Berg; when I first spoke with you about Laura Tyler I needed to find out why she left a job that she had been willing to leave everything behind for. As it turns out, she has disappeared."

"I'm sorry, but what has that got to do with me?"

Since he didn't offer me a seat, we both stood standing, which felt a little awkward.

"Can I be honest with you?" I continued. "I find it odd that after working only one year at your company Laura left Boston abruptly."

"When did you say she went missing?"

"About two weeks ago."

"So how would I be involved in her disappearance if she was long gone from here?"

"I'm not saying you are, but it seems like something might have occurred that Laura was involved in and it followed her to Connecticut."

"You're making a lot of assumptions Tracey," he said with a cold stare.

"Did she happen to mention the name of someone she was dating?"

"No, and just to be clear before you insinuate anything about my relationship with Laura, it was strictly employer/employee and nothing more."

"I never implied otherwise," I said, biting my lower lip.

"If there is nothing else, I have an appointment."

"Just one other thing, why do you think she left Boston?"

"I have no idea and I don't care," he said in a dismissive tone.

I couldn't help notice how Berg changed his attitude when I challenged him. Though he was an asshole, I doubt he had anything to do with Laura's disappearance. Too much time had gone by for him to be a viable suspect.

It was still too early to go back to Amy's apartment so I swung by the Echo Lodge Motel since I doubted I would be up for the drive back to New York tonight. The lodge was pretty much as Charlotte described. I walked in and there was no one around. I raised my voice for assistance and a door opened about ten feet from behind the counter. A young girl no more than 16 years old greeted me. She was wearing her light brown hair in a single braid down her back. As she got closer, I noticed freckles across her nose.

"Hi, I'm looking for a room for one night."

"Sure, it's seventy-five dollars. Will you be paying cash or by credit card?" she asked, yawning.

"Late night," I said jokingly.

"Sorry, I was doing my homework. I'm holding down the fort while my father goes on an errand. My name's Lavender."

"Oh, I sympathize with you Lavender. I never liked doing homework though I probably shouldn't tell you that."

"It's okay. Did you say cash or credit card?"

"Credit card. By the way, can I check in now?"

"Sure, check out time is 11:00 but don't worry if you're not out by then."

"Thank you, you've been a big help."

Lavender smiled, turned and went back to where she appeared from. I took the room key and left. Since I didn't know what Amy looked like I couldn't follow her from Walmart. It was almost five so I went back to her place to wait, hoping she came straight home.

I checked my messages and e-mails while sitting in my car. Nothing needed my attention. I turned on the radio and tried to get a station that played decent music. I finally found one that had 80's music. I kicked myself for not bringing a book on tape that I could listen to.

Around 6:15 a small white car pulled into a spot near Amy's apartment. A young woman with dirty blond hair in a ponytail got out carrying a brown paper shopping bag and walked up the steps to Amy's apartment door. I waited till she got in and knocked. She opened the door halfway with the chain on.

"Amy, my name is Tracey Marks. I'm a friend of Laura Tyler," I lied. "I just need five minutes of your time; it's really important."

"How did you get my address?" she asked nervously through the door.

I didn't want to scare her and confess I was a private investigator but I couldn't come up with anything else quick enough. "Laura is missing and her husband hired me to find her. If you could just let me in, I can explain everything, please."

Amy shut the door in my face. Just as I was ready to plead some more through the closed door, I heard the chain come off, and Amy slowly opened the door halfway and practically pulled me into her apartment. The place was sparse of furniture and wall hangings. It was fairly depressing. There was a couch that looked like it had seen better days and a white wicker chair with a cushion on it. I sat in the chair and Amy sat on the couch

"I'm sorry if I scared you but Laura has been missing for a few days. At this point we don't know what happened to her, if anything. I was talking to her ex-boss, Raymond Berg and he mentioned that you were friendly with Laura." Before I could continue Amy burst out,

"You spoke to him, why did you do that?" the color draining from her face.

"Amy what's the matter?"

"What did he say? Is that how you knew I was here?" she asked frantically.

"No, he has no idea where you are. He just casually mentioned that I might get in touch with you concerning Laura but he doesn't know where you live."

"Are you sure?"

"Yes."

"Why are you so afraid of him?"

"Laura and Berg were in a relationship for a few months when he became physically abusive. When they first started dating he was very charming and she really liked him. It began with verbal abuse, putting her down whenever he had the opportunity. At first she shrugged his comments off, but then it started to escalate and she couldn't ignore it anymore. She confronted him and that's when he became physical. It was hard on her since the affair was a secret. That's why she left but he threatened to hurt her if she went to the police or told anyone."

"Why do you think he mentioned your name to me?"

"He didn't know Laura and I were good friends. He thought we were just work acquaintances."

"There's one other thing, Laura told me that Berg was up to something shady with the company but she didn't tell me what it was, maybe she didn't know."

"It's been a while since Laura left Boston. It's hard to believe after all this time he had anything to do with her disappearance."

"Well maybe he was stalking her. He strikes me as the type that doesn't give up if he wants something," Amy said, looking down at the floor.

"I can't say for sure but I don't think you have to worry about Berg."

"Maybe you're right," she said, not quite with conviction.

"Can you remember anything that Laura told you even if you don't think it's important?"

"At the moment I can't but I'll call you if something occurs to me."

"One other thing, when was the last time you spoke with Laura?"

"When she left. I haven't spoken to her since."

"Thank you Amy, and take care of yourself."

It seemed like her reaction to Berg was unusually strong. I wondered if he hurt Amy and she was afraid to tell me.

CHAPTER 11

It was after 7:00 and I was hungry. I went back to the diner since it was the only place I knew and I was tired.

It was a lot more crowded than earlier. A hostess led me to a replica of the booth I was in earlier. I looked for Charlotte but didn't see her. My new waitress Sandy asked if I wanted to order a drink. A glass of Merlot sounded wonderful. It had been a long day.

"Is Charlotte here tonight?" I asked.

"No, her shift is over sweetheart."

I was still looking at the menu when Sandy brought me my glass of wine.

"How you doing dear, any decisions yet?"

"I'll have the Cobb salad, thank you."

While I waited, I checked my messages. There was one call but no message. Strange, could be marketers. They never leave messages.

After dinner, I went back to the motel. The office light was still on so I went inside. There was a man probably in his forties behind the desk. He had a long scar that went from the left side of his forehead all the way down to his chin. Though some people might think it would ruin his looks, I thought it gave his face character. I would have loved to hear the story behind the scar.

"You must be Lavender's dad."

"Oh you met the darling of Echo Lodge," he said with a twinkle. "I hope she was on her best behavior."

"She was. You can be proud. By the way would you happen to know where I can get coffee in the morning?"

"Which way are you headed?"

"Back to New York."

"There's a Starbucks nearby. When you come out of here, make a left and it will be in a small shopping center about three-quarters of a mile on the right."

"Great. Thank you and if I ever come back this way, I'll be sure to stay here again."

I went back to the room, showered, plopped on the bed and clicked on the TV. While I was watching some weird movie, I remembered I told Danny I would call if I had a chance. Since it was only 9:30, I thought he would still be up. He answered on the first ring.

"Hi Danny, it's Tracey. I hope I didn't wake you."

"I was just dreaming about you. We were on our honeymoon in Paris and we were sitting in a café, sipping wine. We each had on a beret, mine was black and yours was red. Very French."

I started to laugh. "Wow you already have us married though I do like the honeymoon so far. Do we have children I don't know about?"

"Let me go back to sleep and I'll let you know," he chuckled. "Are you still in Massachusetts?"

"Yes, it was a long day so I thought I would leave first thing in the morning."

"Good idea. How did it go?"

"That's hard to answer. I found out some interesting information but I'm no closer to finding her."

"You're determined so I know you will."

"I wish I had your confidence."

"I'll rub off on you. But in order for that to happen, we actually have to get together. How about dinner Friday?"

"Okay, why don't we touch base later in the week."

We hung up and I fell asleep almost instantly. I set my alarm for 5:45 and was on the road by 6:15. I found the Starbucks and bought a coffee and corn muffin for the ride back. There was no traffic and I made good time back to the city. I had to circle around for a while before I found a parking spot near my office. I called Sam as soon as I got in.

"Sam, it's Tracey." I told him about my encounter with Berg and my conversation with Amy.

"Do you think he had anything to do with Laura's disappearance?"

"I don't know; I think the timeline is off. It's been more than a year and a half since she came back from Boston."

"Should we contact Detective Harris?"

I didn't want to be blunt and tell him that Berg should not be on their radar especially without a body or anything to indicate that she was taken.

"Why don't we give it a little more time and stay positive. I need to ask you about something else. Melanie mentioned that you had a disgruntled employee that worked for you."

"What are you getting at?"

"Is it possible he was mad enough to take it out on Laura?"

"That's nuts. People get fired all the time and they don't go around killing people."

"Just tell me what happened."

CHAPTER 12

"I found out that he had been stealing from the company. He was the bookkeeper and had access to accounts. He swore that he wasn't embezzling money but I couldn't trust him anymore."

"How did you find out?"

"My accountant was auditing the books and discovered it."

"Does anyone else have access to the firm's accounts?"

"No, he's the only one."

"Did he threaten you?"

"Well yes, but he was just blowing off steam."

"Did you go to the police?"

"No, I didn't have concrete proof. Since I couldn't trust him anymore, I fired him and let it go at that."

"Okay, I'd like his name and address."

"Is that really necessary?"

"You're paying me to find Laura, let me do my job."

"His name is Peter Franklin. I'll text you his address," he said in an annoyed tone.

"One last thing, are you sure Laura didn't mention any relatives?"

"I don't think so, but I can check Laura's address book if it's still in the house. Now that I think of it she may have, possibly an aunt on her mother's side."

"Great. That would be a big help." Inside I was

boiling. Why didn't he think of this sooner?

We disconnected and my phone beeped. When I answered there was no one on the line. Just then the phone beeped again.

"Who the hell is it?" I yelled into the phone.

"Hey it's me. Are you alright?"

"Sorry Susie. I'm just a little frustrated."

"Why don't we talk about it over dinner. I've got some big news."

"Could you give me a hint?"

"No, you'll just have to be in suspense. I'll see you at Anton's at 7:00."

About an hour later I got a text from Sam with Peter Franklin's address. No news on any relative of Laura.

Mr. Franklin lived all the way downtown in the Village. Instead of taking my car, I hopped on the subway. The train was having a bad day, creeping along the subway tracks and finally limping into the station. Sometimes I wonder which is faster, car or subway. I had to walk several blocks before reaching Franklin's building. I waited until someone opened the lobby door and caught it before it closed shut. I went up to the fifth floor and rang his buzzer. I heard a loud voice from the other side of the door yell, "who is it?"

"Mr. Franklin my name is Tracey Marks and I would like to talk to you about Sam Matthews." I heard the rattling of a chain and the door quickly open. The next thing I know he grabbed my arm and pulled me into his apartment.

"You tell that bastard if he's suing me, he'll regret it. I'll sue him for firing me," yelling at the top of his lungs.

"Mr. Franklin, Mr. Matthews didn't send me, and as far as I know he's not suing you. I'm here because his wife is missing and I'm just trying to get some information."

"So you think I kidnapped her or killed her, are you crazy?" his voice hitting a pitch I didn't even know existed.

"I know you were really mad at Sam. I'd be mad too if he fired me because he thought I was embezzling from his company."

"Of course I'm angry, but I would never hurt someone."

"Well I just heard you threaten Sam; that doesn't sound harmless to me."

"Even if I was mad enough to hurt him, I would never take it out on his wife. She probably has enough problems married to him."

"Why would you say that?"

"He has a bad temper especially when things don't go his way. He's a control freak," he said in a disgusted tone.

I had no idea whether this guy stole from Sam and I didn't care. My instincts told me he didn't do anything to Laura, though I couldn't be certain.

I took the train back to the office and spent the next few hours writing up the conversations I had with Raymond Berg, Amy Brent and Peter Franklin. As I was finishing up I got a text from Sam with the name and telephone number of a Marjorie Litman. He didn't know her relationship to Laura but he said her name sounded familiar.

I called Ms. Litman, though I was hesitant in case she was a relative and had no idea that Laura was missing. "Hello, is this Marjorie Litman?"

"Yes."

"My name is Tracey Marks. Are you by any chance a relative of Laura Matthews?"

"I'm her godmother, is Laura all right?" with worry in her voice.

"As far as I know nothing has happened to her but her husband has reported her missing when she didn't come home a few days ago. He found your name in Laura's address book and thought that Laura had mentioned an Aunt Marjorie but wasn't sure." I didn't want to tell her that it has been more than two weeks since Laura disappeared.

"I'm not a blood relative but I have known Laura since the day she was born. Her mother and I were best friends and Laura calls me Aunt Marjorie."

"Would it be possible for us to meet, it's very important?"

"Of course. When can you come?"

"I can be at your place first thing tomorrow morning. Are you still at the Bridgewater address?"

I told Marjorie Litman I would be there at 9:30 and we hung up. I was excited to finally speak with someone who knew Laura from birth, and hopefully would be able to shed some light on her.

At 4:30 I called it quits for the day and stopped at my place for a quick change and went to the gym. I brought a change of clothes so I could go straight to Anton's to meet Susie. I was certainly curious about her big announcement.

After my workout I arrived at Anton's and was greeted by Olivia, who's the hostess, though I'm not sure if that is her official title. Olivia is the perfect hostess, warm, always courteous even if the customer is being an asshole. She also has these amazing legs that are a mile long. Just a little envious. Since I'm a permanent fixture there, Olivia seated me at a table even though Susie had not arrived yet.

Susie came in five minutes later just as the waiter was bringing me my glass of Sauvignon Blanc. Before Susie even sat down she gave the waiter her drink order, a cosmopolitan.

"Well this must be a special occasion," I said. How long are you going to keep me in suspense?"

"Let's order first."

"What can I get you ladies?" Stephen asked us.

"I'm going to break tradition and instead of the linguini and clams I am going to order the seafood linguini with clams, mussels and shrimp and a beet salad."

"I'll have the trout and the house salad," Susie said. "I'm not as adventurous as my friend here."

Stephen chuckled as he walked away.

"Okay, now will you tell me?"

"You know how I'm always going on and on about why I don't want to move in with Mark, well I've decided to make the leap," she said with a big grin.

"Wow, that's great. I'm so happy for you and Mark. What changed your mind? Last time we talked about it you were pretty adamant against living with him."

"I know, but I thought about what you said and I have to admit it made sense. I'm never going to know if I don't face my fears. I do love Mark and I want it to work, but if it doesn't, it's not the end of the world. At first I was first thinking I would stay with him three nights a week and see how that went, but it's just not the same as being with someone every day."

"I agree. This is the best way to decide if you and

Mark have a future together."

"I know, but I kind of wish we were doing this together, you know the saying, misery loves company."

"I think I'll let you have this one all to yourself. You can be the test case for both of us. So when are you two love birds moving in together, and who's moving in to whose place?"

"We thought since Mark's place is bigger I would move into his, but for now I'll keep my place. This weekend I'll start packing up stuff. If you're around I can use a helping hand. By the way, Mark has someone he wants you to meet. We can do something casual the four of us so it won't even feel like a date."

"Nice try. Right now I'm too distracted with the case." I'm not sure why I didn't mention Danny. Maybe I thought it would fizzle out just like the others, and all the questions I would be subjected to from Susie gave me pause.

"I want to say something but I don't want you to get mad when I give you my two cents."

"Okay shoot," I said.

"I worry about all the excuses you make for not wanting to get involved in a relationship. I know it's hard to trust, but not everyone is going to leave you like your dad and mom. It's not your fault they died."

"I don't want you to worry about me. I'm fine."

"I won't bring it up again. So what's going on with the case?"

I caught Susie up to date with my trip to Boston and I told her about Marjorie Litman. "I'm really looking forward to finally talking with someone who knew Laura since she was born, though I felt bad about telling her Laura was missing. She seemed upset."

"I hope Laura is still alive. It would be horrible if something happened to her," Susie said.

"It's been more than two weeks, but I'm still trying to be positive."

We each had tiramisu for dessert and called it a night.

CHAPTER 13

"The next morning I drove up to Bridgewater, Connecticut to meet Ms. Litman. I allowed plenty of time since the traffic going into Connecticut in the morning could be a bitch. I arrived a few minutes before 9:30.

Marjorie Litman lived on a beautiful tree lined street with large Tudor style homes. I parked and walked up a long path that led to her front door. Ms. Litman must have seen me coming since she opened the door before I had a chance to knock.

I was greeted by a slender, attractive woman, probably in her early sixties but could easily pass for fifty. She wore her silver blonde hair short, which suited her face and was wearing a pair of beige linen slacks, a white cashmere sweater and black flats.

"Come in," she said quickly. "I've been beside myself ever since you called."

"I'm sorry I upset you."

Her house had the wonderful smell of freshly baked bread.

She escorted me into a sitting room that was furnished with white wicker furniture. The cushions were a floral print. A beautiful beige needlepoint rug with a blue colored border covered the floor. I took a seat in one of the chairs and Marjorie sat opposite me on the wicker couch. The sun was pouring into the room.

"Can I offer you some coffee? I just made Banana Nut Bread."

"Thank you. It smells too good to pass up."

Ms. Litman came back with two coffees and two slices of bread. I noticed a slight tremor in her hands.

"As I mentioned, Laura's husband Sam Matthews hired me to find her when she didn't come home. Though he filed a missing person's report, I don't think the police are seriously looking for her. At this point they probably assume she left on her own which is very possible, it's just that we don't know for sure. What can you tell me about Laura?"

"This is very upsetting," her voice cracking. "I will try to help in any way I can. Laura and I haven't spoken in a while. When she told me that she and Sam were getting married at the courthouse, I offered to be a witness but Laura said they weren't having anything after the ceremony so she didn't want me to bother. Of course I was hurt. Though I'm not a blood relative I helped raise her."

"What was she like growing up?"

"I have to say she was not an easy child, always trying to push the limits. As a teenager she ran around a lot, if you know what I mean. Laura is very pretty and I can see how the boys would go after her. Her father was not around much and it was up to Laura's mother, Justine, to do most of the parenting. Justine had her own issues and there were times when she would leave Laura with me and my husband."

"What kind of issues did her mother have?"

"She had been in and out of therapy for a good part of her life. Laura's mother was distant and though she never came out and said it I believe her husband was an alcoholic. I suspected that he was abusive but we never broached the subject."

"Was Laura close to her mother?"

"She wanted to be, but Justine had a hard time showing affection to Laura. I felt bad for both of them."

"That must have been hard on Laura. How did her parents die?"

"They died tragically in a car accident. Laura's father, Tom, had been drinking. That's what the autopsy showed. It was snowing and they were driving home from a party when their car skidded off an embankment. The police said they both died instantly. Though Laura and her parents had their problems she took their deaths very hard. She had no relatives since both her parents were only children and her grandparents died a long time ago. I thought when she went to Boston for the job offer she was finally settling down and getting a fresh start. I was happy for her. And then when things didn't work out, I started worrying again."

"How did you feel about her marriage to Sam Matthews?"

"Laura called me out of the blue. We hadn't spoken in a while and she told me she was getting married. I was concerned since she had only been back from Boston for about a year and it seemed kind of fast. I asked her if she could come by the house with Sam so I could meet him but they never did. I tried reaching out to her several times but it seemed like she was avoiding me. I was hoping it was because she was busy with a new job and getting married, but I think there was something else going on."

"How did she seem when you did speak with her?"

"I felt like she was keeping things from me, but I

can't be sure. We were always close and when she had any problems she would come to me. Now I rarely hear from her."

"Can you think of anyone else she was close to besides her friend Melanie?"

"I really can't think of anyone."

"What about boyfriends?"

"Laura was popular but didn't keep boyfriends very long. There was one young man who she knew from high school. I think they dated for a while but I believe Laura ended it. I believe his name was, let me think a second."

"Seth Green?" I said.

"Why yes, how did you know?"

"Apparently Laura and Seth have remained friends and they talk every so often."

"Well that's odd."

"What do you mean?"

"If I remember correctly, Laura didn't want to have anything to do with him after they broke up. I believe she thought he was too possessive. Well maybe she changed her mind. She called me up once after she was married and we met in the city. I could tell something wasn't right but I couldn't get her to open up. I thought she looked sad but maybe I was misreading the situation. She may have felt bad that we weren't as close anymore."

"Did she say anything about her husband?"

"I asked her how everything was but she just said fine and changed the subject."

"Can you think of anyone or any place she may have gone?"

"When Laura's parents died she sold their Connecticut home but they also had a cottage in the

Berkshires that Laura decided to keep. Do you think Laura could be there?" sounding optimistic.

"I don't know but I'll look into it. Do you know if her husband knew about the cottage?"

"I can't say for sure but that house has been in the family since Laura was a young girl, so it wouldn't surprise me if many people knew. Why would she keep it a secret?"

"Marjorie, thank you for talking with me and I will do everything I can to find Laura."

As I was walking out I noticed a photo on a side table. I picked it up.

"That's a photo of me, Laura and her mother. We all looked happy there," with a sadness in her voice. "Please keep in touch. I can't stop thinking about her. She's like the daughter I never had, and since her parents died, I feel more responsible for her."

Before I left Marjorie Litman gave me the address for the cottage. It was obvious from everyone I spoke with that Laura did not appear to be happy and had secrets she did not want to share.

It was after one o'clock when I got back. I found a spot for my Volkswagen about five blocks from my office. Having a small car in the city gets me into parking spots other cars can't fit into. I stopped at the deli near the office and picked up a tuna fish sandwich for lunch.

I wrote up a preliminary report to Sam which included all my interviews to date, leaving out the information about the place in the Berkshires. If Laura was afraid of Sam and was hiding out because of him, I didn't want Sam to know. It took me about two hours to finish. I e-mailed the report to him along with my invoice for the hours I had expended so far.

I called Melanie and she answered right away.

"Any news on Laura?" as if she had been waiting by the phone.

"Not yet, but I did speak with Marjorie Litman, Laura's godmother. She mentioned that Laura's parents had a cottage in the Berkshires that she kept. Did you know about it?"

"I did, but completely forgot about it. I wonder if she could have gone there."

"Maybe by tomorrow, we'll know the answer."

When I got to my car I noticed a deep scratch on the passenger side. I've gotten nicks and dings, the cost of having a car in the city but this looked deliberate. I guess it could be a random act but I wasn't convinced.

I was glad to finally be home. Between going to Boston and being on the go since I got back I just wanted to take a long shower and get into bed.

While I was making an omelet for dinner, I flipped on the small TV I had in the kitchen and watched the news.

My phone buzzed. "Hey Danny."

"Hi, how are you?"

"Well besides the jerk that keyed my car, I'm doing pretty good."

"Ouch, your day sounds worse than mine. Maybe if I came over, I could console you."

"Well isn't that gentlemanly of you. It's good to know chivalry is not dead."

"That's what I like about you Tracey. You have a way of blowing me off yet making me smile at the same time. Quite an art. But seriously, what is going on?"

"I don't know. I'm not sure if the stuff that's been

happening is just a coincidence or something to do with the case. Nothing I can't handle so far."

"I just want you to know I'm here if you need anything, though I know you can take care of yourself."

"So what happened with you today?"

"I think it was a conspiracy. Everyone was giving me a hard time. The client I saw was not happy with the computer system I set up for him even though it was exactly what he told me he wanted. Another client said I promised him his system would be ready today. That was not my understanding. Very frustrating. So how about I pick you up Friday at 7:00?"

No guy has picked me up for a date in forever. It felt weird but I decided not to make a big deal about it. "Okay, see you then."

I slept fitfully, waking up every two hours. My mind kept playing over and over again the events of the last couple of days. By 4:30 I gave up any hope of getting back to sleep and changed into my running clothes. As soon as I exited my building the cold air hit me. Fall had finally arrived. Once I started running, I felt better. There was something exhilarating about running early in the morning when it is still dark out and the streets are empty.

When I picked up my car, it pained me to see the gash in it. I stopped at Starbucks for a large coffee for the drive up. Though the Thruway is a little bit shorter I took the Taconic State Parkway. It's a beautiful scenic road lush with trees and mountains ruined only by the gray skies. I made it up to the area around by10:30. The cottage was situated on a beautiful lake with no other houses nearby. I almost missed the turnoff. This was a perfect place to hide out and I was hoping that's where I would find Laura.

The first thing I noticed as I drove up the graveled driveway to the house was the beautiful white birch trees. I parked and walked up to the house with anticipation. I was about to knock when I realized the door was open. I walked into the house cautiously. I could hear the sound of my heart beating faster. I called out Laura's name with no response. I walked quietly into the kitchen and looked around. It appeared it had been remodeled at some point. The cabinets were white with stainless steel appliances. The backsplash had white tiles with different flower designs in each one. It was tastefully done. I opened up the refrigerator. The freezer had a can of coffee and frozen English muffins. There were no perishables. It looked like Laura hadn't been here for a while unless she brought food in.

I heard a doorknob turn and a voice yell "Who the hell are you?"

CHAPTER 14

I practically jumped out of my skin. "Wow you scared me." I was looking into the glaring face of a six foot tall man about 35 to 40 with dark brown hair, and piercing blue eyes. He was wearing work boots that were covered in mud and making a mess on the white wood floor.

"My name is Tracey Marks. The door was open. I didn't know anyone was here."

"That doesn't tell me why you're in Laura's kitchen," he said in a belligerent tone.

"I was told that Laura Matthews is the owner of this cottage. I'm a friend of her husband, Sam Matthews. And who are you?" trying to sound friendly, not wanting to get into any major confrontation with this guy.

"I have no intention of telling you who I am until I know what you're doing here."

I didn't want to tell him the truth. "Laura was supposed to come up for a few days. Her husband is out of town and has been trying to reach her but she hasn't been returning any of his calls and he's worried."

He was kind of creeping me out. The thought crossed my mind that I was all alone with this guy and there was nobody around for miles if I screamed. I was trying to appear calm on the outside but my heart was going a mile a minute. I didn't want my fear to show. I hoped it was working.

"As far as I know, she's not around," he said with a little less hostility in his voice.

"How do you know Laura?" hoping not to antagonize this guy.

"I look after the place for her and before that for her parents when they were alive."

"Do you remember the last time you saw or spoke to her?"

"Probably about a month ago when I stopped by to make sure everything was okay and she was here. I haven't seen her since."

"Was she by herself?"

"Well, I can't say since she didn't invite me in for a chat or a cup of coffee," with a flicker of a sneer across his lips.

"Do you happen to know if her husband has ever been here?"

"How would I know who she brings up here, I'm not her keeper."

This guy was being a real jerk. I didn't know how explosive he might be if I provoked him but I needed to ask the next question, "What was your relationship with Laura?"

"My relationship is none of your business," and he turned around and went out the way he came in slamming the door shut.

I was glad to see him go. Looking out the kitchen door I saw him walking down to the dock, where a pickup truck was parked. It looked like he was in the process of taking the dock down for the winter. I wrote down his license plate number.

I walked into the living room which was small but had an airy feeling to it. There was a rose colored couch with a bench opposite it with two needlepoint pillows. I walked over to the fireplace and picked up one of the photos that were sitting on the fireplace mantel. I was staring at a teenage Laura with her parents. Laura looked like her mother; both had blond hair and fair complexions. Her mother's eyes were beautiful, but they had a sadness to them. She was looking straight ahead with no expression on her face. Her father was distinguished looking. He was wearing wire rimmed glasses. I couldn't tell from the photo but I imagined he was thin and tall. Laura was smiling. There was a photo of an elderly couple that could have been Laura's grandparents.

The upstairs had two bedrooms. I started rummaging through the nightstand in one of the rooms. Nothing of significance. A box of tissues and an old People magazine. From all appearances it didn't look like Laura was here recently. The closets had a few items of clothing, an old pair of khaki slacks, a blue button down cotton shirt and a black sweater. There was also a pair of women's sneakers on the floor. The bathroom had some toiletries, a jar of Nivea cream, Tylenol and a comb but nothing that suggested she came often or that a man had been here recently.

I went back downstairs and walked into the living room where I spotted a desk in the far right hand corner. Looking through it there was nothing that caught my eye. One of the drawers was locked. I didn't know if I should try and force it open but my curiosity got the better of me. I tugged hard but it wouldn't budge. I began touching the sides and the back of the desk just like they do in the movies for a possible key. I stuck my hands underneath feeling all around and to my surprise there was a key taped to the bottom of the desk. Inside the drawer was a bank book that had $155,400 in Laura's maiden name. The bank was local, The Berkshire Bank. Her passport was also here. I took photos and placed them back in the drawer and taped the key back where I found it.

If Laura was afraid of someone and was planning to leave why were the documents still here and not in her possession unless she didn't have a chance to get them?

I looked around some more but didn't notice anything that would lead me to believe there was some sort of struggle.

I closed the front door and made sure it was locked. I saw the pickup truck leave and heaved a sigh of relief. I walked around to the back of the house and followed the path leading down to the lake. The dock was gone but lying on the grass unchained was a rowboat that anyone could access. I went over to look at it closer but nothing unusual caught my eye.

On the way back I called Susie and explained what was going on. She thought I shouldn't mention the bank account or the passport to Sam in case he was somehow involved. I agreed.

While driving home my thoughts drifted back to when I was a young girl. Both my parents were teachers and every summer we rented a small house on a lake in North Carolina. The people who owned the house left a canoe and a rowboat for us to use. I loved the summers there. My father and I would spend time together swimming or taking one of the boats out on the lake. He taught me how to put bait on a rod and fish. I remember a time we were fishing and I felt this tug on my line. I was so excited thinking

I caught a fish I stood up, lost my balance and landed in the water. My father couldn't stop laughing.

The blasting of a horn jolted me back to the present. Sam hadn't mentioned the cottage to me, which I thought was strange. I wonder if he intentionally didn't tell me but I was going to find out.

The next call was to Marjorie Litman since I wanted to know about the alleged caretaker.

"Tracey, I'm so glad to hear from you. I haven't been able to sleep well since we last spoke. Did you find Laura at the house?"

"No, she wasn't there but I did run into a guy who says he takes care of the place when Laura's not there."

"Oh yes, Ben Cutler. A pleasant enough fellow. I believe he's a contractor. Whenever the house needed repairs, Justine hired him. When Tom and Justine died, Laura asked him to come by every so often to make sure everything was alright."

"Do you know how often Laura went up there?"

"You have to know something. Laura loved her parents but it was difficult for her to be around them. When she was younger they went up as a family but as Laura got older, she rarely went to the cottage."

"You had mentioned in our previous conversation that you had your suspicions that Laura's father may have been abusive. Do you think he could have been abusive towards Laura."

"I don't think he would ever do anything to harm Laura. He may have been many things but he loved that girl and would never hurt her."

"Did you ever see him hit Laura when he was drunk?"

"Never."

"Did Laura know Ben?"

"Of course. When they bought the cottage her parents became friendly with Ben's parents. Ben would sometimes be at the house when I was visiting. It's just my intuition but I thought he might have been infatuated with Laura."

"Do you think Laura felt the same way?"

"I'm not sure but I don't think they ever dated, at least not that I'm aware of."

"Thank you and I'll be in touch." The more I'm finding out about Laura the more complicated it seems to get.

When I got back I called Sam and told him I needed to stop by his office to speak with him.

His office was on the first floor of a brownstone on 38th Street and Park Avenue. Getting a parking spot was a challenge, and I finally gave up and parked in a garage.

As I walked into Sam's office he was leaning over a very attractive young woman probably in her early thirties with dark curly brown shoulder length hair and they were laughing. I just watched them for a moment before I cleared my throat to announce my arrival.

CHAPTER 15

"Tracey, hi," Sam said in a surprised voice. "Tracey this is Nicole, my receptionist. Let's go into my office."

"How long has Nicole worked for you?" I asked when he closed the door to his office.

"About a year. So what have you found out?" seeming to change the subject quickly.

"Did you know Laura had a cottage in Massachusetts?"

"Yes, I did."

"And you didn't think it was worth mentioning?" annoyed at his attitude.

"I'm sorry but I forgot about it since Laura never went up there."

"Are you telling me that since you have known Laura, neither you nor Laura have been to the house?"

"Yes, that's what I'm saying. Why are you asking me about this? Is Laura there? Did you find her?"

"Laura's godmother told me about the place so I went to check it out. No, she wasn't there, but I was told by someone who looks after the property that Laura was there about a month ago."

"I didn't know she went up there. I'm surprised she didn't tell me, though I may have been out of town on business so she could have forgotten to mention it"

I wasn't sure if I believed him or not.

"Did you know that someone looked after the house?"

"I believe Laura may have said something in passing, but I have no idea who it was."

"Is there anything else you may have forgotten to tell me?"

"No, believe me."

"Have you heard anything further from Detective Harris?" I asked.

"No. The last time I spoke with him he said they're looking into it, but I have my doubts that they're looking very hard."

"Sam I want to be honest with you. Do you think Laura may have left you?"

"No. Just like I told the police, I don't believe she did. I know something must have happened to her."

On my way out, I waved to Nicole. She gave me a quick wave back. I wondered if anything was going on between Sam and his receptionist.

I finally had a chance to check my messages. I had one missed call from Susie.

My cell phone buzzed. It was Seth Green.

"Ms. Marks I was calling to find out if you heard from Laura."

"Seth, I'm glad you called. I'd like to stop by your office tomorrow. I have a few questions I'd like to ask you."

"I'd be happy to answer your questions but the next day or so is very busy, can't it wait?"

"I'd prefer if it didn't. I would really appreciate it if you could squeeze me in. I promise it won't take long."

Reluctantly he agreed to meet me first thing in the

morning. I would have preferred to question him over the phone so I wouldn't have to drive up to Connecticut, but I was troubled by the fact that Ms. Litman thought Laura had severed ties with Seth Green, and I wanted to see his reaction in person.

After I hung up I returned Susie's call. "Hi, what's up?"

"I just wanted to see if you're still available for packing duty over the weekend."

"Sure. How about Sunday? I figure it's the least I can do since you're making a big move and it seems like I'm partially to blame."

I made it to Seth Green's office the following day with ten minutes to spare. I rode the elevator up to the fifth floor and was greeted by the receptionist. She told me that Mr. Green had an emergency and wouldn't be in until 11:00. Could I come back then or reschedule? I was pissed. I wondered whether he really had an emergency. I told her I would be back at 11:00.

I found a nearby coffee shop and had some breakfast since I only had coffee before I left.

When I returned to Seth's office he came out to the waiting room and we went back to his office.

"I hope I didn't inconvenience you too much but it was unavoidable."

I didn't say anything.

"So what was so urgent that you needed to see me right away?"

"Do you know who Ms. Litman is?"

"Her name does sound vaguely familiar. Are you going to keep me in suspense?"

"It's Laura's godmother."

"Yes, now I remember. I had forgotten her name since it's been years since I last saw her. Laura is very fond of her."

"I spoke with her and she has a different recollection of you and Laura. She said that Laura broke up with you and didn't want to see you again." I waited for his response.

"I'm not sure why she would say that. It's just not true," protesting just a little too much.

"Why would Ms. Litman lie?"

"I have no idea. Maybe Laura told her what she wanted to hear because Laura knew she didn't like me."

"Ms. Litman never said she didn't like you. Why would you think that?"

"I just got that vibe from her, nothing Laura said. What are you insinuating?" raising his voice.

"I'm just trying to find out what happened to Laura. You knew her since high school; maybe there's something you're not telling me."

"I promise you I'm not hiding anything. I want Laura found just as much as you do, probably more. Are we through now?"

"Just one more question. Did you know about the cottage?"

"Of course, it wasn't a secret. When Laura and I were dating we would sometimes go up there, though it was infrequent. Anything else?"

"Yes, the last time we spoke you mentioned that your wife didn't know about Laura. I was curious if you're sure?"

"Yes, I am. Now I really need to get back to work."

I showed myself out. I had my doubts whether he

was telling the truth. I guess it was possible Laura told her godmother what she wanted to hear, but the picture I'm getting of Laura doesn't fit with his explanation.

It was after 3:00 by the time I got back to the city. Traffic on I95 was torture and I had to circle the area near my office for fifteen minutes before I found a parking spot.

When I got in I typed up my conversation with Seth and then conducted a database search on Ben Cutler. I inputted his name and the Town of Stockbridge and came up with one possibility. I clicked for the report. In combing through it, a Benjamin Arthur Cutler, age thirty-seven was listed. I found a current address which showed that he and a Stephanie Cutler were the owners. It listed Stephanie's age as thirty five. This was probably his wife. There were two cars registered to him, a Ford pickup truck, the one I had seen which makes sense since he's a contractor and a 2015 Silver BMW. The name of his company was listed as BAC Contracting, his initials. Ben is registered as an independent with voter registration. There were no criminal records listed but there was one DWI under his driver's license record. According to the report he had one civil action brought against him and his company. Doesn't surprise me since contractors get sued all the time. I was surprised he didn't have more. The only noteworthy piece of information was a matrimonial action that was filed in 2011 by a Bonnie Cutler.

I wonder if anything was going on between him and Laura. He did get nasty when I asked about their relationship. I was interested in finding out more about Ben but he wasn't about to help me out. The more I delved, the more interesting things were getting. The big question still looming was whether Laura was hiding from someone or was she dead?

On the way home I picked up salad stuff for dinner. Autumn had officially arrived. I love this time of year, right before the crisp air turns bitter cold and you have to bundle up to keep warm. Wally greeted me with a big smile.

"Hi Miss Tracey. How are you today?"

"Always better when I see you. Any gossip you can share with me?" It was kind of a standard joke between us. Wally was as straight as they come. Even if he knew that Mrs. Miller in 4K was having an affair with Mr. Lucas in 7J his lips were sealed. I loved that about him, but it didn't make for any juicy gossip.

"Are you trying to get me in trouble now?" he said with a mischievous smile. "I almost forgot there was an envelope left for you at the front desk."

"Thanks Wally. Have a nice evening."

On the way to the elevator, I picked up the manila envelope. No return address. I tried to keep my anxiety level to a minimum. As soon as I got into my apartment I opened it carefully. Out came photos of Laura seated with a man at a restaurant. I kept staring at the photos to see if I recognized the person but he didn't look familiar. I put down my packages and changed into my sweats. Studying the photos I couldn't detect where the place was. It was hard to tell if they were having lunch or dinner. It turned the photos over and they were date stamped four weeks ago.

I dialed Sam. "It's Tracey. I'm going to send you a photo and I want you to tell me if the person with your wife looks familiar. I'm sending it now."

"Hold on a second and I'll let you know."

I had been hesitant sending it to him, but I needed to know.

"No, I've never seen this person. Where did you get it?"

"It was mailed to my home address anonymously."

"Does this mean she was having an affair?"

"I don't know what it means if anything. Sam, are you sure everything was fine between the two of you?"

"I thought so. Now I don't know what to think."

I decided to check with her friend Melanie.

"Melanie, it's Tracey Marks. When you have a chance can you please call me back. I'm sending you a photo and want to know if this guy looks familiar. Thanks."

I finally had a chance to prepare dinner and watch one of my favorite TV series, Homeland. Since I missed the episode from last week, I watched it on demand. I love Claire Danes who plays the lead in the series. It's always tense and violent. Right up my alley. About an hour later Melanie called.

"Tracey, I do know him. His name is Peter. I believe they dated for a while a few years ago. I'm not sure how long it lasted. With Laura it was never a problem getting guys, men were attracted to her but they never seemed to last that long."

"Why do you think that was?"

"She had a lot of family issues which may have affected her. And the deaths of her parents probably added to her problems."

"Where did Peter and Laura first meet?"

"I'm not sure. We used to go clubbing together so I think she met him at one of the places we went to, though I can't say for sure."

"Do you remember his last name?"

"It was a long time ago."

"Please try to think. It may be important."

"I remember he had the same last name as a famous golfer. Let me google it and see what I come up with."

As I was brushing my teeth, the phone buzzed. I grabbed it on the first ring.

"I figured it out. It's Mickelson, Peter Mickelson. It's a good thing I play golf otherwise I would be at a loss."

"Great, do you know if he lives in Connecticut or New York?"

"I believe Connecticut. What do you think this means?"

CHAPTER 16

I wasn't sure but I was going to find out. This was the first concrete break I had and I was excited. Sleeping was proving difficult since my mind was racing faster than Superman's. I must have fallen asleep at some point. The next time I looked at the clock, it was 5:00 a.m. I turned on the TV since sometimes that helps me go back to sleep, but no such luck. Since sleep was going to be impossible, I reached for my laptop. I thought I would try to find out where Peter Mickelson lived. With a pretty uncommon name it shouldn't be too difficult. I found an address for him in Greenwich, Connecticut. I thought of showing up at his house unannounced but in case he was married I wanted to be discreet. No point in getting him in hot water if it was just an innocent meeting with Laura. Unfortunately there was no telephone listing. Most people between eighteen and forty don't have landlines anymore. It just makes my job a little harder since I have to go through other avenues to find their cell phone number. I didn't want to ask Joe for another favor since he would probably want more than a dinner commitment so I had to resort to paying for the information through a company that specializes in this sort of thing. I e-mailed them with Peter's name and address. I should have the cell number by the end of the day.

Everywhere I turned, men were showing up in

Laura's life. The more I investigated, the more intriguing I found it. I thought for now I would hold off telling Sam about Peter Mickelson until I knew more about his connection to Laura. Since there wasn't much I could do until I got his cell number, I decided I would work from home. I went to the gym and on the way back I treated myself to breakfast at this cute French café in my neighborhood that made the most delicious ricotta pancakes. When I got home I lied down and turned on the news. The next thing I knew it was 3:00.

For my date with Danny, I wore a pair of black tweed pants with a gray cashmere pullover sweater. Instead of black flats, I wore my only pair of black high heels.

Toby, my night doorman, rang to tell me Danny was downstairs. I told him I would be right down. I grabbed a jacket on my way out.

"Hey," Danny said. "You look great."

"Thanks, so where are we headed?"

"It depends. I think you said Italian was your favorite."

"Well, at least I know you're paying attention." I was glad he didn't ask why I hadn't invited him up.

"That's good since we're going to the West Village to a little place I know that has great Italian food."

We took the subway since it was a lot faster than a taxi. When we arrived at the restaurant, I was surprised how small it was. I think there were twelve tables in the whole place but there was enough space between tables that you didn't feel crowded or that the other people around you could overhear your conversation.

"How do they make any money with so few

tables?" I asked.

"They're always booked. It's impossible to get a table unless you make a reservation two months in advance."

"How did you get so lucky?"

"I kind of know the owner. He's a very good client of mine, and they had a cancellation."

"I guess it does pay to know people in high places."

We were shown to a corner table and the waiter handed us a wine list. We settled on a bottle of red wine from the northern region of Italy.

The chef came over to the table and Danny introduced me to his friend Marco.

"Hi Tracey. Danny mentioned that he was bringing someone really special. I'm honored."

"Likewise," I said.

"I hope you're open to trying one of my specialty dishes."

"Well I usually stick to what I know, but for tonight I'll broaden my palate."

After hearing the specials, we ordered. We started with a grilled artichoke and then we each had a small salad. I ordered Risotto with all kinds of fishes, and Danny had squid pasta with mussels, clams and shrimp. It was delicious.

While we were eating I told Danny about the case. He was completely absorbed and waited until I finished to ask me any questions.

"Not knowing if she is alive is making it more difficult."

"Do you want my thoughts on this?" Danny asked.

"Yes, by all means."

"If she left, how did she leave? Did she fly or did

she take her car? If she flew there must be a record and her car might still be in a lot at an airport. If she drove she had to have left a trail."

"Okay, I can check out airports but if she drove the police are more equipped to follow the trail, and as far as I know they are not taking her disappearance seriously."

"I'm no expert on marriages but I think there would have to be some compelling reason to just leave. When I was growing up there was a family who lived across the street from us. I kind of had a crush on their daughter Mindy. I was ten and I believe she was around thirteen. I was into older women at that time. Anyway, it turns out that Mindy's mother, Mrs. Larkin went missing. At first the police thought she left her husband but why would she leave her daughter. There were rumors that her husband hit her. The more they investigated Mr. Larkin, they began to suspect him. It turns out he was having an affair. They kept bringing him in for questioning and they uncovered some physical evidence. Under the pressure, he confessed."

"What happened to Mindy?"

"She went to live with her mother's brother in upstate New York somewhere. I was crushed."

"Did you ever get over her?" I asked with a straight face.

"Not until you came along," he replied, grinning.

"I'm beginning to think that something awful happened to Laura," I said.

"You may be right."

We left the restaurant but not before having cannoli for dessert.

When we got outside Danny asked me if I liked

jazz music. He took me to the Blue Note, which was near the restaurant. Between the music and all the wine, I was completely relaxed.

While we taxied back to my apartment, I was grappling with whether I wanted Danny to come up. I knew if he did, I would sleep with him. I really wanted to, but I was afraid it would escalate things too quickly.

As we were approaching my block I told Danny how I felt and hoped he would understand.

"I can't say I'm not disappointed but I want you to feel comfortable."

We kissed. It was a great kiss. My whole body was on fire. The cab stopped and Danny walked me to the front door.

"Hi Toby. Just dropping this lovely lady off. I'll call you tomorrow," he winked at me.

I liked Danny and it scared me. I heard Susie's words in my head. I'm not quite sure it's that easy but I wanted to give Danny a chance.

I put those thoughts out of my mind while I was getting ready for bed. I was drifting off when my cell phone buzzed. Before looking to see who it was I answered. "If you keep looking for Laura there will be grave consequences," and then the line went dead.

CHAPTER 17

My heart was in a full gallop. I needed to reach Detective Harris and let him know about the call. I knew it was late but I was hoping he might be on duty. I began frantically looking for his number which I finally found at the bottom of my backpack.

"Detective Harris, please."

"He's not in right now. Can I help you?"

"No. It's important that he contact me. It's about Laura Matthews." I left my number and asked that he call me as soon as he got in. I didn't think I would be able to sleep but the buzzing of my phone jarred me awake. I glanced at the clock. It was 5:30.

"This is Detective Harris, how can I help you?"

"Detective Harris, I spoke to you a few days ago about Laura Matthews. As I had mentioned to you, her husband has asked me to look into her disappearance. Well I thought you should know I received a threatening call a few hours ago warning me to stop looking for Laura. I had also received a threatening note about a week ago with basically the same message."

"You did the right thing by reporting the incident. Did you happen to record the person?"

"No, but from now on, I will. Have you looked into her disappearance at all?" I said sounding exasperated.

"As I told you before I am not at liberty to provide

that information to you, and it would be a good idea to heed the warning you received."

"I just hope it's not too late when you do finally look for her."

I was furious when I hung up. How dare he tell me what to do. Maybe a body does have to show up before Harris does something about it.

When I looked at my phone I had an email from late yesterday afternoon with the telephone number of Peter Mickelson. I was debating whether to contact him today but thought it would be wiser to wait until Monday when he was at work and not home.

Just as I was about to shower my cell phone buzzed. "Hi Susie."

"What's the matter? I can tell by the sound of your voice something's wrong."

"I got a threatening telephone call telling me to stop looking for Laura or else."

"You need to call the police."

"I did. I was told there was nothing they can do about it."

"Did you recognize the voice?"

"No, I think the person was using something that distorted their voice."

"Do you want to quit the case?"

"Absolutely not. I think if they were really serious they would do more than make crank phone calls."

"You may be right but please be very, very careful."

"I will. Are we still on for tomorrow?" I asked.

"I guess so, just some doubts creeping in. Am I doing the right thing or should I call it off before it's too late?"

"You're thinking too much. Everything will be

fine. If you back out now, I'll steal Mark away from you," I said in a playful tone.

"I know you're right; I guess I needed to hear it again, and again and again."

"I'll see you at 11:00 tomorrow." I was determined not to let the threat ruin my day.

On my way to Susie's on Sunday I stopped at Balducci's for bagels and lox. I also picked up a gorgeous looking tomato and cream cheese.

"Oh, you come bearing food, I love you," she said, hugging me. "I'll put the coffee on."

As we sat and ate, I filled her in on the latest developments.

"This is getting really intense. It's like an episode of Law and Order."

I laughed. "Yes, except for the fact that they solve the crime in an hour."

"Just a small technicality. If you need a sidekick, I'll be glad to help out."

"I will keep that in mind."

We packed until five when I called it quits and went home.

"My phone buzzed as I was walking into my apartment."

"Hi Tracey, it's Danny. How are you?"

"Exhausted. I was at Susie's helping her pack." I still hadn't told Susie about Danny. "How was the rest of your weekend?"

"I had an emergency at a client's office. Their system crashed so I had to go in yesterday and get it up and running again. It basically took all day. Today I spent playing catch up with laundry and cleaning."

"I didn't know men did that stuff," I said

teasingly."

"I had a good teacher. My mother was a real stickler when it came to me and my brother doing chores. The only thing I wasn't allowed to do was iron. I think she was afraid I would either burn the clothes or the house would go up in flames."

"Well my mother was just the opposite. She was a neat freak and she wouldn't think of having me do anything for fear I would make a bigger mess. The truth is she thought she was the only one who was capable of doing it right. That was fine by me."

"So are you trying to tell me I'm dating a slob?"

I smiled. "I have to confess I am more like my mother than I want to admit. I'm not as fastidious but I do like it when my apartment is clean."

"Good to know since it may have been a deal breaker."

I could picture him grinning. "I saw this ad for a Roomba vacuum that goes by itself. You don't have to push it around," I said.

"What would be the fun in that. Talking about fun, I have two tickets for Jersey Boys for Wednesday night and would love your company." Have you seen it yet?"

"Are you kidding, I rarely see a play. I'm in."

"Why don't we meet at the Italian restaurant, Lattanzi, at 6:00? I'll text you the address."

Monday morning I took a three mile run getting geared up for my call to Peter Mickelson. Instead of going into the office I waited at home in case I needed my car.

"Mr. Mickelson my name is Tracey Marks and I am looking into the disappearance of Laura

Matthews."

"Who?"

"Laura Matthews, though you might know her as Laura Tyler."

"Yes, of course I know her. What do you mean? What has happened?"

"Can we please meet as soon as possible?"

"Yes, of course. I'll meet you at 10:00 at the coffee shop across the street from where I work."

He gave me the name and address of the coffee shop and I made a beeline to my car. The traffic was pretty light since it was going in the other direction. I made it with two minutes to spare. Peter was already sitting at a booth. Peter was a Matthew McConaughey look alike. Bluntly said, simply gorgeous. I slid in and the waitress came over. I ordered coffee and an egg sandwich since Peter had ordered breakfast.

"Thanks for meeting me. I really appreciate it."

"Sure, what's going on?"

"What I can tell you is that Laura has been missing for almost three weeks. Her husband hired me to find out what happened to her."

"Do the police know?"

"Yes, but I'm not sure they're taking it seriously. There is no evidence of foul play. How do you know Laura?"

"Laura and I dated for a while about three years ago."

"How did you two meet?"

"We met at a bar in the city."

"Why did you break up?"

"I hate to admit this but Laura broke up with me. I don't think it was because of anything I did. I think she liked playing the field and I was sorry we parted ways."

"What can you tell me about her?"

"Laura was trying to find her way. Her parents' death haunted her. From some of my conversations with Laura I got the impression her father was an alcoholic. Her mother was another story. She didn't get along with Laura but I'm not sure why. I think Laura was always trying to get their attention and when they died, she was lost."

"I am impressed by your analysis of Laura."

"Don't be. You just have to be around her for a while and you would come to the same conclusion."

"I'm trying to sort out if Laura left on her own or something happened to her. Did you talk to her or see her recently?"

"No, I haven't seen Laura since she went to Boston, which was over two years ago," he said, avoiding eye contact.

My hand kept fingering the photos that were in my pocket. I took a sip of coffee not sure what to do since I knew he was lying.

The waitress came over with our food. After she left I took out the photos and placed them on the table facing him.

"Where the hell did you get these?"

"First tell me why you lied to me?"

"Okay. Laura called me out of the blue. She said she needed to talk. The reason I didn't mention it was because she had told me not to tell anyone."

"Were you having an affair with her?"

"No, nothing like that," shaking his head. "We met a few times and just talked."

"About what?"

"Different things. For one, Laura was struggling in

her marriage. From what she said I got the feeling she married Sam because she thought it was time to settle down, not because she loved him, but then she had misgivings. I believe Laura wanted it to work but just wasn't happy."

"What else did she say?"

"She liked her job but it wasn't what she really wanted to do. Laura was thinking about going back to school for fashion design. The truth is there wasn't much I could do except listen."

"Are you sure you weren't looking to swoop in and be her savior."

"The thought crossed my mind more than once, but Laura didn't need any more complications in her life."

"How admirable of you."

"Now answer my question, where did you get those photos?"

"Someone sent them to my home anonymously."

"So that means someone has been following Laura. Maybe that person has something to do with her disappearance."

I ignored his comment. "Did Laura say anything to you about being in danger or that she was afraid of anyone?"

"No, though she did tell me about that creep who was her boss at her last job. I don't think she was worried about him being a threat since she was here and he was up in Boston."

For all I know I could be sitting opposite the guy who had something to do with Laura's disappearance.

"When was the last time you saw her?"

"About five weeks ago."

"Have you spoken to her since then?"

"No, now I'm really worried. I don't think she would just leave. It doesn't make sense."

"Oh, one last question. Did you know about the lake house in the Berkshires?"

"Yes. Why?"

"No reason, just curious. If there is anything else you remember or you hear from her please contact me."

I gave him my card and left. I was coming to the same conclusion as Peter Mickelson. The more I learn about Laura the more I believe something happened to her. I could think of a few people who might be suspects if Laura was dead but without a body, it was hard to figure out where to go from here.

CHAPTER 18

On Tuesday and most of Wednesday, I did administrative stuff, including a trip to the library scouring books on missing person cases. Wednesday evening I met Danny at Lattanzi's on 46th in the theatre district. He was waiting outside.

"Hi Danny." He looked really nice, wearing a pair of black slacks and a button down pink cotton shirt with a gray v-neck sweater. I had on a simple black sleeveless dress that came right above my knees with black stockings and black suede boots. I always say dress in black if you're short on fashion sense.

Danny was a perfect gentleman and helped me off with my coat which we checked when we walked in.

"You look ravishing," he said smiling.

"You don't look so bad yourself."

The hostess showed us to a corner table. It was early so it wasn't crowded yet. We each ordered a glass of wine.

"I spoke to my brother yesterday," he said. "He wants me to visit him in Belgium."

"That's great, have you ever been there?"

"No, the last place he was stationed was in Turkey. I went there about two years ago. Before my brother and his wife and nephew were transferred to Belgium they came to the states so I was able to see him then."

"I'm jealous. I've only been as far as Montreal."

"Well, we can remedy that."

"I think it's way too soon for us to go away together. I hope I haven't offended you."

"Absolutely not. I know you better than you think I do. Well, maybe we can start with a day trip and build on that."

"We'll see." Tell me about his wife and your nephew?"

The waiter came over with our wine and we ordered dinner. We shared fried calamari and I had my famous linguini and clams and Danny ordered the Branzino. They had great flatbread that tasted of butter and garlic; out of this world.

"Margo is Israeli. They met when he was there for a few months. I adore her. She's warm and friendly and the kind of person you like to be around. My nephew, Joseph, is really smart and a real wiseass but fun to be with. At this point he knows Hebrew, Arabic, and some French. Unfortunately I don't get to see him very often. Do you have any family in the area?"

"My cousin Alan. He's a second cousin on my mother's side of the family. He and his wife Patty are my family. Alan has an insurance agency in one of the suites where my office is. He's a really great guy."

"Do they have children?"

"No, but I recently found out they're having a baby."

When we looked at the time we had to leave. We decided we would have dessert afterward.

The show was fabulous. I came out humming, 'Can't Take My Eyes Off of You.' I never realized how many great songs the Four Seasons wrote and recorded. When Danny and I left the theatre I turned my phone back on. I had three missed calls, all from Sam. When I listened it took me totally by surprise.

The police up in the Berkshires found a body that they think might be Laura. I signaled to Danny that I needed to call Sam.

"Sam, tell me what happened," I asked with trepidation in my voice.

"I got a call from the police in Stockbridge. I was told that some kids were out in a canoe on the lake and wove their way into a remote area looking for a place probably to smoke weed when they saw a body." Sam was talking really fast. "I need to go up there as early as possible tomorrow morning."

"Do you want me to go with you? I can pick you up anytime you want."

"Can you be at my place at 5:30 a.m.? I want to be up there by 8:00."

I could tell in his voice that he wasn't coping well with the news. Who could blame him?

"Listen Sam we don't know for sure it's her," but the words sounded hollow.

I explained to Danny what was going on and that I was taking Sam up to Stockbridge very early in the morning. I told him I was sorry but I had to cut our date short and I called for an Uber.

Riding home a terrible thought came to me. What if the body found is Laura's. I was probably off the case since the police would now take over the investigation. Maybe I could talk Sam into letting me stay on. Besides needing the money, the case had become really important to me. Maybe it was selfish, but I wanted to be the one who found Laura's killer.

I set my alarm for 4:30. I tossed and turned, my mind in overdrive. By 3:30 I finally stopped torturing myself and got out of bed, showered, and put on coffee. I threw a couple of health bars into my bag and grabbed a bottle of water from the fridge. Sam was waiting outside as I pulled up. He looked like he hadn't slept at all.

"Did you get any sleep?" I asked him.

"I'm not sure. I may have fallen asleep but it wasn't for very long."

Most of the ride up we drove in silence. Sam said we were going to the police station first and the officer in charge was going to take us to the morgue.

When we arrived at the station we were greeted by Detective Carl Graham. We introduced ourselves and he drove us over to the County Morgue. I waited in the outer office while Detective Graham took Sam in the back where the coroner was waiting for him.

My thoughts drifted back to the day my mother died. She had fought a long battle with breast cancer. I was angry and devastated. She was all I had after my father died, and I was naïve enough to believe that after my father was gone, nothing bad would happen to me.

I heard footsteps. I knew as soon as I saw Sam walking towards me that it was Laura. He looked ashen.

"I am so sorry Sam." He didn't say anything.

"I'm going to have to ask both of you to come back to the station so I can ask you some questions."

When we arrived at the station Detective Graham led us to his office.

"Can I get either of you coffee or water?"

I declined and Sam asked for water.

"This must be really hard on you Sam, but I need to find out about Laura. I want you to know that I am going to record our conversation."

"Do I need a lawyer?"

"Not unless you have something to hide."

"Can you please tell me how she died?" Sam asked.

"It looks like your wife was strangled."

I saw Sam wince.

"The autopsy has not been completed yet but it looks like she has been dead for a while, maybe as long as a few weeks. As soon as the autopsy is finished, we'll know more. Did you report her missing?"

"Yes, when she didn't come home I went to the police the next morning."

"Has anyone from the precinct contacted you since then?"

"I spoke to Detective Harris but I don't think he did much. I got the impression they thought she left me. But why would she do that, it didn't make sense, we were only married a year and there were no problems."

"Did you know your wife was at the lake house?"

"No, I didn't."

"Did you find her car?" I asked.

"Not as yet. We're going to search the whole area. We'll need her vehicle information."

"Yes, I'll get that to you," Sam said.

"Was Laura acting differently in the past few weeks?"

"Not that I noticed."

"Was she on any drugs?"

"No, no way."

"What about enemies?"

"What kind of questions are you asking? Why would Laura have enemies?"

"I'm sorry if these questions offend you but I need to ask them. Is it possible she was having an affair?"

"I didn't think so, but now I don't know what to

think."

"Okay, I think we're good for now. Besides the vehicle information, I'll need a list of any friends and colleagues. You can email everything to me. Before you leave, I'd like a DNA sample to rule you out when we process the scene."

Sam and I looked at each other.

"I think you would want to help us find the person who killed your wife."

"Can you give us a minute. This has been a big shock," I said.

"I'll leave you two alone for a few minutes. I'll be right down the hall."

"Sam, I think we should call a lawyer before you do anything. I can call a friend of mine who's a criminal lawyer if you don't have one."

"Okay, go ahead and call your friend."

After talking with a criminal lawyer I know, I told Sam he didn't think it was advisable to take a DNA test.

"What happens if he thinks I have something to hide if I don't take it?"

"He's just trying to intimidate you."

When Officer Graham returned Sam informed him he wasn't going to take the DNA test. I could tell Graham wasn't too happy about it.

"By the way," I said, "I was at Laura's house the other day and there was a guy by the name of Ben Cutler who I was told oversees the property for Laura. Maybe you should question him. Also there's a rowboat on Laura's property down by the lake, maybe the killer used it to move her body."

"You have been busy I see. Any suspects?" he said sarcastically.

"Look, I'm just trying to help."

"Is there anything else you would like to tell me?"

"No." I wanted to tell him to cut the attitude but I kept that to myself.

When we got into the car Sam said he wanted to see the cottage. Since it wasn't a crime scene yet I didn't see any reason why we shouldn't. Besides I wanted to do a more thorough search now that I knew she was most likely killed in the area.

At the cottage I realized we didn't have a key to get in. I tried the front and back kitchen doors but they were both locked. I searched for any open windows on the ground floor but everything was buttoned up tight. I didn't want to call Ben Cutler but I had no alternative.

CHAPTER 19

I googled Cutler's name under contractors and found a phone number. I hated calling him but short of breaking a window, which is probably not the wisest thing to do; there was a possibility that the house could turn into a crime scene. He answered on the first ring.

"Ben, this is Tracey Marks. We met the other day at the lake house. I have some bad news; the police found Laura's body. I'm here with Sam, Laura's husband, and he needs to get into the house. Can you please come over with the key?"

"That's terrible. What happened?"

I don't know. Right now I need you to come over with the key. We'll be waiting," and I hung up.

"Sam, you've never been here?"

"You already asked me that and I told you no," he said angrily.

I let it pass. Ben strolled in forty-five minutes later.

"Thanks for bringing the key over," clenching my fists. "Is this the only key you have?"

"No, I have another one. I didn't know my services are no longer needed," he said with an icy stare.

I could see Sam looking this guy over.

"I understand you knew my wife."

"I knew Laura and her parents. Laura and I have known each other since we were young. I'm sorry for your loss."

"Did you see her recently?" Sam asked.

"I told your friend here that I saw Laura about a month ago but we didn't really talk. I just stopped by to check on the house. What happened to her?"

"They're not sure, they haven't done the autopsy yet," I said.

"Okay, well I guess I'll be going. By the way, do you still want me to keep an eye on the house?"

"For now. I'll let you know if there's a change," Sam said

I was surprised Ben didn't ask where they found Laura. If it was me, I would want to know just out of curiosity.

Before going into the house, I went down to the lake. I checked the area for any traces of a struggle but realized Ben had been all over the place when he was dismantling the dock. I hunched down to inspect the rowboat without touching anything since I didn't want to get my prints anywhere. I also examined the paddles. No blood or anything that looked suspicious but I'm sure the police will conduct a more thorough search.

I found Sam in the living room walking towards the fireplace where there was a photo of Laura with her parents. He picked it up and was staring at it.

"Why didn't she tell me she was at the house?" talking to himself as if he was unaware I was in the room.

"I don't know, maybe she came to be by herself," I said softly.

"I wish I could believe that. Why would someone want to hurt her?"

"Hopefully we'll find the answer."

We both walked through the house, Sam more out of curiosity. I couldn't find any signs of a struggle but I knew the police had devices that could reveal blood that the naked eye can't see.

I wondered where Laura's laptop and phone were. When they find her car hopefully they'll be in there. I purposefully didn't mention the bank book and passport to Detective Graham. He can find it without my help.

"Sam, I think we should get something to eat before we head back."

He silently nodded.

I drove into the town of Stockbridge. It was probably a place Laura knew well coming up here all these years. It was fairly small and quaint as most of these New England towns are. It was basically one street that went through the town with shops on both sides. We stopped at a café. The inside was charming with both square and round marble tables. The walls were painted in a mustard color with French posters. They had a chalkboard listing the menu. I ordered a tuna fish sandwich and a large cappuccino and Sam had a bacon, lettuce and tomato sandwich and a coffee.

"Excuse me," I said to the waitress. "Do you by any chance know a Laura Matthews or maybe you know her as Laura Tyler?"

"Why of course. I knew her parents also. It was so tragic what happened to them. I've been living in Stockbridge more years then I care to admit. My name is Claire."

"I'm Tracey and this is Sam. When was the last time you saw Laura?"

"Do you mind telling me why you're asking?"

"Some kids found Laura's body near the lake."

"Oh my god, are you relatives?"

"I'm a private investigator and Sam is her husband."

Sam said, "Did you see her recently?"

"I haven't seen Laura in quite a while. Last time I saw her was maybe eight months ago."

I gave Claire my card. "I would appreciate it if you could ask around. Maybe somebody saw her more recently."

"Sure. Again I'm so sorry for your loss."

After the waitress brought our food I debated whether to broach the subject with Sam whether he wanted me to stay on the case now that Laura was found. I could wait to see if he did, but it would be a distraction that I didn't want weighing on me.

"Sam," I said, playing with my silverware and praying I wasn't off the case, "I was wondering now that the police are involved if you still want me to investigate Laura's death?"

"More than ever. What happens if they think I did it? You see it on TV all the time. They focus on the husband and don't look for anyone else. I need you to find out what happened to her."

"You're getting way ahead of yourself. At this point they have no reason to suspect you." I didn't necessarily believe my own words but I was relieved that he still wanted me to investigate Laura's death.

On the drive back my mind was swirling. I had so many thoughts going on I felt like my head was about to explode. Sam was quiet and I didn't have the energy to engage him in conversation, besides he seemed lost in his own thoughts. I couldn't wait to get back and put my head on my pillow and sleep for about two days though I knew I didn't have the luxury. I needed to figure out what my next steps would be.

There was no traffic going back. I dropped Sam off at his building. Before he left he asked me how long before they released Laura's body and I told him to contact Detective Graham.

I felt bad for Sam but I knew my feelings couldn't cloud my judgment. Sam was still a suspect in my mind.

After dropping Sam off, I went directly home. Wally greeted me with one of his big smiles. Seeing him was the highlight of my day.

I went upstairs with the full intention of going for a run. I never made it. I fell asleep. When I got up it was dark and the 7:00 evening news was on the TV. I needed to call a few people, including Laura's godmother. I was debating whether I should do it in person, which was probably the right thing to do, but I didn't know when I would have the time.

I was just about ready to leave a message for Ms. Litman when she answered.

"Ms. Litman, it's Tracey Marks."

"I'm so happy to hear from you. I was just in the middle of playing Mah-Jongg with my lady friends."

I was glad she wasn't by herself.

"I'm so sorry to have to tell you that Laura's body was found yesterday." I could hear her crying softly into the phone. I never had to do this before and it was heart wrenching. I didn't know whether to continue or wait for her to say something.

"Ms. Litman would you like me to call back later? I know this is not easy for you."

"Do they know what happened?" her voice

cracking.

"At this point, they don't know much. She was found by some kids in an inlet on the cottage lake." I didn't want to mention how she died. "As soon as they release the body I will call you about the funeral arrangements. Is there anything I can do?" just because I didn't know what else to say.

"Thank you Tracey, so much. You might want to tell Sam that it would be nice if Laura was buried with her parents if that's possible. They're buried at Stepney Cemetery in Monroe, Connecticut."

"I will definitely tell him. You have my number if you want to talk."

I was glad that call was over with. I poured myself a glass of Chardonnay and sunk my body down into the sofa. I still needed to call her friend Melanie and I also wanted to contact Seth Green. I couldn't quite figure out how he fit into the picture. I know from the cell phone records that they spoke, but were they friendly conversations? Did they have a relationship or was it just one sided?

I called Melanie first. No answer. It went straight to voice mail.

I then called Seth. He answered right away. "Seth, this is Tracey Marks. We spoke about Laura. I have some bad news, her body was found yesterday. Before I had a chance to continue, Seth said, "Oh my god, what happened?"

"They don't know yet except she was found near the cottage lake. They still haven't done the autopsy."

"Do they think it was a suicide?"

"Why would you say that? Did she say anything to you?"

"No, but why would someone hurt her?"

"I don't know, would you happen to have any ideas?" trying to provoke him.

"Of course not. Why, do you think I had something to do with her death? I would never hurt her, I..."

He stopped in mid-sentence. "What were you going to say?"

"I was going to say I cared for her. We've known each other since high school and I would never do anything to hurt Laura."

"When was the last time you saw her?"

"I've already told you I only spoke with her on the phone," in a defiant tone. "Can you please keep me informed," trying to keep his cool.

CHAPTER 20

We hung up. I thought that was interesting. I bet he had a thing for her but did he act on it? A few minutes later I got a call from Melanie.

"Hi Melanie, I'm sorry to have to tell you but Laura's body was found yesterday." For what seemed like forever there was silence from the other end of the phone. "Melanie are you there?"

"I'm sorry I just can't believe it. What happened?"

I explained what the initial thoughts on her death were and where she was found.

"I'm just having a hard time processing this. Why would anyone want to hurt Laura?" She started to cry. I gave her a few seconds.

"Do you have any idea what she was doing at the lake?"

"As far as I know she didn't have plans to go up there, but lately I had no idea what was going on with her."

"Do you think she may have gone there to hide out?"

"I doubt it. Too many people know about the lake house. I remember something that Laura told me. It was right before they got married. She was thinking of having the ceremony at the lake house but Sam talked her into getting married at City Hall since neither of them had any relatives. I think Laura would have liked it at the lake even if only a few people came."

"Why do you think she acquiesced to Sam?"

"To be perfectly honest I don't believe she was that excited about the marriage. I think she tried to convince herself that all her problems would disappear if she settled down with Sam. He seemed like the perfect person to marry. He was successful, handsome, charming and he really loved her, or so it seemed."

That fits with what Peter Mickelson had told me. "Do you think she was having an affair?"

"If she was, she didn't tell me. Will there be a funeral?"

"I'll call you as soon as I know the arrangements."

I was completely wiped out from the day. I didn't even have the strength to make dinner even if I did have something in the refrigerator. Instead I made myself a peanut butter sandwich and brought the sandwich and a bag of potato chips into bed with me and turned on the TV. By 10:00, I was out cold.

I woke up at 6:00, put on my running clothes and a sweatshirt and went for a jog. It was really nippy outside. Normally when I run it's to clear my head but now I was trying to get some inspiration on how to proceed.

As I was heading back the sun was coming up. I took a hot shower, dressed in my standard work clothes, including my leather jacket and headed to the office. I was starving, so I went to the coffee shop two blocks from my apartment for a big breakfast. I know everyone who works there since I'm a regular.

Kathy greeted me, "Hi Tracey, sit anywhere you like and I'll bring you over coffee."

Kathy is a single mom about my age with gorgeous curly light brown hair that comes down to the middle of her back, though she wears it in a ponytail while she works. When she smiles her face lights up. Unfortunately being a single mom and working two jobs she doesn't smile too often. I can't imagine what's it like having to work and be the only one responsible for a child.

While I was waiting for my pancakes, I called Susie.

"Hey I was just thinking about you and wondering how things were going," Susie said.

I brought her up to speed.

"Wow, poor Laura. How did her husband take the news?"

"He was a basket case. I need to find out more about this guy Ben. There was something that was a little off about him that I can't explain. I ran a background check but nothing significant came up except that he was married and divorced, but that's not that unusual unless the ex-wife has some interesting information."

"If he might be a person of interest, you should talk to the ex-wife."

"I was thinking of putting a tail on him, but if he did kill Laura what could we possibly gain by surveilling him now?"

"You may be right but there is always the outside chance something will prove fruitful from watching him."

"First I'll see if the ex-wife will talk to me. Depending on what she says surveillance might be the next step."

We hung up and I called Danny. I felt bad about having to cut our date short.

"Hey it's nice to hear your voice," he said. "How did everything go?"

"I'll tell you when I have some time."

"Look I know you are kind of up to your eyeballs in this but I'm leaving on Monday to visit my brother for a week. I thought I could lure you over to my place tomorrow evening with a home cooked meal."

"On two conditions, one, it's just dinner and two, I bring the wine."

"I'll promise you anything," he said teasingly. "See you at 7:00."

When I arrived at the office, I went next door to see Alan. Margaret was not at her post. Alan's door was open. "Hey cous, how are you?"

"So nice of you to stop by," Alan said, with a loving smile across his face. "Sit down."

"They found Laura's body the other day."

"Sorry to hear that. Does that mean you're off the case?" with hopeful optimism in his voice.

"No, my client wants me to stay on since he thinks the police will point the finger at him. He wants me to find the real killer."

"And what do you think?"

"I go back and forth. I just don't know."

"I need you to be really careful Tracey. Promise me."

"Always. How is Patty feeling?"

"She's doing great. Morning sickness has passed. Right now we're going to hold off on any further renovations. Our room is big enough to have the baby stay with us for a while. Don't forget to keep Thanksgiving open. If you have someone you'd like to bring, the more the merrier."

"If I am still alive, I'll be there. Only kidding. By the way, where is Margaret?"

"She'll be in a little late. Tommy is sick so she had

to get a babysitter."

"Tell her I said hi."

I crossed the hall to my office. I turned on my computer anxious to locate an address for Ben's ex-wife, Bonnie. Even if she remarried there should still be a reference under the name Cutler. She was no longer living in the Stockbridge area but was now living in East Canaan, Connecticut, right below the Massachusetts border. I called keeping my fingers crossed she wouldn't flat out refuse to talk with me.

"Hello, is this Bonnie?"

"Yes," she said curiously.

"My name is Tracey Marks. I'm a private investigator looking into the death of Laura Matthews though you might know her by her maiden name Tyler."

"Oh that's terrible. I sort of knew her from my ex-husband Ben."

"Yes, I met Ben at Laura's lake house. I was wondering if I could come by and ask you a few questions."

"Well I don't know how I can assist you but I'll be glad to help in any way I can."

"That's great. Is sometime today convenient? I'm in Manhattan so I could probably be there in about two hours depending on traffic."

"Is one o'clock okay?"

"Perfect."

Bonnie gave me her address and I called an Uber since I needed to pick up my car. Now I was really glad I had a big breakfast.

There was a little traffic on the way up but not bad. Bonnie lived in a garden apartment in a very pretty development. The landscaping was very attractive with purple and yellow flowers planted in front of her building. I love flowers, but don't ask me to name them. Sometimes I buy the ones they sell by the bunch at my corner market to brighten up my apartment.

Bonnie was nothing like I pictured her. She was striking with long jet black hair that she wore in a ponytail. She had lips that I can only dream of. They were full, but natural, not from Botox. She was tall and slender wearing tight jeans and a tight black cotton short sleeve tee-shirt. I couldn't help but stare. I followed her into the kitchen where there was an antique wood table with four wood chairs covered with blue and white cushions.

"I just made a pot of coffee. Can I pour you a cup?"

"That would be great. Black, no sugar, please."

We both sat down. I said, "Did you ever meet Laura?"

"I met her once. It was after her parents died. Ben and I were going out to dinner and he stopped by her place to make sure everything was okay. It turns out Laura was there and he quickly introduced us and we left."

"Did he ever talk about her?"

"He probably mentioned her a few times but nothing that stands out."

"Are you on friendly terms with Ben since your divorce?"

"Why do you ask?" she said curiously.

I needed to be careful about what I said since I was trying to elicit information that could be helpful to me and I didn't want to anger her.

"I went up to the lake house thinking Laura might

be there. Instead I ran into Ben, and he was not too happy to see me, actually he was trying to intimidate me and I'm not sure why. Do you have any ideas?"

"Ben and I did not split up under the best of circumstances. When we first met he was charming and eager to please. That lasted until the day I said I do. He was very possessive to the point of smothering me."

"Was he ever violent?"

"He had a tendency to have outbursts. There were times when I thought he would hit me but instead he took out his anger on the nearest thing to him, whether it was throwing a glass or punching his fist against the wall. The last straw was the day I was meeting a girlfriend for dinner. I waited at the restaurant for about twenty minutes. When she didn't show, I called her. She was surprised that I was at the restaurant since Ben had contacted her and told her I was sick and wouldn't be able to make it. I was livid, as you can imagine. I didn't even bother to confront him. The next day I went straight to a divorce attorney."

"Do you think he would be capable of killing someone?"

"Honestly, I don't know. I guess it's possible in a fit of rage."

"I'm sorry to ask you this but do you think Ben was cheating on you?"

"I don't know, but why would he be so possessive if he was cheating?"

"I'm not sure the two are mutually exclusive."

I thanked her and left. As I was driving back I thought about what Bonnie told me. If Ben killed Laura, what would be his motive?

CHAPTER 21

On Saturday Sam called me in an agitated state. "I got a call from Detective Graham. Laura was two months pregnant."

"I'm so sorry Sam."

"They want me to take the DNA test. What if I'm not the father? Could she have been cheating on me all this time?"

"We don't know at this point that it's not your baby. Let's take this one step at a time. I think you need to consult an attorney."

What I thought I didn't want to say out loud to Sam. If it's not his baby, he'll be their prime suspect and I would also put him at the top of my list.

"I'll ask a friend of mine to recommend a criminal attorney," he said, sounding stressed.

After hanging up, I called Susie. "You got a minute."

"Sure, what's going on?"

I filled her in on the latest developments.

"I don't see any way around it for Sam. He's going to have to submit to a DNA test otherwise he'll look guilty even if he isn't."

"What happens if it turns out it's not his baby?" I said.

"He'll probably be there number one suspect, but they still have to do an investigation. You don't convict someone without evidence, and Sam is a long way off from rotting in jail."

"The thing is I'm not sure he didn't do it. I wish I could be. Did I mention his receptionist? I may be imagining it but I think something may be going on between them."

"Oye, I think I feel a headache coming on," Susie said.

"I forgot to ask you, when is the big move?"

"Today. I might be the one calling you for advice."

I had so much going on with the case and tonight was my dinner date at Danny's place. I didn't know if I was up to it.

The rest of the day, I tried to keep busy. My Superintendent came up around 2:00 and fixed a leaky toilet.

I dressed casually for my date with Danny. I wore jeans and a red linen blouse with short black boots. I took an Uber to his apartment and as promised, I brought a bottle of Cabaret Sauvignon.

As soon as I walked into his apartment I was overtaken by the wonderful smells coming from the kitchen. We embraced at the door. Danny gave me a tour of the apartment. It was very tastefully done in modern décor. It was so different from my apartment, but I really liked it. The living room had a white couch with gray and black throw pillows. On one side of the couch was a light grey upholstered chair and opposite was the identical chair. In the middle was a large square shaped light gray wooden table with books and various art objects on it. Covering the hardwood floor was a textured area rug in shades of gray, black and white. The walls had lovely artwork. There was an Andy Warhol print above the couch, an abstract of the Brooklyn Bridge in blue, green and orange.

"This place is amazing," I said. "Did you have a decorator?"

"I have to admit I did have some assistance, but in my defense, I helped pick out the furniture, well at least some of it."

"Well you both did a great job."

"At first I wasn't sure going modern was what I wanted since I've been in peoples' homes where too modern had a cold feeling to it, but the more the decorator showed me, the more I began to really like the idea. Can I get you a glass of wine?"

We walked into the kitchen. My eyes widened. I loved it. It had gray cabinets with a small island in the middle. The floor was a marbled gray wood. I sat down on one of the cushioned stools.

Danny poured two glasses of red wine and sat down next to me.

"Do you own the place?" I asked.

"I do. I bought it five years ago. It needed a lot of work so I got a good price for it. I redid the bathroom and the kitchen before I moved in and turned the second bedroom into an office. I'm lucky that I can work from home to design the system my clients need for their businesses and then set it up at their offices."

"With my line of work I might be able to work from home but I wouldn't get the same exposure that I have being in an office with other businesses, though that hasn't worked out as I planned."

"How is your client doing?" Danny asked.

"I think he's feeling stressed. Besides having to arrange a funeral, the autopsy showed that his wife was two months pregnant. If it isn't his baby, the police are going to definitely look at him as a possible suspect."

"What do you think?"

"I think if I was him, I'd be worried. He may wind up being the person they focus on without looking at anyone else, though I think there are other persons of interest also."

"So what now?"

"I'm waiting to find out if it's Sam's baby or not. The results may open up all kinds of possibilities."

"Are you hungry?"

"Starved."

"You have two choices of where to eat. We can sit in here or we can sit at the dining room table."

"I actually think it's kind of cozy here."

"Great, here it shall be."

Danny made a fabulous meal. We started off with an appetizer of grilled shrimp that was in a butter, wine and garlic sauce. We then had a salad with mixed lettuces, tomatoes and olives. The main course was a risotto with peas and scallops in a light tomato sauce. I made my usual sounds of joyous pleasure as I was eating. Danny poured us more wine.

I helped Danny clean up under protests from him, and then we took our wine into the living room. Between the food, the wine and the music I felt as limp as a rag doll.

"Shall we dance," Danny said as he stretched out his hand.

"Are you sure you didn't invite me to dinner under false pretenses?" I asked as Danny held me to close to him.

"Shall I call you an Uber," as his hand moved slowly down my back.

"What if I said yes?"

"I would probably open the nearest window and jump out."

The next moment his mouth came down on mine. At first his lips were soft against mine and then my mouth opened greedily and a groan came from somewhere inside me. Danny lifted me up and I wrapped my arms and legs around him. As Danny gently put me down on his bed, he looked at me for a second to make sure this was okay with me. I nodded.

Frantically we were pulling at each other's clothes. Danny's hands and mouth were exploring everywhere. When we finished, we both laid drenched in sweat. A few minutes later Danny began touching my nipples, softly at first, then more roughly, his fingers slowly moving downward, lightly teasing me. I softly moaned and climaxed again.

Danny looked at me and said, "How about dessert?" We both laughed.

While Danny went to the bathroom, I checked my watch. It was almost 12:00. I really liked Danny but I didn't want a sleepover. I started to get dressed.

"Hey, where are you going?"

"Home."

"Is it something I did or said?"

"It's complicated. It's me. I told you I'm not that great with relationships. Trust me it has nothing to do with you."

He walked over to me and put his arms around my waist. "Okay, I don't like it but I understand. We kissed. "Look, I bought some apple strudel at a great Hungarian bakery nearby. Why don't we have some dessert and then I'll take you home."

"That sounds good but I can take an Uber."

"I'd rather take you."

When we got back to my apartment building, Danny double parked and walked me to the front door. We kissed and said our goodbyes. I watched him as he got back into his car and left. The thought crossed my mind that he might be mad at me since I'm not that good at reading signals. I liked Danny but now that we slept together, I didn't want to give him the impression that this was a serious relationship.

On Sunday I called Sam to find out what was going on.

"I spoke to a lawyer who is in the Berkshire's. He said he would take my case if I needed him. In the meantime I'll submit my DNA here and they'll send the results up to the coroner's office."

"Do you know when they'll release Laura's body?"

"I have a call into Detective Graham. Hopefully I'll know more later today."

"I spoke to Marjorie Litman, Laura's godmother. She thought it would be nice if Laura was buried with her parents at Stepney Cemetery in Monroe, Connecticut. Also if you can let me know the arrangements, I'll contact some of her friends so they can attend."

"Thanks, I appreciate that."

"Look Sam, I know things look bleak now but they'll get better."

"I just want you to find out who did this, Tracey."

"I will," trying to sound as if I believed my own words.

Susie called after I hung up from Sam. I met Susie for a drink at a bar/restaurant. No atmosphere, kind of dark, but on the bright side it has a pool table and a dartboard, which can be fun to play if you're hammered. We sat at a wooden booth and we both ordered a glass of Cabernet and shared a Margarita pizza. We wouldn't venture to eat much else here since it's kind of a dive.

"Well, I see that the old ball and chain gave you permission to go out," playfully punching Susie on the shoulder.

"Not funny," she said laughing. "By the way, Mark said hi. We were thinking of having a few friends over after Thanksgiving."

I thought this might be a good opportunity to mention Danny since it was weighing on me that I was keeping a secret from my best friend.

"I have something to confess but you have to promise not to ask me a million questions."

"Yes, I promise," practically falling out of her seat from excitement.

"I met a guy at the shooting range. We've only been on a couple of dates, and you know this could be over by next week with my track record, so don't get too excited."

"Okay I'll try to contain myself but I need some details, like a name for starters."

I told Susie how we met and what I knew about Danny. I could see that she was dying to ask more questions but she was trying to restrain herself.

"One question, on a scale of one to ten, how much do you like Danny?"

"I might give it a seven."

"Wow. For you, that's pretty high. If you don't bring him to our get together, I will never talk to you again," sticking her tongue out at me.

I was hoping I would not live to regret fessing up to her.

Walking back home, Danny called. "Are you all packed?" I said.

"Almost. You know us men we leave things to the last minute, not too much pre-thought involved."

"Yeah, not like us women who start packing days ahead of time and wind up bringing way too much stuff."

"Well, enough of the foreplay, I'll text you when I arrive in Brussels. Stay safe."

"You too."

I didn't want to admit it but Danny was growing on me, though there was a part of me that was glad Danny would be away for a while. I had to stay focused on the case and not have any distractions. My first priority was solving Laura's murder.

CHAPTER 22

On Monday Sam called as I was walking to my office. "The baby is not mine. What the hell was going on with Laura. This is a nightmare," he said. His anger was palpable.

"You must feel awful but this might give us another avenue to explore. The person who got her pregnant may have something to do with her death."

"Yeah but we have no idea who that is, and now the police are going to focus on me for sure now."

"Sam if you didn't kill Laura there won't be any evidence against you. Let's not get ahead of ourselves. Do you know if they processed the crime scene yet? Maybe they can find a DNA match."

"I have no idea. They haven't told me anything except they are releasing the body today. I've made the funeral arrangements."

Before we hung up, he gave me the details. There wasn't going to be a church service, only a graveside ceremony.

Sam certainly sounded surprised that it wasn't his baby. Maybe he truly was in the dark. What the hell was going on with Laura? Why would she have an affair? It certainly seems that she wasn't happy with Sam but was something else going on with her? Again more questions than answers.

When I got to the office I contacted everyone connected to Laura with the date, time and place of the funeral, leaving a message if they weren't available. I felt bad for Ms. Litman since she would have liked a church service for her goddaughter but she was grateful that Laura was going to be buried with her parents. I offered to pick her up so she wouldn't have to go alone.

The day of Laura's funeral was unseasonably warm for the middle of October. It was near 70 degrees and not a cloud in the sky. I dressed in gray slacks, a white blouse and a black blazer. I picked Ms. Litman up at 11:00. She looked a little bit older than the last time I saw her, her face more drawn. She was very quiet on the ride to the cemetery, her hands playing with her handkerchief. I didn't try to engage in conversation, wanting to respect her privacy.

I was actually looking forward to the funeral, knowing it was a possibility one of the mourners could be the killer.

When we arrived, I stopped in the office to get directions to the graveside. Cemeteries, besides being depressing, are a maze to me. The first time I went to visit my parents' graves, it took me almost a half hour to find them.

I spotted Sam standing by himself near Laura's grave. I introduced him to Ms. Litman. Sam expressed his sympathies and Ms. Litman seemed to recoil at Sam's touch and appeared visibly upset. She could be mad at Sam thinking he was the reason Laura and she had not been as close as they once were.

I noticed some people walking in our direction. As they came closer I saw it was Laura's friend Melanie and Mr. Nichols and Jane from the jewelry store. I was glad to see them since I was feeling a little uncomfortable from the tension between Sam and Marjorie Litman. Melanie went over to Ms. Litman while Sam, Mr. Nichols and Jane were talking. This gave me the opportunity to step back and observe from a distance.

I had invited Peter Mickelson and watched as he approached me.

"Hi Tracey. Thank you for contacting me about Laura's funeral. I've been racking my brains trying to remember if there was anything Laura said to me that could be significant. I just don't understand. If she was in danger, why wouldn't she tell me?"

"Maybe she didn't know she was in danger at the time. Peter, I know you told me that your relationship was strictly platonic but was there anything else going on?"

"Look I'm not going to get into this here. I told you before there was nothing physical between Laura and me," as he walked away.

Maybe this wasn't the best time to challenge Peter. Tact may not be my strong suit.

I was surprised to see Ben Cutler even though I had contacted him. He looked a little uncomfortable in his black suit, probably sweating from the heat. I decided not to approach him since our last encounter did not end well.

I then observed two people getting out of a car who looked vaguely familiar. It was Seth Green and his wife. They appeared to be in a heated argument but stopped as soon as they saw me. I would love to have been a fly hovering above listening to their every word.

The last person to arrive was Father McGraw, the priest from Marjorie Litman's Church. She asked him to perform the service since he had known Laura. Father McGraw was short, only about 5'4" but there was a confident air about him that made his stature appear taller. He had a caring face, someone you might confess your secrets to even if he wasn't a priest.

After a few minutes talking to Sam, Father McGraw began the service. I stayed back hoping to keep a watchful eye on everyone's demeanor during the funeral, especially Seth Green and Ben Cutler.

I watched as Melanie and Marjorie Litman were quietly crying. Sam was solemn though no tears were shed at least as far as I could tell. His head bent down through most of the service. Ben Cutler was looking straight ahead and at times staring at Sam with a scowl on his face, wiping his forehead from perspiration. I was surprised that Seth looked genuinely grief stricken while his wife seemed to be looking around, distracted. It did not appear that any friends or family of Sam's were attending the funeral. I thought that was odd.

The priest gave a lovely service speaking highly of Laura and also mentioning her parents. No one else spoke. I walked over to Sam when the service was over and I could see the sadness in his eyes. Since Sam had not arranged for anything after the funeral, people were just milling around, not knowing what to do.

I walked over to Marjorie Litman, who was talking with Melanie. "Sam hasn't planned anything for after the service, would you like to stop some place for lunch?"

"If you don't mind I'm not up to it. Can you drive me straight home?" Marjorie asked.

"Sure. Melanie, maybe we can speak another time."

Before we left, I caught up to Seth Green and his wife.

"Glad you both were able to come. I'm sure Sam appreciated it."

Seth mumbled something. He was probably angry at me from our last encounter. His wife barely acknowledged me.

"By the way, it turns out Laura was pregnant." I deliberately told them to see their reactions.

Seth's hands were balled up by his sides as if he was trying to contain his anger without speaking. His wife said, "how terrible for her husband," without much feeling behind it. I wondered what was going on with both of them.

I walked over to Ben before he left. "Thanks for coming. I'm sure Ms. Litman was happy you were here." With that he got into his car without saying a word. I guess I'm not too popular with some people.

On the drive back to Ms. Litman's house I asked her if there was anything else she remembered about Ben Cutler that she hadn't mentioned to me.

"Why, do you think he hurt Laura?"

"I don't know but I can't rule him out."

"There were some rumors that he might have gotten into some trouble when he was younger. I think a girl accused him of sexual assault but I don't know if it's true or what happened. What about Laura's husband? I know he hired you, but Laura seemed so different after she met him. I blame Sam in a way, even if he didn't have anything to do with her death. Maybe that's not logical but that's the way I feel. In some way, I blame myself also. I knew she was a troubled teenager but I thought it would pass. I should have taken a more active role in her life knowing Justine and Tom had problems."

"You did the best you could," not knowing what else to say. "In the meantime take care of yourself and I promise I will do my best to find out why Laura died."

I dropped Marjorie off and headed back to the office. I was lucky to find a parking spot a few blocks away. On my way I picked up a chicken salad sandwich for lunch.

I mulled over what Marjorie Litman told me. I needed to find out the name of the woman Ben may have assaulted.

"Hey Susie, I need to run something by you, give me a call."

As I was taking the last bite of my sandwich, Susie called.

I related what Marjorie Litman told me. "I think I'll go up to Stockbridge and snoop around and see if anyone remembers Cutler from back then or remembers the incident."

"It's possible this woman might not be the only one he assaulted," Susie said. "You mentioned the waitress you met at the café who's been in the area for many years. Maybe she knows something or she can ask around. Let me know when you plan on going."

After hanging up, I called Sam. "It's Tracey. How are you doing?"

"I'm tired. I couldn't face being alone in the apartment so I'm in the office."

"That's understandable. I thought the service was really nice. What did you think?"

"It was. I'm glad she's buried next to her parents. I just don't understand why she cheated on me. For God's sake, if she was so unhappy why couldn't she tell me?"

"I don't know. Listen Sam, Marjorie Litman mentioned that there was a rumor that Ben Cutler sexually assaulted someone about fifteen years ago. It may be nothing but I think it's worth a trip. It's your money so I wanted to check with you first."

"That could be it," he said sounding almost relieved. "She wasn't having an affair, he forced himself on her and Laura never said anything because he threatened her if she went to the police."

"I guess it's possible. Why don't we see what I find out before we go jumping to any conclusions? By the way, I was a little surprised that only Laura's friends were at the funeral."

"I don't have any family in the area and the only close friend I have is out of the country now."

Sam's explanation about why no family or friends were at the funeral did not seem plausible to me but what reason did he have to lie?

CHAPTER 23

My phone buzzed. "Tracey Marks."

"Oh Ms. Marks, I'm glad I caught you. It's Claire from the café in Stockbridge."

My ears perked up. "Yes. Were you able to find out anything?"

"Well I asked around and it turns out I spoke to a woman who had been in contact with Laura recently. She was quite upset when I told her what happened. She said to pass on her information to you."

"That's great. Thanks so much for asking around. You've been a big help. I hate to ask but I need another favor."

"Sure, I'm glad to be of assistance if I can. I liked Laura and she was always kind and asked about my family when I saw her."

"It appears that Ben Cutler may have sexually assaulted someone about fifteen years ago. Do you know anything about that?"

"No, would you like me to ask around?"

"Yes. Also I'm coming up within the next day or so and I'll try to stop by."

Claire gave me the telephone number for Jessica Benson. I called her immediately. Just as I was waiting to leave a message, she answered.

"Ms. Benson, this is Tracey Marks. Claire asked me to contact you."

"I feel awful about Laura. I couldn't believe it when she told me. It was such a shock."

"Would we be able to meet? I have some questions I'd like to ask you."

"Sure, it just so happens I'm going to be in Manhattan tomorrow. I'm a jewelry designer and I'm talking with some prospective clients. I could text you when I'm free."

"That's great. Just let me know where and what time and I'll be there."

My mind was racing. It seemed like things were brewing but I didn't know if it would lead to finding Laura's killer. I need to think positive since my tendency is to go negative.

It was almost 4:00. I decided to lock up the office and head home to take a run and hopefully clear out the cobwebs. When I got back to my apartment I changed into my running clothes, which now included sneakers that light up in the dark. The park was crowded, people walking their dogs, sitting on benches talking on their cell phones or reading the paper. Nannies watching kids getting ready to leave since it was near dinner time.

The run was harder than usual, but I plowed on glad to be out in the fresh air and getting some exercise. The funeral was on my mind. I didn't know what to make of everyone's reactions. Ben could be the killer. He seemed the most uncomfortable, though Seth Green seemed very agitated when I mentioned Laura was pregnant. Was Laura's killer at the funeral?

Forty-five minutes later I returned but not before stopping at the Corner Sweet Shoppe for a pint of deep chocolate ice cream and to chat with Mr. Hayes. After a quick shower, I decided to call Raymond Berg. I wanted to inform him of Laura's death and try to gauge his reaction.

"Mr. Berg, it's Tracey Marks. I'm calling to tell you that Laura Matthews is dead, someone killed her."

"I'm sorry to hear that. I liked her in spite of what you may think."

"I know you were having an affair with her and I have knowledge that you physically abused Laura and threatened her if she told anyone."

"Well you have to prove that, and since Laura is no longer alive, I think you're out of luck." There was something sinister in his voice.

"It gives you motive to kill her," though I was probably reaching on that one.

"Almost two years later. You don't really believe that. I haven't seen Laura since the day she left. If you have any more questions you'll have to direct them to my lawyer," and he hung up.

It was worth a shot. I didn't really believe he killed Laura and she had posed no real threat to him.

The next day I received a text from Jessica Benson. She was able to meet at 11:00 at the Time Warner Building. Upstairs there's a bakery with a sitting area where you can buy scrumptious baked goods, including croissants and other breads. It also serves food.

I arrived about fifteen minutes early to ogle all the baked goods. While I was waiting, I grabbed two seats from people who were just leaving. As I sat down I recognized Jessica from her description. It's hard to miss her with her shoulder length soft blond curls, dark black oval shaped glasses and her 5'10" stature. I waved her over.

"Nice to meet you Tracey."

"Glad you could come. Can I get you a coffee or anything else? I was eyeing the baked goods before."

We both got coffee. I bought a croissant for Jessica and a sticky bun for myself.

"So what kind of jewelry do you design?" I didn't want to get right down to business since she was kind enough to go out of her way to meet me.

She showed me a few pieces, a silver necklace with an interesting design engraved throughout and beautiful silver hoop earrings. They looked expensive. She told me that she had been designing jewelry for years but it was only of late that there was interest from buyers in New York. She was very excited.

"So how do you know Laura?" I asked.

"About a year ago I was at a jewelry show in Stockbridge. Laura stopped by my booth and we started talking. She told me she was working at a jewelry store on Fifth Avenue so we seemed to have something in common. Whenever she came up she would call and we maintained a friendship. Recently we discussed the idea of pitching my jewelry to her boss."

"When was the last time you saw her?"

"Well, actually it had been a while, but I saw her about six weeks ago. Let me explain what I mean. I happened to be in Pittsfield, a town about fifteen miles from Stockbridge. It was about 2:00 in the afternoon and I was walking around the town browsing the shops and noticed Laura going into a restaurant with a man."

"Are you sure it was Laura?"

"Absolutely. I saw her from behind and I recognized her coat. It's red. I didn't want to intrude so I just called out to her and waved. She turned, waved back and walked quickly into the restaurant."

"Did you think it was odd that she walked into the

restaurant without coming over to talk with you?"

"It did cross my mind that maybe she didn't want me to meet whoever she was with, but I have no idea why."

"Do you remember what the guy looked like?"

"It happened pretty quickly and I don't believe he turned around. From the back all I could tell was that he was taller than Laura and maybe had brownish hair."

"Did you happen to notice if they were holding hands?"

"I can't be sure. Wow, I would make a terrible witness to a crime."

Too bad, I said to myself. "It's perfectly normal since most people don't hone in on details. They say that two people witnessing the same exact scene might have completely different accounts. Can you tell me about your conversations with Laura?"

"Though she was a newlywed, she never talked about her husband or her marriage. So you don't think the person she was with was her husband?"

I just looked at Jessica without saying anything.

"If she was seeing someone she didn't confide in me."

"Did she say anything to you about being afraid of anyone or being stalked?"

"No, I'd remember that. She talked about her job and living in Manhattan. She thought she might go back to school for fashion design. I told her she would be really good at it. Laura had great fashion sense. She always looked put together, not like me."

"Do you know Ben Cutler, the guy who looked after Laura's house when she wasn't around?"

"I did meet him once. I was at Laura's place and

he stopped by, said he was making sure everything was okay. Laura wondered how often this guy came to check on the house."

"What do you think she meant by that?"

"I'm not quite sure. Maybe she thought he came around more than he needed to."

"Do you think he could be the person that you saw with Laura?"

"I really can't say. I'm sorry."

"We found out that Laura was pregnant and the baby wasn't her husband's."

"Oh, that's awful. I wish she would have told me."

"She may not have known she was pregnant. It would have been very early on in the pregnancy."

"Did you hear any rumors about Ben sexually assaulting someone about fifteen years ago?"

"No, but if you want me to ask around I will. I know a lot of people in the Stockbridge area."

"That would be a big help and I appreciate you taking the time from your busy schedule. I've decided to take a ride up either tomorrow or the next day to see what I can find out. Do you by chance remember the name of the restaurant in Pittsfield you saw Laura going in?"

"Yes, it was Elizabeth's. Call me when you're in the area. Maybe we can get together for a drink if you have time."

We left and I wished her luck with her prospective clients.

If only the guy had turned around, I may have been able to figure out who Laura was with. That would have been too easy. Still, the person she was having an affair with might not necessarily be her killer.

CHAPTER 24

My phone rang. "Hi Sam, what's going on?"

"They want me to come in for questioning."

"Sam, you knew this was coming. They have to ask you questions. You're her husband. Just be truthful. If they catch you in a lie, even a small one, they'll be more suspicious. When are you going?"

"Tomorrow morning. I contacted the attorney I mentioned to you and we're going to meet before my meeting with Detective Graham."

"Is there anything I can do?"

"Yes, find out who killed Laura and quickly."

"Believe me, I'm working on it. Call me when you get back."

Before heading home, I tried to work out a plan on how I was going to find out the name of the person Ben Cutler may have assaulted. I thought I would try the clerk's office and see what was on file for him. Maybe I'll get lucky. Probably most of my time will be spent walking around town going into places to see if anyone knows anything. Not very scientific but I couldn't think of any other way. Being a PI is a lot of grunt work; there are no shortcuts. I made a reservation at a motel just a mile outside of Stockbridge.

Monday morning I headed to Stockbridge. I

arrived at about 10:30. I hadn't heard from Sam since he met with his attorney and Detective Graham on Friday. I took that as a sign they hadn't arrested him.

I found my way to the county clerk's office and parked in their lot. I went up to the third floor and meandered through the halls until I spotted the door to the records room. The first things I noticed were computers lined up against a wall. On two big desks were gigantic cloth covered books that looked really ancient. Thankfully there was someone behind the counter that might be able to help me.

"Hi. This is my first time here and was hoping you can show me how to use your computer to do some searches."

"Sure, be glad to. My name is Gary. What do you want to look up?"

"If I have a person's name how do I find out if they have any criminal or civil records?"

Gary was a pleasant guy who was eager to please. He reminded me of someone who at first a woman might not pay attention to but once you start talking with him you forget that he's kind of geeky looking. He showed me how to navigate the computer. First I looked under Cutler's name for any criminal records and I didn't find anything. I knew it was a long shot. Under civil records, it listed his divorce from 2011, a tax lien and two lawsuits, one from a company and the other from an individual that was suing him. I thought the person might be of interest, not because of the lawsuit but because the person may be willing to talk with me. I asked Gary to pull the file.

The man's name was John Cramer. He was suing Ben and his business for work Ben had started but never completed.

I jotted down Cramer's address. I thanked Gary and left.

I sat in my car searching for Cramer's telephone number. The internet website listed John Cramer between sixty-five and seventy and a telephone number. I was keeping my fingers crossed that he was retired, hoping I would find him at home.

He lived on a street lined with ranch houses, all painted white. Everyone's lawns looked recently mowed and neatly kept.

I knocked on the door and a bald man about seventy with a paunch, probably due to age answered. "Can I help you?"

"Mr. Cramer, I'm sorry to bother you. My name is Tracey Marks. This is a little awkward." Before I had a chance to finish he waved me in.

"It's a little chilly standing by the door," he said.

He led me into the kitchen and we both sat down. The kitchen looked like it was modeled in the sixties. It had a formica table with four chairs with beige vinyl seats. The room was nice and toasty.

"Can I offer you a cup of coffee? I was just sitting down myself. It's my late morning ritual now that I'm retired."

"What did you do?"

"I was a traveling salesman. I sold many different things, vacuums, encyclopedias, security systems. When my wife died two years ago, I retired. My only regret is that we didn't get to travel, always thinking we would have enough time. Don't make that mistake young lady. Now how can I help you?"

I kind of felt bad for Mr. Cramer. It was obvious that he was lonely and missed his wife.

He poured me a cup of coffee. "As I started to tell

you, I'm working on a case involving a woman who was murdered." I could see his face perk up. "Her family owned a cottage nearby. You may know them, Justine and Charles Tyler. They were killed several years ago in an automobile accident."

"I didn't know them personally but I knew who they were. I remember reading about it in the newspaper. He was drunk at the time if I remember correctly."

"Well their daughter Laura was recently killed. There was a man who looked after the cottage for Laura, his name is Ben Cutler. I was at the county clerk's offices and I saw that you sued him."

"Don't get me started with that crook. My wife and I hired Cutler to do the bathrooms. It was a nightmare and I won't bore you with the details."

"What happened?"

"He never finished the job. I sued him, but try getting money from a contractor. They're smart. They hide their assets so you can't get anything, or their company goes out of business and they open up under another name."

"Sorry, that must have been very upsetting. The reason I brought him up, I was wondering if you heard any rumors about him allegedly sexually assaulting a girl when he was in high school?"

"I can't say that I have but knowing his character, I'm not surprised."

"Would you happen to know anyone that might have known Cutler when he was younger?"

"I believe he played on the high school football team. If you go to the library in town they have yearbooks. Maybe you can see who some of his teammates were. I believe the coach has retired, but still lives in the area. His name is McIntyre. I can't recall his first name."

"Well you've been a big help. I appreciate your hospitality and you make a great cup of coffee."

"I learned from my wife. I hope you find out who killed Laura," he said to me as he walked me to the door.

"Thank you, me and you both."

Mr. Cramer pointed me in the direction of the library. I wonder how I'll feel when I'm much older. I love being by myself now but will I in twenty years?

The library was on Main Street. I went to the reference desk and asked where the yearbooks were kept. Once I was directed to the right area, I parked myself at a table. I took out the books from 1996 and 1997 and started searching. The coach for the football team was Glen McIntyre. I found Ben Cutler in the graduating class of 1997. He basically looked the same, a little less hair now but the same piercing eyes. I took a photo of the football team with their names listed at the bottom.

When I got in my car I googled Glen McIntyre. Apparently at age sixty, he was still coaching, but now he was the assistant coach. I found an address for him on one of the Internet address sites. Since I was starving I decided to eat before going to see McIntyre. I stopped at the Once Upon A Time Bistro on Main Street.

I sat at a table for two and was handed a menu by a young man who looked to be in his early twenties with short curly black hair. He was tall and slender. His dark framed glasses gave him a very studious look.

The menu was interesting. I ordered a bowl of

New England Clam Chowder and ravioli stuffed with grilled vegetables, served with tomato and baby spinach. While I was waiting I checked my cell phone for messages. Sam left me a message asking me to call him.

"Hi Sam, how did it go?"

"They asked me a lot of questions, but they didn't arrest me."

"That's because they have no evidence."

They found Laura's car at some hotel parking lot in Pittsfield. Apparently anyone can park at the hotel.

"Did they find her laptop and cell phone?"

"They think both of them are at the bottom of the lake since they weren't in her car."

"They're probably checking her cell phone records if they haven't done it by now. They'll dust for prints, but unless someone is in the system, they can't be matched. The same for the baby's father, unless they have a suspect they can't match it. Anyway I am up in Stockbridge now trying to track down someone who knew Cutler from when he was in high school. I think I may have a lead. I wonder if the police have interviewed Cutler yet."

"I have no idea. They're not going to tell me anything."

After hanging up, I called Jessica to see if she wanted to have a drink later. She gave me the name and address of a restaurant in town and we made plans to meet at 8:00.

It was close to 4:00 now. My next step was venturing over to the coach's house. He lived on a dead end street two miles out of town. I parked in front of a white colonial house with green shutters. Above the garage was a basketball hoop. I knocked

ELLEN SHAPIRO

and a very attractive woman about fifty-five years old with short brown hair with blond highlights opened the door.

"I am sorry to bother you but I'm looking for Glen McIntyre."

"May I ask what this is about?"

"I'm a private investigator looking into the death of Laura Tyler Matthews."

"Oh my god, I know her. Please come in. Glen should be home shortly. He's still at the high school. What happened?"

I followed Mrs. McIntyre into the living room. The room had a beautiful dark brown velvet couch with a long brown leather ottoman as a coffee table. Opposite the couch was a club chair with a geometric design in brown, gray and beige with a glass side table. We both sat on the couch.

"She was strangled, and found in an area by the lake where Laura's cottage is located."

"Are the police investigating?"

"Yes, but I was hired by Laura's husband to look into it also. How do you know Laura?"

"Well, this is a small town and Laura's family had been a part of the community for years. It was horrible when they died tragically in a car accident."

I heard the front door open. Mrs. McIntyre yelled out to her husband that she was in the living room. To my surprise, Glen McIntyre did not look anything like I expected. He looked to be around forty-five instead of his age, sixty. He was a nice looking man who kept himself in shape. He was average height, solidly built with a full head of reddish brown hair. His face was lean and he had a square jawline.

"Oh Glen, something awful has happened. You

remember the Tyler family. Their daughter Laura was found dead a few days ago. Oh, I'm sorry, this is Tracey Marks. She's a private investigator looking into Laura's death."

I thought I saw his eye twitch. "Mr. McIntyre, it's nice to meet you."

"How terrible. What happened?" he asked.

"The only thing we know at this point is that she was strangled. The police are investigating."

"Do they have any suspects?"

"As far as I know they don't, it's still early."

"Are you working for the police?"

"No, I was hired by Laura's husband."

It seemed like he was pondering this new information that I gave him.

"Why would he hire a private investigator?"

"I really can't say. Maybe he just wants another pair of eyes on the case. The reason I'm here is that there was a rumor that Ben Cutler may have sexually assaulted a woman back in high school. I was told that he was on the football team that you coached back then and was hoping you remember the incident."

"As I recall there was something that happened with a girl he was dating at the time. I believe her name was Emily, Emily Barnes, but nothing came of it. How is he connected to Laura?"

"He took care of Laura's cottage when she wasn't there."

"Is he a suspect?"

"Probably not but I just need to be thorough. Do you happen to know if Emily still lives in the area?"

Mrs. McIntyre said, "Her parents live here but I don't know what happened to Emily. I can't recall their first names but I believe they are still on

Longworth Street."

"Did either of you know Laura?"

"Not really. I would see her sometimes walking in town and we would say hello but that's about all," Mrs. McIntyre said.

"What about you Mr. McIntyre?"

"No, I never met her."

I thought it was curious that Mr. McIntyre asked so many questions. He was also quick to give me the name of Ben's old girlfriend and deny that he knew Laura.

"Mr. McIntyre, how is it that you remembered Emily's name after all these years?"

"Well at the time I was the coach and I took an interest in all of my players so it isn't something I would forget."

"Do you remember anything about the case or what happened?"

"I believe she accused him of sexual assault but it was his word against hers and if I recall correctly she never pursued the matter."

"Is there anything else you remember about Mr. Cutler?"

"He was kind of a smart ass but a hell of a player. I thought he would get into college on a football scholarship but he injured his shoulder pretty bad in a motorcycle accident, which ended his playing. It was a shame."

"Was he bitter about it?"

"Probably at the time, but you would think he would've gotten over it by now."

You would think, I said to myself. "Thank you both for your time."

When I got back to my car I looked up the name

Barnes on Longworth and found a telephone number. Instead of going there directly, I called Mrs. Barnes explaining to her that I was an old friend of Emily's from high school and was in the area. Did she know how I could get in contact with her? Mrs. Barnes told me that her daughter now lived in New York, Brooklyn. She gave me her address and telephone number. I added that lie to the list of all the others I've told. I was certainly going straight to hell.

CHAPTER 25

I was meeting Jessica at a restaurant called Michaels that was in Stockbridge. I had time to check into the Pleasant Valley Motel and take a shower. It wasn't much to look at but it was clean and the grounds were kept in good condition. I got the key to my room and pulled my car in front of the door to my room. I rested my head on the pillow and the next thing I knew it was 7:20. I took a quick shower, dressed and drove to Michael's.

Jessica was at the bar already drinking. "Hi Jessica, I'm so glad you could meet me." As I was talking I signaled to the bartender and ordered a glass of Cabernet Sauvignon.

"Any luck today?" she asked."

"Ben Cutler was on the high school football team. I spoke with Glen McIntyre who was the football coach back then and he remembers an incident with Ben's girlfriend at the time, but doesn't think anything came of it."

"From what I remember there were rumors McIntyre was quite the ladies man."

"That's interesting. Was that after he was married?"

"I think so, though I don't actually know anyone who he was involved with. Again they were just rumors."

"I can tell you that he looked like he was in great

shape for his age. He still has an athlete's body."

"Changing the subject, the food is really good here, are you hungry?"

The hostess sat us at a table and gave us menus. When the waiter came over we ordered a basket of garlic bread and we both ordered the pan seared Tuscan chicken served with artichokes, olives and sun dried tomatoes with penne.

I was very curious about the rumors involving the coach, but what did it have to do with Laura? Could she have been in a relationship with him even though he was almost twice her age?

"So how did you get into the PI business?" Jessica asked.

"It was kind of a fluke. I always enjoyed reading books where the main character was a PI and watching whodunit mysteries on TV, but it never occurred to me to actually pursue a career in the field. Instead I became a paralegal, but it turned out I hated the work and was bored out of my mind. Just when I was rethinking my career choices, a friend told me a private investigation firm was looking to hire a person to train and he thought of me. The rest is history. I worked with the firm for five years and applied for my PI license.

"That's a great story. I knew from the time I was a little girl that I wanted to design jewelry. Once when my mother wasn't looking, I took a very expensive bracelet of her's to play with and lost it. I thought she was going to kill me; instead, she bought me a jewelry kit where you make necklaces and bracelets out of beads. It was the beginning of my professional career. As I got older I started sketching pieces of jewelry and realized I was pretty good at it."

I enjoyed Jessica's company. I could see why Laura stayed in contact with her. Jessica told me she was gay and was in a relationship with someone who was also in the same profession but more in the marketing end of it.

We left the restaurant a little after 11:00 and I went back to the motel. As soon as I opened the door I knew something was wrong. My laptop, which I had left on the bed was open and I knew I didn't leave it that way when I left earlier. I took a quick scan of the room and saw that the contents of my overnight bag were spilled out on the floor. My heart was pounding in my ears. My mouth went dry. What if the person was still in the room. My thoughts were interrupted by loud arguing. I turned to see a couple a few doors down going at it. It spooked me. I left my door open and walked very slowly into the room. I took out my cell phone and speed-dialed Susie.

"What's the matter?" Susie asked.

"Someone's been in my room." Before I could get the next words out, my head felt like it exploded. I was trying not to lose consciousness. In the distance I heard a door slamming and Susie yelling into the phone. I opened my mouth but no sounds were coming from my throat.

The next thing I knew I woke up on the floor with unbearable pain in my head. For a moment I wasn't sure what happened to me. I tried crawling to the bed but it hurt too much. I frantically looked around for my phone but I couldn't find it. I was so scared my body began to shake and my breaths came quickly. The last thing I heard was sirens in the distance and I hoped they were coming for me.

I must have passed out again because the next

thing I knew I was waking up in a hospital with a throbbing head and a splitting headache.

"Hi, welcome back," the nurse said. "You young lady have a concussion from a nasty blow to the back of your head. We took a scan and it seems everything is fine except for the concussion. Don't try to talk. I'm going to give you something for the pain."

"How did I get here?" I croaked out.

"Someone must have called 911. The police were contacted and they'll be here in the morning. Is there someone I can call for you?"

"No." I vaguely remember calling Susie. "How long have I been out?"

"About three hours. Excuse me there is some commotion in the hallway."

The next face I saw was Susie's rushing over to me with tears in her eyes. I was never so happy to see anyone in my life. I started to talk but it was too much of an effort.

"It's okay just rest. Mark is waiting in the hall. I don't think he wanted to chance it that I would get here in one piece if I drove by myself."

I tried to laugh but it was too painful.

"I knew something was happening to you so I called 911. I was so frightened; I didn't know what to think. Thank heavens you told me the name of the motel before you left. After the police talk to you the doctor thinks you'll be able to go home. Mark will drive your car back and I'll drive us back to the city. I know you feel like shit but can Mark come in for one minute to say hello?"

I nodded yes.

"Hey there, you gave us quite a scare. I hope you don't make a habit of it," he said as he gently touched my hand.

"I think our welcome time has expired. I made a real stink so they made an exception since no visitors are allowed in the middle of the night. I'll see you in a few hours," Susie said, squeezing my hand tightly.

The next thing I knew I heard the door open and a police officer walked towards me. I was thankful it wasn't Detective Graham.

"What time is it?" I asked.

"It's 9:00 a.m. How are you feeling?" Officer Nugent asked. He was very tall and had the beginnings of a beer belly. He was probably around fifty with a receding hairline. His face had scars that looked like they may have been from acne when he was a teenager. But scars and all he had a kind face.

"A little better. I don't feel as nauseous, and my head went from feeling like it was in a vice to a dull throb."

"Can you tell me what happened last night?"

"There really isn't much to tell. Before I walked into my room I knew someone had been there. My laptop was open and my overnight bag was dumped on the floor. I was clobbered before I knew it. Unfortunately, I didn't see who it was."

"Did they take anything?"

"I don't know. I passed out. Did you find my cell phone and laptop?"

"Yes, we dusted them for fingerprints. Hopefully we can find a match. Do you have any idea why someone would want to hurt you?"

"I'm not sure. I'm investigating the death of Laura Tyler. Her husband hired me, and I was up here looking into a guy named Ben Cutler, who oversees Laura's cottage. I was asking around about him so you might want to talk with him."

"You are very lucky. I think the person just wanted to scare you."

"Well I guess that should give me great comfort."

"I need to get some personal information from you and then I'll be on my way. Before you leave you need to stop by the station to pick up your phone and laptop. Your fingerprints are in the system from the background check when you applied for your PI license. If you think of anything else, here's my card."

The doctor came in about a half hour later and gave me the thumbs up to go home. He told me I needed to rest for a few days and no exercise.

We drove by the police station and Susie picked up my phone, laptop and backpack. Once we got on the road I told Susie what had transpired yesterday.

"Well you certainly ruffled someone's feathers. What are you thinking?"

"I'm still wondering whose baby it was. If the person was married and she threatened to expose him that might get someone angry. I'm pretty sure the person was looking through my computer to see what information I had on the case."

"That's what I'm thinking. You probably surprised him or her. Hopefully whatever you were hit with is still in the room, though prints will be almost impossible because so many people are in and out of a motel room."

"Did you call Danny?"

"Danny left last Monday to visit his brother in Brussels. He's in the service with his wife and son. I'll tell him when he gets back. Thank heavens you remembered where I was staying."

"I have to say you scared the crap out of me.

Though the person might have wanted to scare you, you could have been killed. Who am I going to complain to if anything happened to you?"

"You do have a point. My eyes are closing, sorry."

"Hey Tracey, we're home. I would carry you but then I'd wind up in the hospital from a broken back."

We left Susie's car parked in front of the building.

"Hi Wally. Your friend here got herself hit on the head so she needs her rest."

"I'm fine Wally. No need to worry."

"If you need anything just buzz me and I'll come right up," he said with a worried look on his face.

"Thanks, I don't know what I'd do without you."

I still had a bad headache, which the doctor said could last a few more days. When we got inside I slowly lowered myself on the couch.

"I'm going to take a look in your refrigerator to see if there's anything to eat."

"Don't bother. There wasn't anything before I left so unless the food fairy came, the fridge will still be empty. There's no shortage of places to call so don't worry about me."

"Okay, but I'll stop by tomorrow anyway, and glad to see you still have a sense of humor."

After Susie left I undressed slowly, took some aspirin and got into bed. Laying there it finally hit me that I could have been killed. I started hyperventilating. I took deep breaths trying to calm myself. After a few minutes, I was breathing normally.

I fell asleep and when I woke up it was dark. I turned on the TV and slept until morning. My headache was now a minor annoyance and I felt almost human.

I worked from home, giving myself one more day

of rest. First I called Emily Barnes and left a message that I was calling about Laura Tyler, hoping she knew who Laura was. I didn't want to mention Ben Cutler's name since she might not call back.

I wrote up my report on what transpired in Stockbridge including the incident at the motel and sent it to Sam along with my invoice and requesting an additional retainer.

By the time I finished, it was almost 1:00. I was just about ready to scramble some eggs when my cell buzzed.

"Ms. Marks, this is Emily Barnes, you called me."

CHAPTER 26

"Yes, thank you for getting back to me. I'm looking into the death of Laura Tyler, do you know her?"

"Not personally but I know who she is. Her parents died years ago in a car accident. What happened to Laura?"

"She was killed recently and her body was found near her lake home. When Laura first went missing I went up there hoping to find her, instead a guy named Ben Cutler was at the house. Apparently Laura's parents had an arrangement with Mr. Cutler to oversee the property when they weren't there. Laura had the same arrangement after her parents died.

I'm sorry to bring this up but there was a rumor that something happened between you and Mr. Cutler."

"That was a long time ago. What has that got to do with Laura?"

"I don't know if it has anything to do with her death, but I'm looking into all possibilities. I met him twice and he wasn't very pleasant, to say the least. My intention is not to pry and I promise our conversation will be confidential. If you would rather talk in person I could meet you anywhere you want."

"Let's talk in person since right now I'm talking to a complete stranger."

Before hanging up we set up a time to meet at her place tomorrow. I had no idea if pursuing this was a waste of time, but Ben was my prime suspect at the moment. I didn't want to fall into the trap you see on cop shows where the police focus on one person.

I went back to scrambling eggs and took out a sesame bagel that was in the freezer and defrosted it. I saw I had a text from Danny that he was extending his trip and would let me know when he was coming back. I had mixed feelings. I was wrapped up in the case and without Danny here, I had no distractions. On the other hand, I kind of missed him.

As I ate I contemplated my next move. I still wanted to investigate Seth Green. It bothers me that he told me one story and Marjorie Litman told me a different one.

I wasn't feeling like myself yet and was glad there was nowhere I had to be at the moment. I was just about to lie down and watch some mindless TV when my cell buzzed.

"Hey, how are you feeling?" Susie asked.

"Much better. I'm working from home."

"That's smart."

"I spoke with Emily Barnes and we're going to meet tomorrow. I was wondering if the police questioned Ben Cutler about what happened to me."

"If they haven't already, they will, but I wouldn't count on getting any information from them."

"I really want to be the one to find Laura's killer but I feel like I'm spinning my wheels."

"I sympathize with you but I know eventually it will happen. Just have faith."

"Thanks for the words of encouragement. Talk to you soon."

I was just about to nod off when the phone buzzed again. It was Sam.

"Are you all right? Why didn't you call me?"

"I'm much better. My friend picked me up from the hospital. I must have really ticked someone off."

"I wouldn't want anything to happen to you because of me."

"I'll try not to get whacked again, Sam. Did Detective Graham ask you if Laura had a will?"

"Yes, and I told him I didn't know, which is true. I looked through the apartment but couldn't find one. That probably makes me more of a suspect. This just keeps getting worse and worse."

I tried to put a positive spin on it but Sam was right; it didn't look good.

The next morning I drove to Brooklyn into an area called Dumbo which stands for Down Under the Manhattan Bridge Overpass where factories were converted into very expensive apartments. The millennials who worked in Manhattan starting moving to that part of Brooklyn since it was a quick commute. Now the area is considered trendy.

After riding around for a few minutes, I found a parking spot. Emily buzzed me in and I walked up to the second floor. Her apartment was a loft, all open with beautiful hardwood floors and large windows. There was very little furniture, a leather couch and two cushioned chairs with chrome frames. The kitchen was sleek and modern.

Emily was tall and thin. She looked like a model. Her hair was chestnut brown, very thick which she wore in a long braid. Her eyes were huge and dark.

She was wearing jeans and a white tee-shirt. Her feet were bare except for the red nail polish on her toes. She sat on the couch and signaled me to sit in one of the chairs.

"Thanks for seeing me. I know bringing up the past must be painful."

"I rarely think about that night anymore."

"Can you tell me what happened?"

"Ben and I had been dating for a few weeks. I was sixteen and he was, I think about a year older. We were at a party and we both had some wine. I have to admit I was very attracted to him. There was a bedroom upstairs that we went into. At first, everything was fine. We were kissing and he was touching my breasts on top of my blouse. Then he put his hand on my thigh. It was summertime and I was wearing a sundress and my legs were bare. I told him to slow down. I didn't want to have sex but he wasn't listening. He pulled my panties down and that's when I started really freaking out. I screamed and he put his hand over my mouth, and I thought I was going to suffocate. Then I realized he was unbuckling his pants. At that point I was petrified he was going to rape me. I tried pushing him off me but he was too strong, and then I heard someone open the door and it must have frightened Ben since he quickly got off me. I ran out of the room and out of the house."

"That must have been so scary for you. Did you go to the police?"

"I did. He was brought in for questioning but it was his word against mine. And the person who opened the door was a friend of Ben's and said he didn't see anything, just heard voices. I made the decision not to press charges. You see what happens on TV and I didn't want to go through that. I just wanted to forget."

"Do you know if there were any other incidents involving Ben?"

"Just talk. Ben was a good looking guy and there were lots of girls that were after him."

"Would you happen to remember if Laura Tyler was one of them?"

"I don't, I'm sorry."

"Did Ben have a temper?"

"When I first started going out with him he was sweet. But he was the kind of guy that liked to get his way and he definitely had a nasty streak."

"Do you think he could have killed Laura?"

"I have no idea."

"Well if anything else comes to mind, please let me know."

On the ride back I went over everything I knew about Cutler. He was arrogant and from what his ex-wife said he had a temper and was possessive. But what would be his motive to kill Laura? Ms. Litman said she thought Ben may have been infatuated with Laura when they were younger. If he still had feelings for her maybe he tried to act on them, and if she didn't want to have anything to do with him, it could have made him angry, but angry enough to kill her?

I was a little tired but I thought I would go into the office for a while. I was keeping my fingers crossed that I wouldn't bump into cousin Alan since I couldn't lie to him, and he'd be really upset if he knew what had happened to me.

After stopping for coffee and a corn muffin, I made it safely into my office. I checked my phone for messages and was happy to see a text from Danny. He was having a good time and missed me. I texted him back that I was keeping New York safe, fighting crime at every corner.

My phone buzzed. "Tracey Marks."

"Ms. Marks, my name is Janet Green, Seth Green's wife. I would like to meet with you."

I was totally caught off guard and baffled why she wanted to see me. "Sure we can meet. I'm busy for the rest of the day but I can see you tomorrow."

"Why don't I come by your office say around 11:00?"

"Fine, I'll see you then."

Well, I didn't see that coming. I was beyond curious as to what she had to say and was really looking forward to our meeting.

I called Sam asking him to find out if they brought Ben Cutler in for questioning. He said he would contact the police and get back to me.

My phone buzzed. "Hi Susie."

"You want to meet for a drink before heading home?"

"I'm a little tired. Can we do it tomorrow?"

"Are you sure you're all right. How's the head?"

"No headaches, so that's a good sign. When I see you tomorrow I'll explain what's going on."

The next day I was raring to go. I was getting a little antsy since I hadn't been at the gym for a few days, but I thought I would wait one more day just to be on the safe side. I was in my office by 9:00.

Sam called. "I spoke with Officer Graham. He told me they brought Cutler in for questioning but he had an alibi for that night."

"Did they say what his alibi was?"

"Oh yeah, his wife. He was home all night with her

and she apparently corroborated his story."

"You have to be kidding me. So they're not going to question him any further?"

"I guess not."

"I have Seth Green's wife coming in this morning, and I have no idea why she wants to talk with me. This should be interesting."

I had some time before I met with Janet Green so I googled her. She had a page on LinkedIn. Apparently she designs decorative boxes and trays. I went to her website, which was fairly detailed. When I searched one of my databases under her name, nothing of interest popped up.

I heard a knock at the door. "Come in Mrs. Green. Nice to see you again, have a seat. Can I get you a cup of coffee?"

"Sure, milk no sugar."

Janet Green was dressed in a short black dress and heels, a little overdressed for our meeting but maybe she was going someplace afterward.

"So what can I do for you?" as I handed her coffee.

"I believe my husband lied to you."

I sat there stunned, where was this going? Mrs. Green's eyes were darting all around.

"Seth told you that he and Laura Tyler were friends. I don't believe that's true. I think it was more than a friendship. He may have had a thing for her."

"What does that mean?"

"I'm not sure; I think he was infatuated with her."

"And why are you telling me this?"

"I thought you would want to know."

"That's not what I mean. Why would you want to say something that might get your husband in trouble?"

"Because it's true."

I couldn't believe what I was hearing.

"I'm not saying he killed Laura. I know Seth, and he doesn't have it in him to kill anyone. He couldn't even squash a spider. Once I overheard him talking to someone on the telephone and at the time I didn't know it was Laura. It sounded like he was trying to convince this person to meet with him."

"Did you ask him about it?"

"No. I didn't want him to know."

"Do you think he may have been following her?"

"Maybe, sometimes he came home later than usual. Whenever I asked him where he was, he always used the excuse it was business meetings."

"Are you planning on leaving him?"

"No, why would I do that? It was probably just a crush and as far as I know nothing happened between them."

"But aren't you angry at him? Otherwise why would you be here?"

Janet Green did not respond to my question but her silence told me all I needed to know. This woman was seething with anger. I would have been in divorce court already.

"When I first came to your house looking for Seth you told me you didn't know who Laura Tyler was. Is that true?"

"Yes, at that time I had no idea who she was," looking down at the floor as she spoke."

"So at what point did you find out about Laura."

"I confronted Seth after you came to the house and asked about her. He fessed up except he told me it was a friendship from high school and nothing else."

"Did you believe him?"

"I was skeptical but I didn't push it."

"Well, I appreciate you stopping by. I hope everything turns out well for you."

"Do you plan on talking with Seth about this?" Janet asked.

"At some point, why?"

"I would prefer if he didn't know I came to see you."

"I guess I can arrange that."

Well, that was an interesting conversation. I wonder what her motives are. She could be lying to get even with him or maybe she had something to do with Laura's murder. Just because she's a woman is no reason for me to dismiss her as a suspect. I needed to talk with Seth but I wasn't going to give him any warning.

CHAPTER 27

I was getting a clearer picture of Laura from what I've learned so far. We know she ran around with different men, never keeping a relationship for any length of time. Her parents, though they may have loved Laura, did not seem very attentive to Laura's needs. After they died there was no chance she was ever going to get their attention. Maybe she thought marrying Sam was a way of getting what she never had.

I went home, changed and went for a run to clear my head. When I got back I called Melanie.

Melanie said, "I'm glad you called. I can't stop thinking about Laura. I don't understand if she was having problems why she didn't confide in me."

"I wish I had an answer for you. I want to ask you something. After her parents died, was there a change in her?"

"As I had mentioned to you, she was devastated."

"But eventually she went back to school and life went on. Did you notice any difference in her then?"

"Laura was a big party girl before her parents died, but after they passed away she stopped the party scene. She still dated quite a bit but there was no one she stayed with for any length of time. Why are you asking?"

"I was just trying to understand Laura's behavior. Someone had seen her in Pittsfield with a man who was not her husband. Unfortunately, the person only saw the back of him. Also, we know that the baby wasn't Sam's."

"I'm guessing Laura was unhappy but I believe she was unhappy before her parents died. I should have done more for her. I hope you find out who killed her."

I thought to myself, so do I.

I met Susie at a cozy bar called Dead Poet on Amsterdam Avenue. We found a table and ordered drinks and a basket of chicken wings and nachos. Bar food might not be great for you but every once in a while you just need some happy food.

"How's the head?"

"It's fine but I'm going to need a shrink soon. This case is driving me crazy. Just when I think it's Ben Cutler who killed Laura, a wrench gets thrown in. First, he has an alibi for the night of the attack, which might be bogus since his wife is his alibi. Then Seth Green's wife comes in to see me and practically throws her husband under the bus. She told me that Seth was pursuing Laura."

"She told you that?"

"Yes. She said she overheard Seth on the phone practically begging Laura to see him. Well, she didn't actually know it was Laura at that moment. According to Seth they remained friends after dating in college and talked every so often. I don't know who to believe. Part of me thinks she is a scorned wife but I also think she may be telling the truth. There are too many unknowns, so how do I figure this out?"

"First you have to go back to Seth Green and hear what he has to say. Then make a list of everyone involved, including Mrs. Green and maybe something will hit you."

"Mrs. Green?"

Like you said she could be a scorned wife who might have just been jealous enough to kill Laura."

The weekend came and went. On Monday I drove up to Seth's office to pay him a surprise visit. "I'm here to see Seth Green."

"Do you have an appointment?"

"I don't. Tell him it's Tracey Marks, and it's urgent." Seth came out a few minutes later and ushered me into his office and closed the door."

"Did you ever hear of calling Ms. Marks? I'm in the middle of a deadline."

I ignored his remark. "I thought you would be jumping at the chance to help me find Laura's killer."

"I am, but not when you think you can just drop in anytime you feel like it."

"I'm trying to catch a killer. I'm not here to placate you."

"What is it you want to talk to me about?"

We both sat down. "I've gotten conflicting accounts of your relationship with Laura. I need to know the truth. Look, I don't want to have to get the police involved in this but I will if I'm not satisfied with what you say to me."

He picked up the pen on his desk and started playing with it while nervously looking out the window.

"Okay, I wasn't completely honest with you. We did talk, that's the truth. I wanted more and she didn't. That's all there was to it."

"So what you're telling me is that you accepted

what she told you. You didn't follow

Laura and confront her, maybe trying to persuade her using force?"

"No, of course not, I loved her."

"Maybe that's why you followed her. You were jealous and wanted to know if she was seeing anyone else besides her husband."

"That's crazy."

"No, it's not. Someone was stalking her and I can't think of anyone besides you."

Seth had a poker face on. No reaction.

"Did your wife know you were in love with Laura?"

"Not that I am aware of."

"Did you know that Laura was pregnant and her husband was not the father?"

"I had no idea, I swear," his eyes darting around.

"Maybe she told you and in a blind rage you killed her, knowing that now she was pregnant, you had absolutely no chance with Laura."

"No, no, no. I would never hurt her. You have to believe me."

"What if your wife found out that you were obsessed with Laura? What do you think she would do?"

"Are you suggesting she would harm Laura?"

"I'm not suggesting anything. I'm asking you a question. Do you think she is capable of killing Laura?"

"That's absurd."

"When's the last time you spoke with Laura?"

"I don't remember exactly, maybe six weeks ago, maybe longer."

"Did she say anything out of the ordinary or

sounded weird now looking back at it?"

"Not that I can recall."

"I want you to know that I will find out if you are lying to me or not telling me everything you know." With that, I left.

I believed Seth was stalking Laura but I am not sure he was capable of killing her, though I didn't completely rule him out.

In my mind, Sam was still a suspect. The scene in his office practically leaning over his receptionist Nicole nagged at me. Surveillance was part of my training but I was never the lead investigator. The few times I had to conduct surveillance for clients I farmed it out. It's tedious and boring. Since I didn't want to spend Sam's money hiring someone to tail him, I thought I would take a crack at it.

When I got back to the office I contemplated where I should start the surveillance. I had no idea where Sam parked his car which could be a problem, especially in city traffic. Also he may not be in his office at the end of the day. I could call him on some pretext to find out if he's there. If the starting point was at his apartment in the morning then I would have to follow him all day and that was not going to happen. I decided I would track him from work later today.

Danny texted me that he would be coming home early tomorrow morning and wanted to know if we could have dinner that evening. I texted him back I could.

I left work and went to the gym. It felt good pumping iron again and working up a sweat on the treadmill. I was looking forward to seeing Danny tomorrow but also realized that while he was away, I was so busy I hadn't had time to think about him.

I slept for about two hours knowing I didn't know how long I was going to be out tailing Sam.

Around 5:00, I called him. "Hi Sam, have you heard anything from the police?"

"No, they're not telling me anything. What about you, any luck?"

"I spoke with Seth Green. He admits that he was making a concerted effort to get Laura to go out with him but she wasn't interested. Are you in the office?" I asked, very casually.

"Yeah, I'll probably be here for a while."

"I'll talk to you soon," and I hung up.

I decided to leave now in case he left his office early. I took two bottles of water and a peanut butter sandwich with me and got my car.

When I reached Sam's block I circled around several times before spotting a car leaving about a half a block down from Sam's office. I parked and waited. I had to keep a diligent watch since I didn't want to miss him coming out. Unfortunately it's not like on TV where everything goes according to plan.

Around 6:45 Sam and his receptionist came out. I made a split decision to take the car instead of following on foot. They walked two blocks to a parking garage. A few minutes later Sam's gray Audi emerged from the parking garage. Since I didn't want to be right on top of him, I let one car stay between us. Following them was making me anxious since I had very little control of the situation and not a lot of experience. My phone buzzed but I let it go to voice mail.

They drove up Third Avenue. All of a sudden the car in front of me stopped at the yellow light and I was stuck. Shit. Come on, come on, willing the light to hurry up and turn green. When it finally did, I changed lanes hoping to catch up with Sam. I saw his car a few blocks ahead where he was caught at a light. No wonder I never liked surveillance. You have to have a certain temperament, which I apparently don't have.

At 61st Street, Sam turned right. It looked like he was searching for a parking spot. I stayed in my car and followed him waiting to see where he went. They walked into a restaurant nearby called Isle of Capri. I couldn't see inside the restaurant from the street so there was no point in loitering outside. Instead I waited near his car. I found a spot a few cars behind Sam's on the other side of the street. I knew it would be a while so I settled in. Is it common for a boss to take his receptionist to dinner? I had my doubts. Maybe his relationship with Laura was not as wonderful as Sam claimed it was. If he knew Laura was cheating would it be a reason to kill her? Probably not, unless he somehow found out she was pregnant and that he wasn't the father.

I was starving. I ate my peanut butter sandwich and washed it down with a bottle of water. I looked to see who had called but there was no number listed. My sandwich felt like a rock in the pit of my stomach thinking about the person who threatened me, but when I listened to the message, it was someone who wanted to make an appointment to see me and would call back. Their number was blocked.

I turned on the radio to keep me company so I wouldn't doze off from boredom. I almost missed Sam and Nicole as they walked hand in hand to Sam's car.

I slowly drove out of my parking spot. As soon as I saw Sam start to move, I began to follow. I stayed a few car lengths back since there was no car in front of me. As I was about three quarters down the block a car pulled out right in front of me and stopped at the end of the street as the light turned red. By the time I started moving again, Sam was gone.

CHAPTER 28

I wanted to kill the driver I was so frustrated.

There was still a chance that Sam took Nicole back to his apartment so I headed over to his place. His car was nowhere on the street. I knew his building had an indoor parking garage but I had no way to access it. I waited a little while hoping he still might show up but no such luck. I should have found out Nicole's last name and then I could have pulled up an address for her. I was pissed at myself for not thinking about it beforehand. Since there wasn't anything I could do at this point, I called it a night.

Well, that was a bust. I knew that surveillance in the city with only one car was a long shot, but I was still disappointed, though I don't think it was a complete waste of time. I can say with almost certainty he's having an affair with Nicole. I thought I would hold off saying anything to Sam, at least for now.

The next morning I was in the office by 8:30. My phone buzzed. "Tracey Marks."

"Ms. Marks, my name is Brian Curtis. I was wondering if we could meet. There's a discreet matter I would like to talk with you about and I don't want to do it over the phone."

"Where did you have in mind?"

"I'm up in Stockbridge. There's a diner on Main Street in Brewster, called Bob's Diner. I thought we could meet there. Is today possible?"

"How did you get my number?"

"I looked it up on the internet. You're not that hard to find."

"I can meet you at one. How will I know you?"

"I'll be wearing a black tee-shirt. You can't miss me."

That was really strange. I wondered about all the cloak and dagger.

My phone buzzed again and saw it was Danny.

"Greetings. Nice to have you back on U.S. soil. How was your trip?"

"It was really nice. Spending time with my nephew Joseph was a lot of fun. Being there for two weeks, I felt like I got to know him better. How are you?"

"Good, but busy."

"Are you still up for dinner tonight?"

"I think I can manage that. Why don't we go someplace local. Anton's is a great Italian place near me."

"I'll meet you there at 8:00. I'm still a little jet lagged so I may take a nap."

"Cute," I said and hung up.

At around 11:00 I drove up to Brewster. I'd taken my gun out of the safe and placed it in my ankle holster. I had no idea what I was getting myself into and I didn't want any repeat performances of my stay in the motel.

When I got there I waited in the car for about fifteen minutes. I saw a guy getting off a motorcycle walking into the diner. He was wearing what I would call biker clothes, all in black, including the leather jacket. I wouldn't want to tangle with him.

I was a little nervous as I entered the diner. The guy was already seated at a booth.

"Are you Brian?" He looked like he had gone a few rounds. I'm no expert on noses but his looked like it had been broken more than once. He could have been a wrestler. He was big and stocky with a thick neck. He had tattoos up and down his arms.

"Yes, have a seat Tracey."

I guess we were on a first name basis. We both ordered coffee when the waitress came. "So what's this about?" I said trying to sound tough and business like.

"First I want to know that everything I say is confidential."

"If you haven't committed a crime, then I can say that."

"As I mentioned I live up in Stockbridge and of course Laura Matthews death was well publicized. I witnessed an incident between her and Ben Cutler."

As I was listening I was trying to get a read on him. While he was speaking he looked me straight in the eye but revealed nothing. "What happened?" I asked.

"I was going to see Mr. Cutler at his office regarding some construction work he was planning to do for me. As I was opening the door I heard shouting. I didn't go in but I saw Cutler grab a woman roughly by the arm. She kicked him and he let go. As she was running past me I heard him yelling, "you'll be sorry Laura.""

"Did you hear what they were arguing about?"

"No, I must have come in at the end."

"Did he say anything to you?"

"Nope, he was all business."

"How well do you know Mr. Cutler?"

"I don't really know him at all. He was recommended to me and that's the extent of it."

"Do you have any sort of grudge against him cause I can't figure out why you would go out of your way to contact me."

"Look lady, I was just trying to be a good Samaritan."

"Why didn't you go to the police, why come to me?"

"I have my reasons, but if you must know I've had some run-ins with them. Nothing major."

He didn't seem like the good Samaritan type. Maybe there was more to it than he was telling me.

"How did you know I was investigating Ms. Matthews' death?"

"Stockbridge is not a big town. Word gets around."

"One last question; why come all this way when you could have told me this over the phone?"

"I think we needed to see each other in person, eye to eye, don't you think?" And with that, he got up and left.

CHAPTER 29

Cutler's name kept coming up. I wasn't sure I believed Brian, but what would be his motivation to lie unless someone put him up to it. I wanted to call Cutler and hear his side of the story but I wasn't sure he would take my call since he's been hostile to me from the beginning. I guess I didn't have anything to lose but I decided to sleep on it.

When I got back I wrote up my conversation with Brian Curtis. There was something about him that didn't sit well with me. Maybe I was just being paranoid.

When I arrived at Anton's, Danny was waiting outside. I noticed he was carrying a small shopping bag. We hugged and went inside. Olivia showed us to our table. I saw the smile on her face when she thought I wasn't looking. John came over and we gave him our drink order.

"So how was the trip?"

"It was great. I got the whirlwind tour, but the best part was biking with my nephew, Joseph and spending time with him at the cafes. All of us went to the Musee des Instruments de Musique. It houses instruments from all over the world, including Scottish bagpipes and a collection of traditional Tibetan instruments. But I'm glad to be home. I got you something."

As Danny was reaching down, our waiter came

over.

"I think I'll have my usual linguini and clams and my friend is going to have the same. Oh, and we'll share the beet salad. Thanks Sam."

"Can I get you each another glass of wine?"

"I'll have a glass of Merlot."

"Cabernet Sauvignon for me," Danny said.

Danny took out a gift wrapped box. It was a silk scarf in wonderful colors of blue, lavender and gold. I put it around my neck. "Very chic. Thank you, it's beautiful."

"You're welcome."

"How are Josh and Margo? Are they enjoying their time in Brussels?"

"They are. Josh is trying to figure out if he's going to stay in the Army and make it a career. There are plenty of job opportunities for him if he decides to leave the service. He could probably do consulting work overseas if they don't want to come back to the states. So how is everything here?"

I filled him in on what was going on with the case, including the incident at the motel. As I was recounting the incident Danny's eyes opened wide and he had a worried look on his face.

"I'm perfectly fine. It was just a slight concussion."

"Thank heavens for Susie. I think I'll take the scarf back and give it to her."

"Very funny."

"So what's the plan now?"

"I don't have one at the moment."

We both had dessert and coffee. When we walked out I was debating whether to invite Danny up.

"Do you have a secret life you're hiding from me? Is there somebody in your apartment that you don't want me to know about?"

"No, no. It's just that it's hard to take things slowly if we're sleeping together."

"Well, you can look at it this way. We enjoy each other's company and sleeping together can be optional."

"I like that plan, so now what do we do?"

"I don't know. What are you thinking?"

"I'm thinking I want you to come up and we'll see what happens."

"That is a plan I can get behind."

We walked back to my place. I thought it better not to think too much. When my apartment door shut behind us we stood in the hallway kissing. I pulled away and led him into the bedroom.

"Nice room," he said. That was the last words spoken for the next forty minutes or so until we laid tangled in each other's arms.

"Well, now we know what happens," I said.

"Maybe we need a chaperone," kissing me softly on the lips.

We spent the next hour taking our time, wanting to please each other. "You know there has been something that's been bothering me about the case."

"That's your first thought after I gave you some of my best moves," he said jokingly.

"Guilty as charged. I think the first two warnings I got were from someone who wanted to scare me off. Maybe I was uncovering something he didn't want me to pursue. I'm just not sure if it's the same person from the motel."

"You look like you're ready to nod off, should I go?"

I was too tired to think. The next thing I knew

Danny was dressed and leaning over me.

"What time is it?" I asked him.

"It's 6:00 a.m. I have to go back to my place and get ready to see a client by 9:00."

He kissed me gently on the cheek and left. I was debating whether to get up or go back to sleep for a while. Sleep won out. It was 8:30 when I next woke. I looked at my cell phone for any missed calls but there were none.

I put on the coffee maker. I guess I nodded in the affirmative last night. I wondered how wise it was to have Danny stay over. Though I feel comfortable when I'm with him, I didn't want a serious relationship at this time. I was afraid that Danny wanted something more than I did.

I went to get my laptop to check something and it wasn't in the dining room where I thought I left it. Instead I found it on the kitchen counter. That's weird, but I've been so busy lately I probably put it there absently.

I made a list of all the people I've spoken to who may have had reason to want me off the case. I think I can eliminate Melanie, Laura's boss, Mr. Nichols and Jane, from work. I probably could rule out Raymond Berg. I was leaning towards Seth or his wife and Ben Cutler.

As I was contemplating that thought, my phone buzzed.

"Ms. Marks, this is Detective Graham in Stockbridge. I'd like you to come up to my office on Friday since I have some questions for you. How about 12:00?" and hung up.

I was actually glad he called since I had been wondering if they made any progress on Laura's death. I also thought it would be a good opportunity to speak with Ben Cutler in person.

I returned to my thoughts of possible suspects. I began to think Laura was either dead when Sam first came to my office or not long after. Seth Green could have been the one trying to scare me since he was stalking Laura and didn't want me to find out. I can't figure out Janet Green. Though she came in spilling the beans about her husband, I'm not sure how or if she is involved.

I called Susie and got her voice mail.

A little later she called back. "Sorry I missed your call. What's up?"

"I'm going up to Stockbridge on Friday. The detective on Laura's case has some questions for me. Are you interested in taking a road trip with me?"

"Actually I would. Mark is away on business until Sunday and I've never been to Stockbridge."

"Well, you can check it off your bucket list. I'll pick you up at 9:00. We can stop at this diner on the Taconic Parkway and get some breakfast along the way. Also stick a pair of panties in your backpack along with a toothbrush just in case."

"Great, this should be fun."

One of the many things I love about Susie is her upbeat personality. She can bring a stuffed animal to life. Me, on the other hand, would not last one hour in a room full of Happy People Anonymous.

The traffic was very light on the Taconic. Susie and I stopped at the O's diner for breakfast. From the outside it looked like it had been there for fifty years and from the inside it looked like nothing had changed since then. The booths were old and worn. At least it appeared clean.

We both ordered eggs, whole wheat toast and coffee. "So what do you think Detective Graham will ask me?"

"He'll try to get as much information out of you as he possibly can. If you want to find out what he knows you'll have to play a little hardball. You've done a lot of work on this case and he probably needs you more than you need him. I would work it from that angle. Do you want me to come in with you?"

"I think I should speak with him alone. He might not be as willing to share if you're there."

We made it up to Stockbridge by 11:30. "I'd like to show you Laura's house after I speak with Graham, and at some point head over to Ben Cutler's place. I need to get a better read on him."

We drove over to the police station. Susie waited in the car with her John Grisham novel while I went in to butt heads with Detective Graham.

"Can you tell Detective Graham that Tracey Marks is here to see him?"

"Do you have an appointment?"

"I do."

"Have a seat. He'll be with you shortly."

About ten minutes later, Detective Graham came out and took me back to his office.

"Can I get you any coffee?"

"No, thank you."

"Word has it that you have been snooping around asking a lot of questions," looking not too pleased.

"I didn't know that was a crime."

"You're interfering with a police investigation and I don't like it."

"That's not my intention to interfere but maybe we can help each other out."

"And how do you suppose we can do that?" clenching a small rubber ball in his hand.

"Well we can share what we each know, which could help both of us."

"What makes you think I need your help?"

"For starters did you know that Ben Cutler threatened Laura?" The look on his face revealed nothing.

"Where did you hear that?"

"I can't tell you that but it's from a reliable source." I wasn't sure if that was true but he didn't have to know that. "It seems that his name has been popping up. Also, there were rumors that he allegedly sexually assaulted a young girl when he was in high school." After a pause I said, "did you find anything at the house that might be important?"

"Like I told you before this is a police investigation and I don't want you sticking your nose where it doesn't belong."

I was pissed. Now that I knew where I stood with Detective Graham I had no intention of telling him anything else. "I haven't heard back from Officer Nugent, who is handling my attack. Do you know if he has any leads?"

"You'll have to get in contact with him directly."

I stood up to leave and started walking out.

"Remember what I said, keep your nose out of it."

"What an asshole," I said to Susie as I got in the car.

"What did he want?"

"He wanted to read me the riot act, making it clear it's his investigation and to keep out of it."

"He can't stop you from snooping around."

"Hopefully not."

We drove over to Laura's place. I still had the key from when Sam and I were locked out of Laura's house. I checked the back to make sure no one was lurking around down by the lake. I didn't want any surprises.

"This is a really nice summer home," Susie said. "I hope Mark and I can afford a house like this one day."

"Why don't we split up. You can take the bedroom and I'll check the garage," I said.

The garage was fairly neat. There were all kinds of tools hanging on the walls and an empty refrigerator near the stairs that led into the house. There were a few boxes sitting on shelves mounted on the wall. The first box I took down was filled with old clothes. I checked through it just to make sure nothing was in the pockets. The next box was filled with books, mostly classics like Jane Eyre, Silas Marner, and Little Women.

"Hey, come up here. I need you to look at something," Susie yelled.

I sprinted up to the bedroom and saw a shoebox on the floor filled with pictures. "Where did you find this?"

"I almost didn't. I had to use the step stool to reach the shelf. It was sort of hidden way in the back under a blanket."

I started sifting through the photos.

"Is there anybody specific you're looking for?"

"I wish I knew." There were loads of photos of Laura when she was a little girl, some with friends when she was a teenager and a few as an adult. There were some photos of her parents, a few with Marjorie

Litman and other people who I didn't know. There was one that caught my attention. It was taken at a restaurant or a bar, I couldn't be sure. In the photo Laura was with the assistant coach Glen McIntyre that I had met and another woman with long dark hair and beautiful large brown eyes.

"Shit, I can't believe it."

"What, what is it?" Susie said.

CHAPTER 30

"It's the assistant coach. He told me he never met Laura."

"Maybe he didn't remember. If he was at a bar drinking he might not recall meeting her."

"Yeah, I guess that's possible but I'm not so sure. He has his arm around Laura's shoulder. I wonder who the other woman is?"

"It could be he didn't want to mention it in front of his wife."

I took the photo and put it in my pocket. I was wondering if taking it was a crime, but who would find out.

I went through the rest of the photos but nothing else stood out. I put the box back where Susie found it and we both went back downstairs. The last box in the garage was also filled with books.

"I'm curious if Laura's passport and bank book are still in the drawer."

The key was where I placed it last and so were the passport and bank account.

"You want to have lunch? I'm starved," I said to Susie.

I took Susie to the café in town where Claire waitresses. Maybe she knows the mystery lady in the photo. I spotted Claire as soon as we walked in.

"Tracey, how are you?"

"Good. This is my investigator Susie. Any chance

we can still get lunch?"

"Sure. Our menu is the same for lunch and dinner."

We both ordered burgers and fries. "How would you like to be my #1 investigator? If it wasn't for you, I might never have found the photos," I said to Susie.

"First, I would be your only investigator, and second, how much does it pay?"

"You can't put a price on training with the best PI in all of Manhattan."

"Well, don't we have a swell head. I think I'll stick with my day job."

"Wise choice," I said laughing.

"Can I get you anything else?" Claire asked as she set down our food.

"I was wondering if you knew the woman in this photo?"

"Can't say as I do, but I recognize the coach. If you need to find out who the woman is there's an artist's studio two blocks from here. The woman who owns it, Joan Rubin, has lived here all her life. She might know her or might know how to find out who she is."

"That's great. Thanks for all your help."

I gave Claire a very generous tip. "Well, it's 4:30. Let's see if the studio is still open."

"Okay boss," Susie said, giving me a salute.

The door didn't list any hours. As we entered, we heard a chime.

"I'm up here," someone shouted.

Susie and I climbed the stairs and were greeted by a slender woman who looked to be in her late fifties with long gray hair. She looked like a hippie from the sixties with her long skirt and sandals.

"Welcome, how can I help you?"

"Wow, your artwork is beautiful," Susie said. "Are these landscapes of the area?"

"Yes, they are. Feel free to look around."

While Susie was browsing, I plunged forward. "Claire from the café told us we should talk with you. I'm a private investigator and I am investigating the death of Laura Tyler Matthews. I have this photo and was wondering if you know who this woman is?"

"That was terrible about Laura. What a tragedy. You're not from around here?"

"No, I'm from New York City, where Laura lived. Her husband hired me."

"Why do you need to know who she is?"

"I'd like to answer you but then I would be violating confidentiality." I could see her contemplating what I said.

"Let me think about this and I'll contact you."

"Look I'm sorry I can't tell you why. There are other people involved. If I could, I would."

"What about McIntyre?" Joan asked.

"He just happens to be in the photo but he is not a target of my investigation." I hoped my nose wasn't growing longer as I was speaking. "Well, thank you for your time."

"Excuse me, how much is this painting?" Susie asked.

"It's $350. Would you like it?"

"I would. Can I give you a check or I can come back after I go to a cash machine?"

"No, that's fine. I trust you. I'll wrap it."

"Isn't it pretty?"

"It is." It was a watercolor of a beach scene; kids playing in the sand; frolicking in the water; and people sitting on beach chairs, shaded by umbrellas.

Further out was a boat with someone fishing. "Do you think Mark will like it?"

"I hope so. I know exactly where it's going," Susie said.

"Why the hell couldn't Joan tell me who the woman is. It's almost 5:30 and we still haven't talked with Cutler."

"Why don't we stay over and talk to Cutler in the morning. Mark's not coming home until Sunday afternoon. We can check in somewhere and then get drinks."

"That's a great idea. I don't think I have it in me to interview one more person today."

"Let's have us some fun," Susie said.

We drove over to the Pleasant Valley Motel where I stayed last time I was here. We went into the office and rang the bell.

"Hey, aren't you the person who got attacked when you were here?"

"Yeah, that's why I brought my bodyguard with me this time," I said with a deadpan face. He looked at Susie, scratching his head and raising his eyebrows.

"We'd like to check in for one night, preferably not room 104."

"Oh I get it; that's where you were clobbered."

"That guy's a real genius," Susie said as we walked to our room. "How about we freshen up and ditch this place?"

"Sounds good to me. Why don't we check out Pittsfield? It's only about 10 miles from here," I said.

We found the restaurant Elizabeth's on East Main Street, the one Jessica Brown had seen Laura going into with a man. It was located in a house, one of the charms of small town living. The website said it was

Italian. Good to know, in case we got hungry.

"I need your advice on something though I can't believe I am asking you," I said as we settled in at the bar.

"Shoot, advice is my specialty," Susie said.

"Hey gals, what can I get you to drink?" the bartender asked.

"I'll have a Merlot and my friend here will have a Cabernet," I answered.

"He's really cute."

"Let's try to focus here," I said.

The bartender set down our drinks and put a basket of pretzels in front of us.

"What's your name?" Susie asked.

"It's Leo. Are you women from around here?"

"New York City," Susie and I chimed in.

"Well enjoy your drinks."

After he left, I said to Susie, "The problem is I slept with Danny, and we had one sleepover sort of by accident. I'm afraid he's getting too serious and it's way too soon. Just because we slept together doesn't mean I want us to be joined at the hip."

"You do have a problem. I see no other solution except to talk with him and tell him how you feel and hope for the best."

"That's your answer. I could have told myself that."

"Well, you don't have to pay me."

"Seriously, that's all you got?"

"Unfortunately yes, but before you throw under the bus, I'd love to meet him."

I signaled to Leo, "Do you by any chance recognize any of these people?"

"Any reason you're asking?"

"This woman," I pointed to Laura, "is dead and I'm looking into her death."

"Are you a cop?"

"No, a private investigator," I said handing him my card.

"So she was murdered?"

"Yes, she owns a summer home in Stockbridge."

"Oh yeah, I heard about her. Why are you looking into it?"

"Her husband hired me."

"She looks familiar," pointing to Laura, "but I don't recognize the other two."

"Where do you know her from?"

"I'm not sure. It could be from here or the newspaper article about her death."

"Thanks Leo. Can I buy you a drink?"

"Normally that's frowned upon but since it's before the dinner crowd I'll join both of you."

I was hoping he wasn't pouring himself the best scotch on the shelf.

"By the way, this is my investigator Susie."

"I've never met female investigators."

"Well, today is your lucky day," Susie said.

"How's the food here?" I asked.

"Really good. Usually we're booked on Saturday evenings but you could probably get a table if you have dinner by six."

Leo left to wait on some guys at the end of the bar.

"That was a good move to show him the photo."

"I thought if Laura was having an affair with a married man they wouldn't want to be seen around Stockbridge."

Leo came back and told us the guys at the end of the bar want to buy us our next drink.

"Tell them we're good." Two minutes later both guys were standing behind us.

"Hello ladies." The guy who spoke was practically breathing down my neck reeking of liquor and cigarettes. The other guy was just standing there with a smirk on his face.

"You mind if we join you?" putting his hand on my back.

"Actually we do. We're not looking for company and get your hand off my back now," I said.

"Oh, the snooty type. You think you're too good for us. Maybe your friend here feels differently."

I saw Leo walk over. "Look guys the ladies don't want company so why don't you just leave it at that."

As they were leaving, the ringleader whispered in my ear, "you'll be sorry cunt."

"You would think a nice place like this wouldn't get jerks, but the liquor brings it out in them, sorry," Leo said.

"I think it's time we go," Susie said.

I paid for our drinks, including Leo's, and gave him a generous tip.

"Well that was interesting or maybe disgusting depending on how you look at it," Susie said as we were walking to the car.

"Hey ladies, where you headed," blocking our path.

"Look guys, I'm sure you're a lot of fun but we've had a long day and it's almost past our bedtime so please move."

The two jerks that hassled us inside did not budge. I was debating what to do.

"You know ladies there's a great place right down the road that has dancing. We can take a ride over."

"Why don't we meet you there. We'll follow you."

"Isn't this one funny, Arty?"

I looked at Susie and said, "start walking to the car." As we did the jerk closest to me grabbed my arm and Susie kicked him right in the shin. I pushed him hard and as we ran to the car, we heard the idiot yelling, "you bitches, you'll be sorry."

When we were safely inside the car I said to Susie, "you were awesome."

"I can't believe I did that. I don't know what came over me."

"You were great. I can't wait to tell Mark," I said.

"I'm not sure we should tell him. Between this and you getting clobbered at the motel, he might not want me to play with you anymore." And then we both laughed so hard tears were running down our cheeks.

We headed back to Stockbridge to get some dinner where we had an uneventful but nice dinner at the Once Upon A Time Restaurant.

CHAPTER 31

The next morning after breakfast, we headed over to Ben Cutler's contracting business hoping he was there.

We pulled into Cutler's parking lot. His truck was parked outside.

I told Susie to chime in if she thought I could use her help. When I opened the door he looked up from whatever he was doing.

"You again, you're not welcome."

"I need to talk with you. This is my investigator, Susie."

"I'm in a hurry, so make it quick."

"I heard you had a pretty heated argument with Laura a few weeks ago just before she was murdered. You threatened her."

"Who told you that bullshit?"

"It's not bullshit and you know it. So what happened?"

"Get the hell out. I don't have to talk with you."

"That's true but I think the police would be interested in hearing what I have to say. It doesn't look good, especially after being brought in for questioning about my attack."

The sneer on his face turned to contempt.

"She came up one day during the week and found me in her house."

"What were you doing there? Obviously Laura

didn't think you were there just to check on the place."

"I was looking around, call it curiosity. I had this thing for her but I knew she wasn't interested. It was harmless."

Susie asked. "How did she react?"

"As you can imagine, she was mad. I couldn't blame her."

"So what happened at your office?" I asked.

"She wanted her keys back and I got angry. I grabbed her arm. It was stupid, but I still wanted to take care of the house for her. She wouldn't see reason."

"So if she fired you, why were you taking down the dock when I first met you?"

I wanted to get the dock down for Laura before the winter came in. That was all there was to it."

"Maybe you knew she was dead already. Why should I believe anything you tell me? I heard there were rumors about you when you were in high school, an incident with a girlfriend."

"I don't care what you believe or what you heard. Now get out."

"You have any questions?" looking at Susie.

"No, I'm good."

"I think Cutler had the hots for Laura and was frustrated that she didn't feel the same way," Susie said as we were walking to the car.

"Ben has a temper and could have accidentally killed her. I don't know if I believe his story. What's your take on it?"

"Not sure what to make of it either. It's possible if she didn't want anything to do with him it might have made him angry, but enough to kill her? I don't see it unless, as you said, it was by accident."

"Before we hit the road, I want to call Officer Nugent. Maybe he would be willing to tell me what's going on with Laura's investigation."

"Officer Nugent, this is Tracey Marks. I haven't heard from you and I was curious if you made any progress on my case?"

"Unfortunately, we don't have any viable leads. Mr. Cutler had an alibi and there were no witnesses."

"Were you able to figure out the weapon used?"

"Unfortunately, no. And in a motel room, there are a million prints.

"What about on my computer."

"The only prints were yours. The person probably wore gloves."

"Were there any cameras on the outside of the motel?"

"I checked and they don't have any. That would be too much to ask."

"By the way is there any news on Laura Matthews' investigation?" I said holding my breath.

"I don't think they've made much progress but I'm not part of that investigation."

"Do you know if they established where the crime scene was?"

"They're not sure but they think it's probably down by the lake in back of her house. Unfortunately, it's been trampled over."

"Okay, thanks. And please let me know if you turn up anything on my case."

"They think the crime scene is down by the lake on Laura's property," I said to Susie after I hung up.

"That makes sense. If she was meeting someone she knew, she would be caught off guard."

"But why go to all the trouble of moving her body, why not just leave her? Isn't the killer taking a chance he might be seen?" I said.

"Well, one thought would be that they didn't want the body found right away. They probably waited till it was dark and then either transported the body in a car or in the rowboat that was on the property."

Before heading home, we took in some of the sights including a tour of the Norman Rockwell Museum.

I dropped Susie off at her place around 8:00. After parking my car I picked up some Thai food for dinner.

Before eating, I did some sit-ups and push-ups since I hadn't exercised in three days. Danny was weighing on my mind. Why do things have to be so complicated? I texted him and asked him if we could meet Monday for a drink after work. He texted back to let him know what time and where.

Monday morning, after stopping for my usual coffee and muffin, I peeked my head into Alan's office and said hi to Margaret.

"Did you ever get those earplugs?"

"What did you say?"

I laughed as I waved goodbye.

Sipping my coffee I pondered what I found out this past weekend in Stockbridge. Cutler was still high on my list. McIntyre, the assistant coach, was now in the picture. Was he somehow involved with Laura? He lied, telling me he never met her. I can see how Laura could get involved with him. Though he was much older he was good looking and he kept himself in shape. Maybe he represented a father figure to Laura.

I called Sam. "Tell me you have some good news," he said.

"I did find out some interesting things but I'd rather not say yet. But I need to talk to you about something. Can we meet?"

"Can you come by my apartment tomorrow morning, say about 8:30?"

"Sure, I'll see you then."

My phone buzzed. "Hello, is this Ms. Marks?"

"Yes, speaking," not recognizing the voice on the other end.

"This is Joan Rubin. We met at my art Gallery on Saturday. You had inquired about a woman in a photo you showed me."

"Yes. Thank you for calling."

"I can tell you the name of the woman but I need you to keep me out of it, meaning she can't find out I gave you her name."

"I can promise you that."

"Her name is Michelle Gordon. I don't have her number but I know she lives in Chatham, New York; it's not that far from Stockbridge."

"I think I pass the exit driving up the Taconic."

"Well, good luck."

I pulled up a report from my database on Michelle Gordon. It gave a current address and cell phone number but no indication of whether she was married. It listed her age as thirty-nine.

I googled Michelle and it turns out she is a web designer. I went to her website. It said she had been in business for over fifteen years. There was no address, just a post office box and a telephone number. I'm thinking that her office is probably in her home.

So what now, call her or take a trip up there? This could be a delicate situation and I might get only one bite at the apple. I decided to go up there tomorrow after I meet with Sam.

At five, I left to meet Danny. I was dreading this conversation. I met him at a pub not too far from his place. I arrived before him and ordered a glass of wine at the bar, hopefully to get rid of my jitters. When Danny arrived he ordered a beer and we moved to one of the wooden tables. It looked like the kind of place you can throw your peanut shells on the floor.

We both started speaking at the same time. We laughed and played 'no you go first' and I won.

"I had to go to Stockbridge over the weekend. The detective on Laura's case politely demanded my appearance at his office on Friday. So while I was there I talked to Ben Cutler, basically threatening him if he didn't tell me what his argument with Laura was about. He buckled but not sure if he was being forthright or making up something to appease me. Also Susie found a photo at Laura's house and I am trying to track down the name of the woman in the photo. It might be a lead.

"It sounds like you had a busy weekend. I met a buddy of mine for drinks who I haven't seen in six months. Are we fine?" he said looking into my eyes.

"Yes, I've been thinking about us, and you know how I said from the beginning I didn't want to get serious, I want to make sure we're on the same page. I like the way things are now, I just can't promise you how I'll feel in the future."

"I'm fine with how we are at the moment, and I'm

willing to be patient, but I can't promise for how long."

"Thanks, I appreciate that."

We spent the next two hours talking, eating and drinking. When we left it was almost 8:00. We kissed outside and I caught a taxi home.

The next morning I went to Sam's place with the purpose of confronting him about his relationship with Nicole. I knew it would not be a pleasant conversation. We sat in the living room.

"So what's going on?" he said.

I thought I would ease into the conversation. "Have you heard anything more from Detective Graham?"

"No. I'm not sure if that's a good sign or not."

"Sam, are you having an affair?"

"No, why would you ask me that?" averting my eyes.

"Someone happened to see you with your receptionist having dinner."

"It was just dinner, nothing else," turning his back and walking into the kitchen. I followed.

"Do you always hold hands with someone you're just out to dinner with?"

His mouth opened and he sighed. "Okay, but it's not what you think."

"You don't know what I think."

He sat down. "When Laura and I first got married everything was wonderful, but for no reason, things started changing. She became distant, less affectionate, and she wouldn't tell me what was going on no matter how hard I pushed her. Weekends she would take off for a day and not tell me where she was going. After a while I stopped trying and that's when I started the relationship with Nicole. Maybe I gave up too easily. I just didn't know what to do anymore. I tried everything but she wouldn't budge. She wasn't even pretending to care what happened to us."

"Why didn't you tell me all this before?"

"Would you have believed me and taken the case?"

He had me there.

"I swear I have no idea what was going on with her, but I did not have anything to do with her murder. I need you to believe me."

I left Sam's place thinking about what he said. I didn't know whether he was lying or not but from what I have learned about Laura, his story was plausible.

CHAPTER 32

Before heading up to Chatham I stopped at a Starbucks for coffee. I exited at 102 off the Taconic, and with the help of my GPS, I found Michelle Gordon's place. It was a stone house situated on a few acres with cornfields in the distance. There was a vegetable garden on the side of her home.

I rang the bell. At first, I thought she was out since it was a while before the door opened. Michelle looked exactly like her photo on her website. "May I help you?" she said.

"My name is Tracey Marks and I'm looking into the death of Laura Tyler, actually Matthews. Can I come in and speak with you?" I handed her my card.

"Yes, of course."

She led me into a large kitchen. The floor had black and white square tiles and the cabinets were white with stainless steel appliances. In the sitting area there were two small leather couches and a beautiful stone fireplace.

"Please sit. I was just going to have coffee. Can I get you a cup?"

"That would be great, black, no sugar is fine."

"Are the police looking into her death?"

"Yes, but I was hired by her husband."

"May I ask how my name came up in your investigation? The police haven't even questioned me."

"I found a photo of you, Laura, and Glen McIntyre in her summer home. I knew McIntyre since I had been at his house regarding someone else connected to the case. I showed the photo to a few people and someone mentioned your name. Did you know Laura well?"

"Not really. I met her through Glen."

"May I ask how you know Glen?"

"I designed a website for him. He started a side business and he hired me to design his website."

I could tell she was being very guarded with her answers. "What do you know about the relationship between Laura and McIntyre?"

"As far as I know, they were friends."

"Do you think there was anything else going on between them?"

"You would have to ask him. I can't help you there."

Okay, I was getting nowhere fast. I needed a different approach.

"I certainly understand your reluctance to talk with me but I promise whatever you tell me is in confidence and won't be repeated to anyone else. You have my word. What I know is that he was a real ladies man and he fooled around." I added the last part.

"I think your sources are pretty accurate, but I still cannot confirm about Laura."

"Were you having an affair with him?"

"We dated a few times but I decided I didn't want to get involved with a married man. It's a no-win situation."

"How often did the three of you get together?"

"It was just that once."

"When Glen introduced you to Laura, were you dating him?"

"No it was over by then but we got together a couple of times afterward. I still help him out with the website."

"Is there anything you can tell me about Laura?"

"Not really. As I mentioned we only met that one time. I think I've told you everything I can. It's a shame about Laura. I can't imagine who would want to kill her."

"I can't either but I'm going to find out."

On the trip back I thought about what Michelle told me. Though she didn't actually come out and say that Laura was having an affair with McIntyre she didn't deny it either. Could McIntyre be the father of Laura's baby and if he was, did Laura threaten him with an ultimatum that got her killed?

My phone buzzed. "Hello."

"Ms. Marks, this is Peter Mickelson. I remembered something that Laura told me, though I don't know how important it is."

"What is it Peter?"

"Laura had mentioned that when she got back from Boston she went to see a shrink or a therapist."

"Did she say why?"

"She didn't go into details, just that she had to sort through some stuff."

"Do you know how long she was seeing this person?"

"I don't. To tell you the truth I got the feeling no one knew she was seeing a therapist, not even her husband."

"You don't by any chance have a name or where the practice is?"

"I don't know the person's name, but I believe his office was in Connecticut."

"Thank you, Peter. You've been a big help."

"I hope you find the bastard that killed her."

Me too, me too, I said silently to myself. When I got back to the office I took out the cell phone records I had obtained from Laura's phone. I made a list of all the Connecticut phone numbers. There were about fifteen, two of which I already knew, Seth and Melanie. There was no other way to do it but call each number and hope one belongs to the therapist. I was getting discouraged when on the eleventh try I had a hit.

"Dr. Michaels' office, may I help you."

"Yes, is this the Dr. Michaels who is a therapist?"

"Yes."

"I would like to make an appointment?"

"The doctor can see you next Tuesday at 3:00."

I certainly didn't want to wait that long. "Is it possible to see him sooner, it's kind of an emergency."

"Let me speak to Dr. Michaels and get back to you. I need to ask who referred you."

"Laura Tyler Matthews."

"Thank you. I'll get back to you as soon as I speak with him."

"I started pacing back and forth. I was hoping this would be a big break in the case. I decided not to tell Sam until I knew more.

I wrote up my conversation with Michelle Gordon and then called Susie. "Laura was seeing a shrink. I found out the name of the doctor and I'm waiting to hear back when he can see me."

"Slow down girl. I know you're excited but how do you know he will share any of their conversations?"

"Well, Laura is dead, so why wouldn't he?"

"For one you're not a relative, let alone a close one, but if he's giving you a hard time tell him you'll get permission from her husband."

"Do you think that will work?"

"If she wasn't dead I would say no, but the fact that she is I give it a 50/50 chance."

"Okay, that makes me feel a little better."

"I gotta go. I have a client coming in for a consultation in five minutes. Talk soon."

I wonder what the police know. They haven't said anything to Sam. I wouldn't be surprised if they are quietly building a case against him. Though they might not have any physical evidence, they could probably build a strong circumstantial case.

I was shutting down my computer when my phone buzzed.

"Ms. Marks, this is Dr. Michaels' office. He could see you tomorrow at 4:00."

"Thank you so much." I was mulling over the idea of getting Sam's permission in writing before I went, but I was still hoping I could get the doctor to talk to me without it. Also I wasn't sure how Sam would react knowing Laura was seeing a shrink and what she might have revealed.

Jerome Michaels' office was on the second floor of an office building in Greenwich, Connecticut. The receptionist told me to take a seat. On the dot of 4:00 a door opened and Dr. Michaels introduced himself and brought me into his office. He looked like the actor who played Mr. Big on Sex and the City. I sat in a comfortable leather chair and he sat opposite me.

"How can I help you?"

"Actually I'm not here as a patient though I could probably use some analysis. I'm here about Laura Tyler Matthews. I was told she had been a patient of yours. Did you know she was killed?"

"Yes, I read about it in the paper. I was very sorry to hear of Laura's death. How can I help you?"

"I was hired by Laura's husband, Sam Matthews, to find out who killed her."

"I thought the police are investigating?"

"They are but I was originally hired when Laura went missing, and at that time the police were not taking her disappearance seriously. She died near her summer home in the Berkshires. I was hoping you might be able to help me out. There may have been things she told you that would lead me to the person who killed her."

"I see. But there are confidentiality issues involved. I'm sorry I can't help you."

"I thought because she's deceased, you might be able to waive those issues."

"I would need to discuss this with her husband. If you ask him to call me, I would be glad to set up an appointment to meet with him."

"Is there anything you can tell me? I really don't want to get her husband involved in case he had anything to do with her death."

"I'm sorry but I could lose my license."

"Look why don't I just talk and you can just listen."

Since he didn't say anything, I continued.

"Laura was unhappy and may have been for a long time. I think she used male relationships as a way of making herself feel better but it didn't work. She married Sam thinking things would change but they didn't. She could have been depressed. How am I doing so far?"

He didn't say anything so I pushed on. "She may have had an affair or maybe she had a one night stand but either way she got pregnant and it wasn't her husband's baby. Am I on the right track?"

The doctor's face did not give anything away.

"Ms. Marks, I appreciate everything you are doing to find the person who killed Laura but there is nothing I can say."

"Just one more thing, when was the last time you saw Laura?"

I could see him wrestling with what he should tell me.

"Approximately three months ago."

"Thank you for your time doctor."

I got all I was going to get. I think he confirmed what I said but I'm not sure it would help me to find Laura's killer. So Laura left around the time she got pregnant. What does that say? She trusted Peter but not her husband. Did she trust anyone else? Where do I go from here?

When I turned my phone back on, I got an urgent message to call Sam.

"What's up Sam? Is everything alright?"

"No, they're arresting me for Laura's death. I'm being charged with second degree murder, and was told by my attorney that it's impossible to get the judge to let me out on bail. He's going to try but it doesn't look good."

I was stunned and Sam sounded like he was practically in tears.

CHAPTER 33

"Do you know what evidence they have?"

"David Morgan, the attorney I hired, said he's going to talk with Detective Graham and try and find out what the police know."

"What do you want me to do here? Do you need me to go to the house or talk with anyone?"

No, not yet but I want you to get in touch with Mr. Morgan and let him know what you have found out so far. I'll tell him you'll call him tomorrow."

"Of course. If you need anything else let me know. Sam, I have to tell you that Laura was seeing a therapist. I spoke with him, but I couldn't get much information because of doctor/patient confidentiality. I'll tell Mr. Morgan when I speak with him. I'm doing everything I can to find out who killed Laura."

When we hung up, I felt sick. Poor Sam. I was devastated for him but I needed to keep focused more than ever.

I called Susie. "They arrested Sam and he doesn't think his lawyer can get him out on bail since it's a murder charge. How could they do that?"

"They must have found some more evidence even if it's circumstantial. Does he have a good lawyer?"

"I believe he does. His name is David Morgan."

"I'll see what I can find out about him."

"Sam wants me to talk with his attorney and let him know what I found out so far. I'm really curious what the police have uncovered. I think they were focusing on Sam from the beginning without looking at anyone else. Though they might have a circumstantial case against him, I doubt he killed his wife. I just don't see him as a killer."

"You may be right but for now you have to concentrate on the leads you have. You might be able to use Mr. Morgan's resources to assist you with your investigation."

"That's a good point."

"By the way, have you spoken to Danny about the relationship?"

"I have. I think he's okay with it for now but he can't promise me that it won't change at some point."

"How do you feel about that?"

"I don't know. Right now all I can think about is Sam and finding out who killed Laura. I'll sort out my feelings another time."

When I got home, it was already dark. I was stressed from the day and decided to go for a run. I took my usual route in the park, which was a two mile loop. About halfway around I had the weird feeling someone was following me. I looked around but saw nothing unusual. There were some other runners, nobody suspicious. Walking back to my apartment I noticed a guy in a hooded sweatshirt about a half a block behind me that I spotted when I left the park. My heart started racing. I slowed up and ducked into the nearest store hoping he would just pass by without looking in my direction. He kept going. I waited for my breathing to return to normal and headed back to my place. I think my imagination is working on overdrive.

I was exhausted by the time I got to my

apartment. I was worried about Sam and I was worried about finding the killer. I took a long, hot shower trying to unwind.

In the morning I contacted David Morgan. "Mr. Morgan this is Tracey Marks, Sam said I should give you a call."

"Yes, I was wondering if we could meet on Saturday. I'm coming into the city for an art exhibit. I thought it would be more convenient for you then coming up to Stockbridge."

When I hung up I texted Danny and asked him if he wanted to meet for a late lunch on Saturday. He texted back that he had lunch plans, but Sunday was fine.

I was wondering if Danny was playing hard to get after our talk, or maybe he was having lunch with another woman. Why are these thoughts popping into my head? It's not like me. I texted him back that Sunday was fine.

On Saturday I met David Morgan at 11:30 at Elio's on Madison Avenue. Mr. Morgan was nothing like I pictured him. He was about fifty, average height, wiry built with gray hair that probably made him look older then he was. He had wire rimmed glasses and was dressed kind of preppy with khakis, a blue shirt, brown loafers and argyle socks.

The waiter came over and took our order. We both had lox and bagels and coffee.

"What was the evidence they had on Sam?" I asked.

"Besides the fact that it wasn't his baby, he was having an affair. Apparently they had a tail on him.

Also, they interviewed neighbors in their building and it turns out one of the neighbors overheard them arguing around the time Laura went missing."

The waiter set down our food and filled our coffee cups.

"I know it looks bad but I have been working this case for weeks and the police are building a case around Sam and haven't looked into anyone else."

I filled Mr. Morgan in with what I had learned so far. "I believe Laura was troubled and there were several men in her life. Any one of them could have killed Laura out of jealousy or maybe the baby's father was married and she threatened him, or he felt threatened. Do they have any physical evidence?"

"If they do, they haven't shared it with me. You seem to have done a lot of legwork which may prove fruitful. In the meantime I'm going to see what I can find out about Sam's finances and exactly what physical evidence, if any they have on him. Can you send me the reports you sent to Sam and any other information you may have withheld from him?"

"Sure. I would like to be kept informed as to what you find out. So what's going to happen to Sam now?"

"He's going to be held in the Berkshire County jail until trial. He can't receive calls but he can call you. There are visiting hours. Why don't we speak in a few days," Mr. Morgan said.

It was 1:00 when I left David Morgan. It was the first week of November but it was still seasonably mild. I rarely get to leisurely walk around the city so I decided to take advantage of the nice day. After browsing the shops, most of which I can't afford, I picked up salad stuff and stopped at a seafood market near me.

I changed into my sweats when I got back. My phone buzzed. It was Peter Mickelson. "Hi Peter, what's going on?"

"Nothing much. I was just checking if you were able to locate the therapist Laura went to."

"I did, though he didn't have much to say because of the confidentiality laws."

"That's too bad. I was hoping he might have some information that would help you."

"While I have you on the phone, did Laura mention the name Glen McIntyre?"

"I don't think so. She did say that she was seeing someone but she didn't tell me his name."

"Did you get the feeling she was afraid of anyone, maybe her husband?"

"No. She did mention a run in with that Cutler guy. I think he was hassling her but she didn't seem bothered by it."

"I'm curious, why you didn't bring it up on any of the previous times we spoke?"

"Like I said it wasn't anything that she seemed troubled by so I must have forgotten."

"Okay, thanks. If there is anything else you remember, call me."

It seemed that Peter was the only person Laura trusted. I wonder if there was other stuff she confided in him that he hadn't shared with me. Why didn't she trust Melanie? I was going to try and find out.

On Sunday I met Danny at Firenze, an Italian restaurant on Second Avenue and 81st Street. Danny made a reservation so we didn't have to wait, though it was only half full. Danny looked great in khakis, a black sweater and a black leather jacket. He reached across the table and put his hand over mine.

"You haven't aged a bit since the last time I saw you," he grinned.

"Right back at you," giving him my best smile. "They arrested Sam. His attorney said bail is not possible."

"What evidence do they have?"

"Can I get you something to drink?" the waiter asked.

"Yes, I'll have a Cabernet Sauvignon," I said.

"And I'll have the same."

"Would you like to order now?"

Danny and I looked at each other. "Just give us a few minutes," I said.

"As far as I know it's all circumstantial, but they could have other evidence they're not sharing. His attorney is trying to find out what they know. I met him yesterday and he seems pretty sharp but Susie is checking into him. Sam was always a possibility. I have a lead I'm working on and hopefully it will pan out. So how have you been?"

"Good. Work is busy. I got a call from a friend I haven't seen in a very long time. She and her husband separated and she needed a shoulder to cry on, so we met yesterday."

That's why he couldn't meet with me. "How is she doing?"

"A little bit of a wreckage, but she'll bounce back. Kathy and I were neighbors growing up. We played together when we were kids. Kathy was always strong willed, adventurous and fun to be with. I probably did things I wouldn't have dared on my own. As we got older, we went our separate ways. We both went off to college but stayed in touch. She wound up getting pregnant and confided in me that she was torn between keeping the baby and getting an abortion. I didn't know how to advise her. In the end she kept the baby but the marriage only lasted a few years. Eventually she met someone else. Ron and Kathy have been together for about nine years but I guess there were too many issues that couldn't be resolved."

"Did you ever date her?"

"No, though in some ways I admired her because she always seemed to know what she wanted and wasn't afraid of anything."

After lunch we took a walk on Madison Avenue. Though Kathy seemed to have her share of problems I could respect someone like her. I wish I had a little more adventure in me. I have to admit outside of my job, I live a fairly tame life.

We stopped at a cute French restaurant/cafe on 77th Street for dessert. I had a Pear tart and Danny had a piece of chocolate cake. We each had a cappuccino.

We went back to my place where we completely enjoyed each other's company, and around 11:00, Danny left.

CHAPTER 34

Monday morning I went to the gym and then headed to the office making a quick stop for coffee and a banana nut muffin.

As I was turning my computer on, my phone buzzed.

"It's me. I did a little checking into David Morgan. He has a great reputation. Also he has written some very interesting articles for the Massachusetts Bar Association. It looks like Sam is in good hands."

"That's a relief. I'm hoping Mr. Morgan can find out what else they have on Sam. I'm going to see what I can dig up on Glen McIntyre."

"What about Ben Cutler. Is he still on your short list?"

"He is, but right now I'm interested in finding out more about McIntyre. I'll probably have to pay him a visit at some point. How are things on the home front?"

"So far, so good. You'll be the first to know if there's a bump in the road."

"I have no doubt. Dinner later in the week? See ya."

I called John Cramer in Stockbridge, the retired gentleman who had told me that Cutler had been on the football team. I thought since Mr. Cramer had lived in Stockbridge his entire life he may have heard some gossip about McIntyre. He answered on the first ring.

"Mr. Cramer, this is Tracey Marks. We met about a week ago."

"Oh yes, the young lady who was interested in Ben Cutler. How are you?" How is the investigation into Laura's murder going?"

"Fine. About Laura's death, I know this might sound a little out of the blue but I was wondering if you ever heard rumors about the assistant coach, Glen McIntyre?"

"What kind of rumors?"

"That he was having an affair."

"I'm kind of reluctant to talk about it. Not that I have any allegiance to the guy."

"I understand but it may be important."

"This is a fairly small town and it's hard for secrets to be kept under wraps. McIntyre had an affair about three years ago. Rumor has it the woman wanted to end it but he didn't so he harassed her. She finally told his wife. I felt really bad for Mrs. McIntyre. It stopped and I guess his wife forgave him since they're still married."

"Can you tell me the woman's name?"

"I'm sorry, maybe you can get her name from someone else since I don't feel comfortable telling you. Is he a suspect?"

"Not that I'm aware of but he may have information that I might be interested in."

"Well if I think of anything else I'll contact you."

I called David Morgan, hoping he might be able to find out who the mystery lady is. "Mr. Morgan, please?"

"He's not here at the moment. Can I have him call you?"

"No thanks."

I called his cell number. "Mr. Morgan, it's Tracey Marks."

"I'm glad you called. I just heard from Detective Graham. Apparently Sam's car was picked up on camera going through a toll on the New York State Thruway."

"So is that a problem?"

"His wife's car was also spotted on the Thruway on the same day and only a few cars in front of his. It looks like he was following her."

"Was it around the time she was murdered?"

"Not exactly. It was about two weeks prior to her death. But if you look at it from their point of view, it throws more suspicion on Sam."

"I can see that. Did you ask Sam about it?"

"Not yet, but I will."

"By the way, I discovered something interesting about Glen McIntyre. He's the assistant coach at the high school in Stockbridge. I subsequently found out he knew Laura, though when I spoke with him he denied meeting her. About three years ago he had an affair with a woman and it turned pretty ugly. The woman felt she had no choice and told McIntyre's wife. I'm wondering if you can find out the woman's name."

"Probably, I'll have someone look into it."

I can understand Sam following Laura if she was being discreet and acting weird. I'll let the attorney ask Sam about it.

I called Melanie and asked her if I could stop by around 2:00 since I needed to discuss some things with her. Fortunately there was very little traffic once I got out of the city.

"I'm glad you called," Melanie said when I walked

in. "I can't stop thinking about Laura. Why would anyone want to kill her?"

"I don't know yet." I needed to be careful what I divulged to Melanie even though I didn't believe she had anything to do with Laura's death. "The last time we spoke you told me that you were not as close as you were at one time. Do you know why that is?"

"Can I get you a cup of coffee?"

"If you're having, I'll join you."

"I tried to find out what was going on with her, but I think I pushed her further away. I felt our friendship was slipping."

"Sam Matthew told me that a few months into the marriage, Laura changed. She became distant and would go off on her own for no apparent reason."

"Well, how do we know he's telling the truth?"

"I don't, except for the fact that other people I've spoken with corroborated her behavior."

"I see."

"I believe Laura was having an affair with a married man, very likely the same person who's the father of her baby. Is it possible she thought you wouldn't approve and that's why she may have avoided you?"

"Laura knew my feelings about having an affair with a married man, so yes, it's possible. Now I wish I hadn't been so judgmental. Maybe if she knew she could count on me she wouldn't be dead."

She handed me a cup of coffee and sat opposite me at the kitchen table. "Don't be so hard on yourself. Can you think of anyone else she confided in?"

"I can't. You did say that she had spoken to Peter Mickelson. Did he mention the affair?"

"No, but he recently told me that Laura was seeing

a therapist."

"Wow, I didn't see that coming. She must have really been in a bad way. Poor Laura. I know I can't change things but it hurts that Laura didn't feel comfortable sharing what was going on in her life."

"It appears that Laura was distancing herself from the people closest to her. Her godmother, Ms. Litman, told me that in the last year of Laura's life she saw Laura only once. Ms. Litman knew something was wrong but Laura stopped confiding in her."

"Do you know what's going on with the investigation?"

"The police aren't telling me anything." I wasn't going to mention Sam's arrest.

"I have my suspicions that Seth Green might have something to do with her death," Melanie said.

"Why do you say that?"

"Even after they broke up he was always following her around, trying to interject himself into her life. Laura and I would be out at a bar and he would show up."

"Did he hassle her in any way or make her feel uncomfortable?"

"Laura was fairly easy going. If she was upset about Seth, you'd never know it. I remember one time we were at a college party and Seth walked in about an hour later. He had been drinking and was practically all over Laura. I said something to him, like get lost but Laura just took it in stride. It didn't appear to bother her. Like I had told you, I was very surprised when you had mentioned Seth's name. I still wonder after all these years if Seth was still in love with her."

"Thanks for your time. If you think of anything

else, please contact me."

On the way back I went over my conversation with Melanie. I had some doubts about Seth. I only have his word that he took Laura's recent rejection in stride. I still go back to what I originally thought, if he found out that Laura was pregnant with someone else's baby, would he snap? When Melanie mentioned Peter Mickelson, I questioned whether he knew anything else about Laura that he kept to himself. Since Laura apparently trusted him, why didn't she tell him about the baby, and if she did, why not divulge that information to me?

When I turned my phone back on, I had a missed call from a number I didn't recognize. Since it was already after 5:00 I headed home instead of the office. I called the mysterious caller. When he said hello, his voice sounded vaguely familiar.

"This is Tracey Marks. You called me."

"Yes, it's Ben Cutler. I thought you might be interested in some information I have."

Well, this was a total surprise. "Go ahead; I'm listening."

"You don't sound very appreciative considering I'm helping you out here."

"I guess my hesitancy might have something to do with our history."

"I know you've been snooping around asking questions about me."

"That's my job." I wanted to say more but I held my tongue since I didn't want to get into a pissing match with him if he really did have information that could help me.

"This isn't something I can tell you over the phone. I need to see you in person."

He had my curiosity peaked but I was also hesitant about going up to meet him in case he was the one who attacked me at the motel or killed Laura.

Sensing my concern, he said we could meet at a diner he knew that was a mile outside of Stockbridge. We made arrangements to meet tomorrow.

The next call was to Susie. "Hey listen I got a call from Ben Cutler. He said he has some information that he can only give me in person, I'm going to meet him tomorrow at the GB Eats in Great Barrington. I'm telling you just in case."

"I'm glad you did but I doubt he would be stupid enough to try anything, at least not now."

"Thanks, and I was going to give you my dog if anything happened to me."

"Wait, you don't have a dog."

"Exactly."

After hanging up I sat down and wrote up my conversation with Melanie. It was bothering me that I hadn't figured out who took the photos of Laura and Peter Mickelson and sent them to me. Obviously they wanted me to know about the photos. The most likely person would be Seth Green. He knew I was investigating Laura's disappearance and he admitted pursuing her, though he came short of saying that he followed her. But why send the photos to me?

The next day I was in the parking lot of GB Eats by 10:45. I didn't see his pickup truck. I went inside and sat down. The décor was very simple but pretty. It had square wooden tables and chairs. The walls were a light gray with wainscoting about a third of the way up the wall. Lights hung from the ceiling. The menu was on a giant chalkboard that was posted up front against the wall. The waitress came over and I ordered coffee and pancakes while I waited.

Ben came in a few minutes later. I signaled him over. The waitress came back with my coffee and Ben waived her away.

I wasn't interested in chit chat with him but I decided to let him take the lead.

"I heard that Laura's husband was arrested."

"He was."

"That's interesting. Do you know what evidence they have?"

"You would have to ask the police. I'm looking for Laura's killer."

"So you don't think her husband did it?"

The waitress brought my pancakes and refilled my coffee.

"You don't mind if I eat while we talk," as I smothered my pancakes with butter and syrup. "I'm keeping all options open."

"Does that include me?" Ben said.

I looked at him without saying anything. He could take a hint.

"What did you want to see me about?" He took out a cell phone and put it on the table.

"What's that?"

"It's a cell phone."

"I know what it is, but why are you showing it to me?"

"I found this in the shed at the house. I guess it does pay to snoop."

Shit. I can't believe I didn't look in the shed. "Why not give it to the police? It might be evidence."

"I'd rather give it to you. Why make their life easier? Besides, we don't know what's on it."

"Did you find anything else?"

"Most of the shed was filled with boating stuff and lawn chairs."

"Where did you find it?"

"It was hidden behind some old towels."

My leg was jackhammering off the floor. I was trying to control it since I didn't want Cutler to see how upset I was. "How well did you know Laura?" I asked him, trying to sound casual.

"I knew her since she was about eleven. That's when her parents and my parents became friends. I was a couple of years older than her so we didn't hang out. Laura had a lot of boyfriends but she was never satisfied with just one. She liked to play the field."

"Did you want to be her boyfriend?"

He laughed but his face had a steely look on it.

"I might have wanted to date her but she ran around with a different crowd and was not interested in me."

"Did that make you mad?"

"I did pretty good with the women. I never had a problem in that department if you know what I mean."

He was making my skin crawl. "But she was the one you couldn't have. Didn't that tick you off a little bit?"

"If you think you're going to get me to declare my undying love for Laura, and that I couldn't live without her so I killed her, don't hold your breath."

"I may not be able to get you to admit it but it doesn't mean it's not true."

"I think we're finished here. I'm trying to help you out and I'm practically accused of killing Laura."

"Am I going to find your number on this phone?"

"Maybe, maybe not." and he walked out.

CHAPTER 35

After I finished eating I paid the check and left. Laura was definitely living a secret life from Sam. Hopefully some of her secrets will be divulged after I obtain the cell records. On the way back I thought about contacting Joe for the phone records but I hesitated since I didn't want to owe him; instead I decided to contact the company I used in the past and pay for the information. With that done, I headed to the office. Somehow I knew I would be back in the area before too long.

I was lucky to find a parking spot two blocks away. I texted Susie that I was alive and well, and would meet her at 6:30 at Anton's. I was debating if I should tell Sam about the phone but I quickly nixed the idea. It was better to have some information that might help his case before mentioning anything to him or his lawyer.

I thought tomorrow evening I would make a surprise trip to Seth Green's house demanding more answers. I know he is hiding something from me and I'm determined to find out what it is.

I walked into Anton's and was greeted by Olivia, looking stunning as usual. Susie was already seated.

"Hi." I noticed Susie had started without me, sipping a glass of red wine.

"Have you ever noticed Olivia's legs? They are gorgeous," Susie said.

"Every time I walk in here. I would kill for those legs. What kind of wine are you drinking?"

"Chianti, very good."

"Have you ever met a wine you didn't like?" Our waiter Paul came over and I ordered a glass of Cabernet Sauvignon.

"No. But in my defense my palate is not as sophisticated as yours. So what happened with Cutler?"

"He found a second cell phone of Laura's that had been hidden in the shed. I could kick myself for not looking there. What if I never found out about the phone? The killer's voice could be on it. I didn't want to think about what else I missed."

"Don't beat yourself up over it. You can't expect to be perfect. I think you're doing great for your first time at bat."

I just rolled my eyes. "I can hardly wait to see who she was talking to. I think at least one number will be McIntyre's."

Paul came back with my wine.

"Are you gals ready to order?"

"Of course, I'm starved," I said. I ordered my usual and Susie joined me.

"Was Ben Cutler being a dick? I can imagine him gloating."

"He was but I didn't care. I think he was ticked off that I wasn't falling all over him."

"Poor boy. Did he say why he didn't bring it to the police? It is evidence."

"I got the feeling he doesn't like the police a whole lot, which I'm thankful for. I asked Sam's attorney to find out the name of the woman the coach was having the affair with. I'd like to talk with her before I confront him."

"If he killed Laura is that a good idea?"

"Do you have a better one?"

"How are you and Danny doing?"

"Pretty good. I saw him Sunday and we actually spent most of the day together. It was nice. I just didn't ask him to spend the night."

"Well, that's progress."

The next day I headed up to Seth Green's house around 5 p.m. I didn't see his car so I waited. I wanted to catch him before he went into the house since I didn't want his wife to overhear our conversation.

Around seven his car pulled into the driveway. I got out and called to him.

"What the hell are you doing here?" he said. If looks could kill, I'd be dead.

"You're lucky I didn't ring the doorbell since I don't think you'd want to have this conversation in front of your wife."

"She's not here but I expect her back any moment."

"So let's make this quick. I know you took the photos of Laura and sent them to me."

At first he looked like he was going to deny it but then changed his mind.

"I was following her. I know it was stupid. I know she didn't care about me but that didn't matter to me. I just wanted to know who she was seeing. I couldn't help myself but I would never hurt her."

"How often did you follow her?"

"It was only a few times but he was the only guy I

saw her with."

"Did you ever follow her when she went to the lake house?"

"Yes, once on a Saturday. She basically stayed in for most of the day, except to go out for lunch by herself, and then she headed back to the city around 7 p.m."

"Did you happen to see any cars around the house or anyone who might have looked suspicious?"

"No. Like I said she was by herself."

"Why send the photos to me?"

"I was hoping the person she was with might have had something to do with her disappearance. That was before she was found. I thought maybe you could track him down. Did you?"

"I can only tell you I don't think he had anything to do with her death."

"Look I'm sorry I didn't tell you, I guess I was scared."

"Did you send me a threatening note or place an anonymous telephone call trying to scare me?"

"No. No way. I swear it wasn't me."

"I'm going to ask you one last time. Is there anything else you're not telling me?"

"Absolutely not."

"I hope so for your sake."

I thought I would give him something to think about if he wasn't being completely honest with me. He seemed sincere but then he could be a good liar.

When I got back in my car I had one missed call. It was from David Morgan. He left me the name and address of Marsha James, the woman Glen McIntyre had the affair with three years ago.

After arriving home I googled Marsha James. The

only thing that came up was a LinkedIn site with a photo of her. It was small and I'm not sure I would be able to recognize her if I saw her on the street. It lists that she is a Vice President at a bank in Great Barrington. I searched my database and found an address and cell number. It did not appear that she was currently married. It listed her age as forty-five. Well at least McIntyre didn't rob the cradle.

My phone buzzed. It was Sam calling, "Hi Sam, how are you holding up?" Probably a stupid question.

"What do you think? I'm trying to hold on to my business but I don't know how I can do that if I'm in here much longer. Someone who works for me is trying to keep us afloat."

"Have you spoken to Mr. Morgan recently?"

"Yes, we speak every day. David doesn't think they have any physical evidence, just circumstantial, but people have been known to be convicted on that alone, which scares me. Were you able to find out anything?"

"I've been following some leads. It appears that the assistant coach may have been having an affair with Laura but I'm not one hundred percent positive. But if it turns out he is the father of the baby that might point to someone else besides you."

"Does my lawyer know?"

"Yes, I filled him in on the situation and I'm going to see what I can find out."

"Well, that's a little encouraging."

"I'll probably be up there in a day or so to interview some people. Can I bring you any books, magazines, any papers from work?"

"Nicole is coming up tomorrow."

"Okay but I'll stop by to see you when I can."

After hanging up I called Marsha James. There was no answer so I left a message giving her enough information that hopefully she'll call back. As I walked outside my building my phone rang.

"Tracey Marks."

"Ms. Marks this is Ms. James returning your call."

"Yes, thank you. This is a little awkward so I thought it would be better to speak in person. I'm looking into the death of Laura Tyler Matthews."

"Yes I heard about it."

"It appears she may have been having an affair with Glen McIntyre." I kind of left it hanging waiting for a response.

"I see." There was a long pause before she went on. "I'm not sure how I can assist you."

"I'm not sure either but I would really appreciate it if we could meet. There are some questions you might be able to help me with."

"I'm going to be leaving the office at 3:00 today. I can meet you at 4:00 at the Starbucks in Great Barrington. They have some tables so we can sit."

"Great, thank you. I'll see you then." I felt like I was spending more time up there than I was here. At least I'm being compensated for it. I'm actually enjoying the hunt. I can see how easy it is to get so involved in a case you become obsessed with it.

At 1:30 I headed to Great Barrington. At this point I knew the Taconic Parkway as well as I did the streets of Manhattan. It's an easy ride since the further north you go there are rarely any cars on the road. When I arrived I parked and went inside. I ordered a cappuccino and sat down while I waited till they called my name. On the dot of 4:00, Marsha James walked in. I recognized her since she told me she'd be wearing a blue leather jacket. I have to say McIntyre has good taste in women. Marsha was about 5'8", slender, brown hair cut short with blond streaks and light blue eyes. She could probably pass for thirty. I stood up and walked over to her. "Can I get you something to drink?" I offered.

"No, I'm fine. I've had too much coffee already today."

I could tell that Marsha was not exactly thrilled to be talking with me. She was playing with her hands and there was little eye contact.

"I won't keep you. I'm pretty sure Laura was having an affair with McIntyre. I have no idea if he had anything to do with her death but I know you had some problems with him, and I thought you might give me some insight since you knew him on a personal level."

"I'm curious how you found out about me and Glen."

"As I have been told by several people I've talked to in the area, word gets around. It's hard to keep secrets."

"You'd be surprised. As you already know I had an affair with him. He was married and I wasn't."

My name was called and I grabbed my cappuccino from the counter. "I want you to know I am not judging you."

"I decided the affair needed to end. At some point I started to feel guilty about being with a married man. I was in love with him so it was difficult to end it but my mind was made up. Glen did not take it well. At first he thought he could talk me into seeing him again, but when he realized that wasn't going to happen, something changed in him. He became verbally abusive. He would call me at all hours and began to follow me around. I'd see him sitting in his car outside my house at night. I thought about getting a restraining order but I didn't want anyone knowing about the affair since I thought I was partially to blame. I told his wife, which I regret doing, but at the time I didn't feel I had any other options. He was scaring me. Later on I sent his wife a letter telling her how sorry I was. I never heard from him again. As far as I know they're still married."

"Do you think if Laura wanted to end the relationship or threatened him he is capable of hurting her?"

"Maybe, but not on purpose. I don't think he would intentionally kill her."

"One last question, did you ever ask him to leave his wife?"

"I wanted him to leave her but he made it pretty clear that was never going to happen. That's what made up my mind to end it."

"Did he say why?"

"At some point I figured out it was the thrill of the affair that he liked more than me. Though he never came out and told me, I believe there were others before me and maybe after. It was never his intention to divorce his wife."

"Thank you for talking with me."

Before I left I thought about whether I should go see McIntyre now to confront him or wait and see what shows up on the cell phone records. It was probably a good idea to have a strategy before talking to him.

As I was sitting in my car looking through my emails, I saw the cell phone records had come in. I started sifting through the printout. There were only a few numbers that were listed, though some of those numbers were called several times in the last two months.

At home I made a list of the numbers and began searching each one to see who they belonged to. The first number I checked was Jessica Benson's, the woman I met who was a friend of Laura's. The next number was Glen McIntyre's, no surprise there. The third number was Peter Mickelson's. That made sense since she was confiding in him. The fourth number was to Dr. Jerome Michaels, the therapist. There were two other numbers, one I was having trouble finding out who it belonged to, and the other was to a Leo Melber. At first I didn't recognize the name but then it came to me. Leo was the bartender Susie and I met in Pittsfield. It may be a different person but I suspected it was the same Leo. Why were he and Laura talking? As I was pondering this new information, my phone buzzed.

"Hey Tracey, I was thinking about you," Danny said, "and I thought it would be nice to hear your voice."

"Is it everything you thought it would be?" I laughed.

"Much more. How are you?"

"Very busy. The case keeps getting more intriguing by the moment. I feel like Stockbridge is my home away from home."

"Anything you can share?"

"It appears Laura had a second phone. Why would someone have another phone unless she had something to hide?"

"Anyone interesting show up?"

"I can't really go into it though there was one number that I believe came from a burner phone so I'm not sure if I can find out whom it belongs to."

"Are you too busy to get some dinner Saturday?"

"I think I can squeeze you in."

"I'm writing you down in ink so you can't change your mind."

I didn't realize it was after 8:00 when I hung up from Danny. I had planned on running but I was too tired so I fixed myself a sandwich and watched some mindless TV.

In the morning I called my friend Joe to see if there was any possibility of tracing the owner of a burner phone. He told me it wasn't traceable. That was what I thought but it still bummed me out.

My second call was to Susie. "You're not going to believe who came up on Laura's phone records?"

"You really have my curiosity peeked but please don't make me guess."

CHAPTER 36

"It's Leo, the bartender we met."

"Well, well, well that is very interesting. Any other surprises?"

"One number from a burner phone which I can't get. The others I know about. I'm going to talk to Leo and also with McIntyre but there is no way McIntyre is going to submit to a paternity test unless it is court ordered."

"I agree. The police have already arrested Sam so they won't be looking at anyone else. You can try and scare McIntyre into admitting the truth but I think he is too savvy to fall into that trap. When are you going?"

"I'm not sure. I don't want to give Leo advance warning by calling him but I also would rather not talk to him when he's tending bar."

"This might be a fallacy but I believe bartenders work late so they probably sleep in. You can probably catch him at home one morning. Just call the restaurant and find out when he's working and go the following morning."

"Good thinking. I would ask your boss for a raise. You deserve it."

"And when I'm fired, I'll work for you and you can pay me the big bucks."

"On second thought, don't ask."

I called the restaurant and found out that Leo was

working tonight. I decided to go up in the morning and keep my fingers crossed that he would be home and then catch McIntyre at the school. It would also give me an opportunity to see Sam.

I left the office around 3:00 and stopped at the market to pick up something for dinner. I was trying to eat healthier these days but the heart wants what the heart wants, and I needed comfort food. I went for frozen macaroni and cheese though I chose the one that has no artificial ingredients. I then meandered over to the Corner Sweet Shoppe to say hello to Mr. Hayes.

"Hi Tracey, how are you?"

"I'm good. I came to indulge myself, so I'm going to get a pint of pistachio and a pint of chocolate, chocolate chip."

"I think you might get a tummy ache if you ate both in one sitting," he said with an amused smile on his face.

When I got home I changed and went for a run; otherwise, I would feel too guilty eating all those delicious calories.

The next day I was on the road by 7:30 with coffee in hand. Leo lived in a garden apartment complex right outside Pittsfield. The complex was small and looked well maintained. I had no idea if he lived by himself or had a roommate. I arrived at 10:15 and boldly rang the doorbell. It took a minute or so and then I heard footsteps and the turn of the knob. Leo was staring at me, trying to figure out who this crazy person was interrupting his sleep. It took a few seconds for my face to register.

"Hey, what are you doing here?"

"I need to talk with you. Can I come in?"

He waved me in. "Let me put on some pants."

While he was in the bedroom I strolled around, a typical bachelor place, sparse of furniture. The focus of the room was a giant TV screen.

"So this is a surprise," he said. "How did you find out where I lived?"

"That wasn't very difficult."

"Ah yes, you're a private investigator. I need coffee badly." I followed him into the kitchen while he put on the coffee maker.

As he was doing his thing I said, "When we talked at the restaurant you barely identified Laura when I showed you her photo, let alone that you'd spoken to her, but we know that's not true. So what gives?"

He handed me a cup of coffee and sat down.

"How did you find out? Oh, I keep asking you the same stupid question I know the answer to, silly me."

"Why don't you start from the beginning?"

"The first time Laura came into the restaurant was about six months ago. She always sat at the bar content to order a drink and sit alone. We began talking. I'm a good listener and she seemed lonely. Before you get the wrong idea, I was not interested in Laura. I'm gay and she knew that."

"So what did she talk to you about?" Leo seemed reluctant to tell me. "Look Leo, Laura is dead and I'm trying to find out who killed her and I need your help."

"I thought her husband was arrested."

"I don't believe he killed her."

"Okay. At first it was just small talk, where she lived, what she did, the house she had up here. I let her take the lead. I rarely asked her any questions. Eventually she talked about her parents and the car accident. You could see by the look on her face that it still haunted her. The more she talked about her life, the more I realized how lonely she was. You would think that someone that pretty wouldn't be lonely. I know that sounds shallow."

"Did she talk about her husband?"

"That's what was really strange, she never mentioned him, though it slipped out one time. It caught me by surprise since she wasn't wearing a wedding ring."

"Did she ever come in with anyone?"

"I don't want to get anyone in trouble if I'm not sure. One evening she came in with a guy. They sat at a table, not at the bar. His back was to me, though at some point he turned in my direction and I caught a glimpse of him. It was quick so I don't know if I would recognize him if I saw him again."

"Could you sense anything about their relationship from their behavior?"

"To tell you the truth I wasn't paying too much attention since I was focused on the customers at the bar, but the few times I looked over at Laura's table, they appeared to be arguing but I can't be sure."

"What makes you say that?"

"Of course I couldn't hear anything but it looked like he was doing most of the talking and his side of the conversation was pretty animated. Laura seemed quiet and didn't seem engaged. Then she abruptly got up and went to the ladies' room. The next time I looked over Laura and the guy were both gone."

"How did you know it wasn't her husband?"

"I didn't. It was just a feeling I got."

"Did she say anything about what happened the next time she came in?"

"No, but I asked her about him. I could tell she didn't want to talk about it so I dropped the subject. I thought maybe he was married. Though if she didn't want me to know about him, why come into the restaurant with him."

"Maybe she did want you to know. Can you think of anything that she might have said during your conversations that were odd or strange at the time?"

"She said there were times she was scared and sensed that something bad would happen, but when I tried to get her to open up and tell me more, she shut down. Listen, I'm hungry. I'm going to have some eggs. Would you care to join me?"

"Sure, I skipped breakfast this morning so I'm famished."

As Leo was scrambling eggs and toasting bread, he told me a little bit about himself. He became a bartender to put himself through school. He was studying communications and was hoping to get a job in the TV industry. Eventually he planned on moving to New York City. I liked Leo. He was easy to be with. I could see how bartending suited him.

As we ate I asked him how often Laura came in by herself.

"I'd say about once every two weeks. She called me a few times to find out if I was going to be at the restaurant. There was something about her that I can't explain. Being both pretty and mysterious, I can see why men would be drawn to her."

"Did she ever come in with anyone else?"

"Not that I can recall."

I thanked Leo for breakfast and left. Did I learn anything new from my conversation? We knew also confided in Peter Mickelson. Both gave similar accounts. I could see how she would be drawn to Glen McIntyre. He was older and possibly Laura saw him as a father figure. That's understandable since her own father was an alcoholic and not emotionally available to Laura according to her godmother.

I headed over to the high school hoping McIntyre was there. Last night I ran a search on him which gave me his license plate number and description of his car. The parking lot was huge. It took me a while before I located his car. I maneuvered my way into a spot where I could keep an eye on his car. It was only 1:30. If the team had football practice after school I could be here for a while.

There wasn't much I could do in the meantime. I checked for messages and emails. Nothing. I hadn't come up with a plan on how I was going to approach my conversation with McIntyre so I had to wing it. If he didn't want to talk to me I could threaten him, which I wasn't comfortable with but I may have no choice. Sam was my priority.

I was just about to make a phone call when I spotted the coach walking toward his car.

"Mr. McIntyre, it's Tracey Marks. I met you at your home regarding Laura Tyler's death."

"Oh yes, how can I help you?" he said with a surprised look on his face.

"I was wondering if we could speak for a few minutes."

"Well I don't have much time since I'm on my way to an appointment."

"This won't take long and I would really appreciate it."

He looked as if he wanted to blow me off but thought better of it.

"Why don't we sit in my car," he said.

I would have preferred my car but thought the chances of McIntyre attacking me in broad daylight were fairly low.

"Since you don't have a lot of time I'm going to cut to the chase. I know you and Laura were having an affair." He started to say something but I just went on. "I have Laura's cell phone records, I have a photo of you and Laura together and you were also seen with her in a restaurant in Pittsfield," though that was a little white lie, "not to mention the fact that you lied to me in your house when you said you had never spoken to her."

"That all may be true but so what," he said with a cocky attitude.

"She was pregnant when she died." McIntyre's eyebrows raised.

"For your information young lady you might want to find out who else she was sleeping with."

"What do you mean?"

"Do I have to spell it out to you? I wasn't the only one she was screwing. Laura liked to play the field, pardon my pun, but you get what I'm saying."

I wrestled with what he just told me. "How do you know she was with other guys? Why would she tell you that?"

"I think you are under the assumption that my relationship with Laura was exclusive. The fact is it was casual and that suited me just fine. I had no intention of getting involved in a serious relationship. I made that mistake once and I wasn't going to let it happen again."

"That still doesn't answer my question."

"Well I guess you'll just have to take my word for

it. Though I can tell you this, I don't think one man could satisfy her."

"Why should I take your word on anything you tell me. You cheat on your wife and the lies probably roll off your tongue."

"Now you're just being insulting," he said with a smirk.

"Did Laura threaten you, said she was going to tell your wife about the baby and you became so infuriated you killed her. Maybe it wasn't intentional but that doesn't matter."

"You have some imagination. Now get the hell out of my car before I throw you out. And if you have any intention of causing me any trouble, you'll be sorry."

"Is that a threat?" I yelled as I slammed the door shut.

CHAPTER 37

Well that was interesting. Maybe I pushed him too hard. I got into my car and sat there mulling over my entire conversation with McIntyre. What if McIntyre was right? I couldn't ignore that possibility. But if he was correct, the possibilities of who killed Laura just jumped and that was a scary thought. If he was feeding me bullshit, I would still have to find a way to call his bluff.

I turned on the radio and listened to some soft rock to clear my head. When I was young and had trouble falling asleep my father would tell me to close my eyes, think of something that made me feel happy and that would keep all the bad thoughts away. If only it was that simple now.

My next stop was the County Jail which was in Pittsfield. When I got there I had to show my credentials and lock my belongings in a locker.

I was shocked when I saw Sam. He looked thinner and his face was drawn. Sam was always so meticulously dressed and now he was in an orange jumpsuit. We spoke in a small room.

"Sam, there are things that I have found out about Laura that may be hard to hear."

"Just tell me," sounding tired.

I continued. "First of all, Laura's behavior was not because of anything you did. From several people I have spoken to, including Melanie and Mrs. Litman,

Laura had trouble in her relationships with men, never staying in one relationship very long. There were several men in her life who I've spoken to that may be potential suspects. Is there anything you remember about Laura's behavior or something she may have said in passing that would be crucial to your case?"

"I've already told you, Laura stopped communicating with me. I have no idea what she was up to."

"Okay. What did Mr. Morgan tell you?"

"That I have to trust him. I don't think they found any physical evidence."

"I'm doing everything I can Sam, believe me. Please try to keep your spirits up. I know it's hard to do but you have to try." I wasn't sure if Sam was even listening to me.

I said goodbye and told him I would keep him updated with any news.

When I got home I was looking forward to relaxing, maybe with my new Michael Connolly book. My phone buzzed. "How did it go?" Susie said

"I'd rather tell you about it in person. I thought if you had some time tomorrow late morning we can meet for breakfast or brunch."

"How about 11:00 at the little French café near you?"

I ate some leftover Chinese food and settled in with my Michael Connolly book. By 10:00, I was sound asleep.

Saturday morning I got up early and went for a run. Wally was outside.

"Hello Miss Tracey. I haven't seen you for a couple of days."

"I've been working all sorts of crazy hours. How are you doing?

"I'm alright. Watch out for that dog poop. I hope it wasn't one of the tenants in our building."

"I doubt it. They wouldn't want to mess with you."

"Be careful out there."

I waved goodbye. It was the second Saturday in November and the mornings were definitely getting chillier. I jogged to the park and did my three mile loop.

When I arrived at the café it was crowded. Susie and I had to wait about fifteen minutes before being seated. We were lucky to get a corner table where no one was close enough to hear our conversation.

"Would you ladies like to order?"

"Yes, I'll have your famous French toast with fresh strawberries and a side of bacon very crisp."

"That sounds scrumptious. I'll have the same," Susie said.

"I don't know how you do it. You eat like a horse, you don't work out and yet you're a peanut," I said.

"Just lucky, I guess. So tell me all about the interviews with Leo and the coach."

I had just finished relaying to Susie everything that transpired when the waitress brought our food and refilled our coffee cups.

"From what everyone has said about Laura it's possible the coach was telling you the truth," Susie said.

"So where does that leave me. It could be any psycho she picked up."

"That's true but I think it's someone connected to Laura or knows you're working on the case. If it was some random person why would they bother to keep tabs on you, they wouldn't even know you existed."

"That makes sense. I still think McIntyre might be lying."

"Have you ruled anyone out?"

"I ruled out her previous boss Raymond Berg. I just don't see a motive, besides Laura was back in New York for almost two years before she was killed. Ben Cutler might be a possibility. He definitely had a thing for her but it didn't appear to be mutual. Not to mention the incident when he was in high school where he sexually assaulted someone."

"Didn't you tell me that Seth Green has pined for her since college?"

"That's true. But Seth knew Laura since high school and he had genuine feelings for her. I just don't see him hurting her. And why would he have waited so long?"

"Maybe the last straw was the baby. All hope for having her went out the window," Susie said.

"One small problem with your theory, we don't know if he knew about the baby."

"Good point. What about Peter Mickelson?"

"That's interesting. It never even occurred to me that he might be involved. He seemed so sincere and open about Laura and his feelings for her. I'll have to have another chat with him. Put some pressure on him. Maybe he'll spill his guts, admit what he did and beg for mercy."

"Wouldn't that be nice. Good luck with that."

"The problem is we still have too many suspects. Maybe we can do like they do on TV, get them all in one room and let them duel it out."

"Or maybe you can disguise yourself as Columbo and figure it out."

"That's probably the best idea you've had so far," sticking my tongue out at Susie.

"How's it going with Danny, and when am I going to meet him? Or maybe we can double date? That would be fun."

"Is that even a sentence? Give it a few more weeks until I'm pretty sure I'm not going to throw him overboard any time soon."

"Okay, but you know how good I am at reading people. If there is something wrong with him, I can save you a lot of time in this relationship."

"I'll keep that in mind."

When I got home I did my Saturday cleaning ritual. It was almost 5:00 when I finished and had the time to mull over my conversation with Susie. I wondered why I dismissed Mickelson so readily without questioning the possibility that he was lying to me. I decided I would pay him a visit on Monday. I also needed to check with Sam's attorney to see if he had found out anything that could benefit him.

I met Danny at a little Italian bistro that makes homemade pasta. I dressed in jeans, a red pullover sweater, and black boots. I grabbed my leather jacket on the way out. When I got to the restaurant, Danny was seated at the bar. I watched from a distance before announcing my presence. He appeared to be laughing at something the woman next to him was saying. He then leaned in and whispered something in her ear. She laughed. I slowly walked towards the bar curious what that was all about.

"Hey," I said. "Did I miss out on something funny?"

"Tracey, hi, this is, I'm sorry, what's your name?"

"Diana."

"Diana is waiting for her girlfriend. She was telling me a story about a guy who had tried to pick her up at a bar with some bad one liners."

"Did it work?" I said with a straight faced.

"No, of course not but I thought it was amusing."

I signaled to the bartender. "Can I get a glass of Cabernet Sauvignon please." Diana had long curly dark hair with an olive complexion which gave her a Mediterranean look. She was very pretty.

Danny started to get up to let me sit down.

"It's fine, I would rather stand. Do you know how long before we're seated?"

"When I came in, which was about twenty minutes ago, I was told they were running a little behind so it might be ten or fifteen minutes."

"So Diana do you live around here?" I asked."

"Oh no, I live in Brooklyn. My friend lives in the area. You'd think I would be the late one but with Megan, you never know. She could be a little flakey. Here she is now."

Megan was striking. I noticed Danny staring. Who could blame him, even I was ogling her. She looked like a model with beautiful straight blonde hair, white ivory skin and a perfect nose. Nobody should be that gorgeous. On the bright side, she was flakey.

Diana introduced us. "Sorry I'm late Diana. The time got away from me. I was studying for my biology exam. Can I get a Cosmo?" she shouted to the bartender.

"Megan is pre-med at NYU."

Danny and I exchanged glances. At that moment Danny's name was called and we were shown to our table.

"Beauty and brains, it should be outlawed," I said.

"You're acting like you have never encountered a smart, beautiful woman before."

"I wouldn't talk. I saw your eyes nearly come out of their sockets."

"You got me there. So you're telling me when you're at the gym and you see a gorgeous guy with a great body, you don't stare for just one moment."

"It's possible. Okay, truce."

"By the way do you know how beautiful you are?"

"So how was your day?" ignoring Danny's remark.

"Uneventful. I spoke to my brother. He and his wife decided they're going to stay for a few more years. He really likes being in the service and they are enjoying Belgium. It gives them the opportunity to travel around easily."

"Do you envy them?"

"Not really. I like what I do and there's always the possibility Uncle Sam could transfer Josh to a place that might be dangerous. Danger is not my idea of fun."

"I never asked you how you escaped marriage for so long."

"I guess I never found the right person, though I was engaged once," he said.

"Do tell all the details immediately."

"Have you had a chance to look over the menu?" The waiter asked.

"I know what I am having, the homemade Lobster Ravioli and your house salad."

"I'll have the same," Danny said. "And I'll have another glass of Cabernet Sauvignon. Would you like another glass of wine?" Danny asked me.

"Why not." When the waiter left I said to Danny, "you were going to tell me about your engagement."

"It was your classic story, we were both young and probably what I thought was love was lust. I called it off before it was too late."

"How did she take it?"

"I'm not sure. I never heard from her again."

"I guess she was quite mad at you."

"I was young and probably could have handled it better. So what's happening with the case?"

"Well the good news is I have eliminated some people from my suspect pool but the bad news is I still have too many, though I'm getting a clearer picture of Laura. Apparently from several of the people I spoke with, Laura didn't stay too long with any one guy. It looks she may have been into the bar scene and picked up the wrong guy. I just don't know and I'm getting very frustrated."

"Did the cell phone records help?"

"Not really. Unfortunately, the burner phone is a dead end. I asked a friend of mine if there is any way you can get a number from a burner but it's impossible. I'll try to see if there is anything that can be done but I doubt it."

The waiter arrived with our salads and wine.

"So what's your next step?"

"Beats me."

"I have every confidence that you will solve Laura's murder. Listen, I was thinking that maybe in the very near future we could go someplace close for an overnight trip. I know your concerns and I respect them but that's why I am suggesting maybe a place no more than a few hours from here."

"I'll think about it but I can't promise anything. Did you have any place in mind?"

"No, I thought I would leave it up to you."

Our food came. "This is so good," as I inhaled my ravioli in about three minutes. "I guess I lack some social graces."

"That's one of the things I like about you."

"You say that now. It might not be so attractive when I'm old and gray and sauce is drooling from my mouth."

"I'll take my chances."

After a delicious lemon tart and coffee, we wound up at my place. Danny left around 2:00 in the morning.

I thought about the scene at the bar. It seemed like such an intimate gesture whispering in her ear. I wondered what he said and why I didn't ask him.

CHAPTER 38

The following morning I called Susie. "Hi, I hope I'm not disturbing you."

"What's going on?"

I explained what happened at the restaurant.

"Maybe you're making too much of it. You know every time you date someone for a while you come up with a reason to ditch them. Don't be too hasty. He could be one of the good guys."

"I hope you're right."

"Mark and I are going to brunch later. Do you want to come?"

"No. I think I'm going to spend a leisurely day at home. I'll talk to you soon."

On Monday I called Peter Mickelson and told him I had some questions about Laura that he might be able to help me with. We agreed to meet in Greenwich on his lunch hour.

Before I left I did a search under Peter's name and address. According to the report Peter owned a condo and did not appear to be married. Maybe there was an ex-wife. He leased a 2016 Black BMW. There were no civil suits or judgments against him. I then contacted someone to run a Connecticut criminal check. Unfortunately I might not get it back until after my meeting with him.

When I arrived, Peter was already seated at a booth.

"I was surprised you called but I was glad to hear from you. Any news?"

"Unfortunately not, but I have some promising leads." No need to tell him the truth.

"Well that's positive. Were you able to find out anything from the therapist?"

"Not really. As I mentioned there were confidentiality issues so he couldn't talk. There is something I wanted to run by you. When we initially spoke you told me that Laura wanted to end the relationship but you didn't. It appears that seems to be a pattern with her. She would meet someone, date them for a little while and then leave. By the way, how did you meet Laura?"

"I met her at a restaurant in Greenwich. I was sitting at the bar waiting for a buddy of mine to show up from work. Why do you ask?"

"Well I'm just trying to get a clearer picture of Laura. I was curious about why she confided in you. Do you have any idea?"

"I'm not sure. When she broke up with me it wasn't because of anything I did. I think she genuinely liked me but had a hard time being in a relationship. Maybe at the time there wasn't anyone else she felt she could talk to."

"That makes sense. Did you think you had a shot at getting back together with her?"

"I guess I was hoping but like I had told you she just needed someone to talk with."

"I know that's what you said but maybe being with her brought up old feelings you had for her. Weren't you pissed that she used you to unburden herself but didn't want to be with you?"

"What are you getting at? That I killed Laura?"

"I'm just trying to understand what was going on. I know I would be pretty mad if she was dumping her problems on me after breaking off the relationship for no good reason."

"First of all I'm not you, and secondly, I don't care what you think. I wouldn't hurt Laura. All I've done is tried to help you and this is the thanks I get."

"If I recall you told me you had not seen Laura since you broke up."

"And I told you that Laura asked me to keep our meetings private. It just so happens I was out of town for a week on business around the time Laura disappeared. I have to get back to work now." With that he got up and left.

What did I expect, a confession? I still didn't get the feeling that Peter killed Laura, though I know I should ignore my feelings and just follow the facts. The waitress came over. I ordered a tuna fish sandwich since I felt bad for taking up a booth.

My phone buzzed. "Tracey, it's Sam. Do you have any news?"

"I wish I did Sam. I'm looking into Ben Cutler. He definitely had a thing for Laura but she didn't appear to be interested in him."

"That might give him a motive. Plus he could easily have been watching Laura when she went up to the house."

"That's all true Sam but it's up to me and your lawyer to find something since the police aren't out there looking for anyone else. The good news is that Mr. Morgan can make a case against Cutler as an alternative person who committed the crime. The fact is at this point all they have is circumstantial evidence. Hopefully we will find the killer before this ever gets to trial."

"I'm banking on it."

If I was in Sam's position I would probably be under the covers. The waitress came with my sandwich and coffee. It's possible that Cutler gave me Laura's second phone to throw me off. Is there anything else I might have missed at the house or on the property?

On the way back I realized that I never did a search in the area where they found Laura. I wonder if Sam's lawyer conducted his own search.

After squeezing my car into a spot probably meant for a motorcycle, I stopped for a cappuccino before heading into my office. I peeked my head into Alan's office. "Hi Margaret, how's it going"

"Good, listen do you have a second?"

"What's up?" I said.

"I'm not sure if it's anything but I stopped by the office yesterday to pick up a file to work on at home, and I noticed your door wasn't completely closed. I peeked in but everything seemed to be fine so I didn't call you, otherwise I would have."

"Thanks for telling me."

That's weird. Why would the door be open unless the cleaning people might have accidentally left it open Friday night after they left. I checked my safe. My gun was still there. I searched my desk drawers but nothing seemed to be missing and my laptop goes home with me. I'll have to contact the cleaning service to make sure it's locked when they leave. Except for my gun, there's nothing worth taking. My phone buzzed. "Tracey Marks."

"Ms. Marks, it's Officer Nugent up in Massachusetts. How are you?"

"I'm okay. Did you find anything?"

"Unfortunately not, that's why I am calling you. He probably wore gloves and we weren't able to establish the weapon he used."

"Thanks for telling me."

"You take care now."

I placed a call to Sam's attorney. "Mr. Morgan, it's Tracey Marks."

"Hi Tracey, what's going on?"

"I was wondering if you searched the area where Laura's body was found?"

"I was going to have my investigator go over tomorrow. Are you interested in meeting him there?"

"That would be great but I thought I could meet him at Laura's place first since I'm not exactly sure where her body was found."

"Okay, why don't you meet Jack at 10:30. Is that too early?"

"No that's perfect."

"I'll text you his number in case of anything."

"Did you find out anything that could help Sam?"

"It's still early; we're working on it."

"The guy I told you about who looked after Laura's place found a second cell phone Laura had in the shed. I had someone pull the cell phone records for the last two months. I recognized all the numbers except for one that was from a burner phone. I was told there is no way to find out who it belongs to."

"You should have given me the numbers and I would have obtained the cell records for you."

"Thanks but it wasn't a problem. I was hoping some number would show up that I wasn't aware of but no such luck."

After hanging up I called Melanie. "Melanie, it's Tracey. How are you?"

"I'm so glad you called. Are there any developments in the case?"

"Not as yet. I wanted to ask you about the times you and Laura went out. Did she pick up guys at bars?"

"Well you make it sound like we would screw anybody. The fact is we would go to a restaurant and sit at the bar. If we met someone who we thought was nice we might give them our telephone number."

"Melanie, my apologies I didn't mean it the way it came out. Do you know if Laura would go home with someone she met at the bar that night?"

"When she was with me I never saw her leave with anyone but I can't say what she did when she was by herself."

"I was curious about Peter Mickelson. Do you know how long they dated before she broke it off?"

"I can't remember exactly but I believe it was longer than her usual trysts. Laura didn't trust men, maybe because of her father but that's pure speculation. So she wound up dumping them for no reason."

"Thank you, that's what I thought." I promise to call if anything major happens."

Melanie confirmed what I thought about Mickelson. Though she broke up with him she probably trusted him more than anyone else.

When I got home I changed into my running clothes. Instead of running in the park, just to be on the safe side, I went to the high school near me and ran three miles around their track. I was looking forward to meeting Jack and searching the area where Laura's body was found. I didn't think the actual place where Laura was killed had been determined.

I was on the road by 7:30 the next day. I picked up a coffee and a banana nut muffin for the ride. One of these days I'm going to have to vacuum the car floor since there are muffin crumbs everywhere.

I was at Laura's place by 10:00. I went inside the shed hoping to find something that would lead me to the killer. Instead I found tools, lawn chairs, seat cushions, rowing paddles, a couple of fishing poles and a tackle box. I opened the box to find nothing but fishing hooks and other related fishing paraphernalia.

"Hello." I heard from outside the shed. I closed the tackle box and stepped outside. Jack was a big guy, maybe 6'4" and built solid. He had a buzz cut with a small gold hoop earring in his right ear. His skin was the color of cocoa. He wore rimless glasses with lenses that change depending on the weather. He looked to be between thirty-five and forty. Though he was big he carried himself gracefully.

"Jack, it's nice to meet you."

"Likewise Tracey."

I knew we were assessing each other.

"I've been looking in the shed. That's where Ben Cutler, the guy who looked after the place for Laura, found another cell phone. I could use a hand."

"Okay let's have a go at it."

Since the shed was fairly small Jack and I maneuvered around trying not to bump into each other. To give us more room we took the lawn chairs and the boating equipment and put that stuff outside. We were almost finished looking through everything when I heard Jack say, "what have we got here!"

CHAPTER 39

"What is it?" I said excitedly.

He held up his hand which had a piece of paper in it. "It looks like a threatening note to Laura."

"What does it say?"

'I'm tired of playing your games. All these years you have teased and taunted me and I've just followed you around like a puppy dog. I warned you that I wasn't going to take no for an answer anymore. You'll be sorry.'

"This person didn't by any chance sign their name?" I asked. Jack looked at me as if to say, 'what do you think?'

"This could be Cutler but it could also be someone else. I know if I confront him, I'm sure he'll have some sort of explanation."

"Unfortunately we don't know when it was written. If it was done five or ten years ago, it might not help much, but if it was written recently it could make a difference. Even if he doesn't admit to it we can get a handwriting analysis done."

After I took a photo of the note, Jack slid it in his jacket.

"I'm glad Cutler wasn't thorough. He probably found the phone and didn't look any further. Let's finish up here and then drive over to where Laura's body was found," I said.

We took Jack's car. After spending more than an

hour thoroughly combing the area and widening the search we didn't come up with anything. It was disappointing but I was happy we found the note.

"Are you up for some lunch?" Jack asked me.

"I am always up for eating."

Jack took me to a local seafood place about five miles from Stockbridge. We settled at a table that overlooked the water. Unfortunately it was too cold to sit outside. The waitress handed us menus.

"So," I said to Jack, "how long have you been a private investigator?"

"About fifteen years. I started out working for several attorneys in the area doing criminal investigations and then Mr. Morgan asked me if I wanted to work for him full time."

"Does he have enough work to have a full time investigator?"

"He pays me well so I guess the answer is yes. We may have some downtime but not much."

"I kind of envy you. Most of my work is pretty routine but I really like working this case. It's like putting together a puzzle. I hate to admit this, but this is my first missing person case. I took it knowing I had no experience and could royally screw it up."

I explained to Jack what I had done so far, investigating Laura's death.

"Well from what David told me, you have done a really good job uncovering as much as you have."

To tell you the truth I had no idea how I was doing but Jack's words were music to my ears.

"So what can I get you folks?"

"Do you like steamers?" Jack asked me.

"I don't know. I've never had them before. I eat linguini and clams all the time so I'll give it a try."

"We'll have a bucket of steamers and I'll have a bowl of your Lobster Bisque."

"I'll also have a bowl of your Lobster Bisque. If the steamers don't agree with me, I'll order something else. Can I also have a glass of Sauvignon Blanc."

"I'll have the same and an order of cornbread."

A few minutes later the waitress brought our wine and our soup with oyster crackers.

"This soup is so good," I said. Jack laughed.

"How did you get into criminal work?" I asked him.

"The person I trained with did mostly criminal work. I found that I was pretty good at it so I decided to stick with it. Eventually I got my license and as I mentioned starting working for criminal attorneys."

"The PI that I trained with had a general type investigation firm. They did a lot of matrimonial cases surveilling spouses who might be cheating. We also handled disability cases where someone claimed they couldn't work. We tried to catch them walking without their crutches or whatever else they claimed. The truth is I hated surveillance. It was boring and you can sit for hours waiting for the subject to come out. I like doing background checks and finding people who moved or who are trying to avoid alimony. The firm did very little criminal work so I wasn't exposed to it."

"Well you seem to catch on pretty quickly."

"Do you think what we have so far will help Sam?"

"It will definitely help when the trial starts."

It was not the answer I was hoping for. In my mind, my plan was to prove he was innocent before there was a trial.

The waitress brought our steamers and cornbread.

"Now this may be a little messy. Watch me. First

we take it out of the shell. See this black covering over the tail, you pull it off, then you dip the clam in the saltwater and then in the melted butter. Once you get use to the taste of the clams you don't even need the butter. Now your turn."

I was very skeptical about the whole process. It seemed like a lot of work, but I forged ahead and did as I was instructed. On the way down it was a bit slimy, nothing like the clams I have with my pasta. By the fifth one, I was actually enjoying myself. I liked the ritual of taking the black rubber off the tail and dipping the clam into the water to clean it and then into the butter.

"Hey, at the rate you're eating these clams we're going to have to order another bucket," Jack said, smiling.

After finishing I ordered a piece of apple pie and coffee.

"While I'm here I would like to take a run at Cutler. Would you care to join me?" I asked as Jack watched me devour my pie in three bites.

"Sure, why not."

As I was taking money out of my wallet, Jack waved me off.

"My boss would fire me if I took your money. Besides it was worth the money watching you eat."

"I'm not sure how to take that remark but thank you for broadening my taste buds."

We left the restaurant and headed over to Ben's office.

"So how are we going to play this, good cop bad cop?" Jack asked, grinning.

"Does that really work? Ben knows me so maybe I should take the lead and we'll see what happens. He may clam up, no pun intended, if you question him."

"That works for me."

Ben's truck was outside his office. There didn't appear to be anyone else around.

I knocked on the door and we went in. Ben looked up with a surprised expression on his face.

"What are you doing here and who's your friend?"

"This is Jack Baldwin. He's a private investigator in the area."

"I'm busy. Why don't you make an appointment with my secretary on the way out?"

"That's very funny. I found something in Laura's shed that might be of interest to you." I held up the note for him to read. "Does it look familiar to you?"

His face gave him away and then he tried to recover.

"I've never seen that."

"Look Ben, I know you wrote the note, you know you wrote the note, so let's not play games."

"Prove it. Now get out."

On the way out I turned and said to Ben, "I will prove it."

"So what are your thoughts?" I asked Jack.

"I think you rattled him. Even if he's not the killer, it'll keep him up at night."

"Would you have done it any differently?"

"No. You would have scared me."

"So where do I go from here. I have one or two possible suspects but unless I can find some physical evidence or get a confession, it won't help Sam."

"It will at trial."

"You and Morgan are looking at it differently than I am. I want to solve Laura's murder before it goes to trial. I don't want Sam to have to go through that ordeal. I just don't know what else to do."

"Look why don't I go through all the reports that you sent David and see if I can come up with anything."

"That would be helpful."

"So are you on your way back to New York?"

For some reason I wasn't really anxious to leave. I liked working with Jack. The truth is I was totally turned on by him. I looked at him and he returned my gaze. What would be the harm? It's not like Danny and I were exclusive. It would be a one and done.

We went back to Jack's place and screwed our brains out for about two hours. It was after 7:00 and I needed to get on the road.

"You're welcome to stay here for the night."

"Though that offer is mighty tempting, I think I'll pass."

I stopped for coffee to keep me going for the ride back though I was really wired from the day and probably didn't need any more caffeine coursing through my body. I called Susie and told her about the note and confronting Ben.

"I think you probably shook Cutler up."

"That was the idea. But waiting to use the note at trial is not what I had in mind. I want it analyzed now. I'm going to call Jack in the morning and see if he can get a sample of Ben's handwriting. I need to figure out if he killed Laura and how I'm going to prove it."

"That's a tall order. Unfortunately the police aren't going to look at Ben when they already have Sam."

"I know. I'm just frustrated. By the way, I have to tell you something else. I slept with Jack."

"How did that happen?"

"It was the steamers."

"What are you talking about?"

I explained how we went to lunch after talking with Cutler and my newly found love of steamers. "They must have been an aphrodisiac. I looked at Jack and I wanted to jump his bones. Did I tell you how sexy he is?"

When Susie stopped laughing, she said, "I am speechless, but it's oysters that are an aphrodisiac, not steamers."

"Oops. Oh well."

"I hope you don't think you cheated on Danny. It's not like you're engaged to him."

"I know that. I really like Danny and I don't want to do anything that might screw it up."

"He's not going to know so don't worry about it. I have to ask, how was the sex?"

"Fantastic."

CHAPTER 40

The ride back was easy and there was no traffic. I was home by 9:30. I got into bed with a pint of pistachio ice cream and watched one of the episodes from the Netflix series, Grace and Frankie. I needed some light entertainment.

The next morning I was feeling guilty for having a half pint of ice cream for dinner. My mission to eat healthier was going down the tubes. I decided to rectify the problem by starting the day with a substantial breakfast of oatmeal topped with yogurt and blueberries. I put on the coffee, showered and sat down to eat.

Proving Cutler was the killer was going to be a real challenge. First the note has to be analyzed and to do that I needed his signature to compare it with. An idea came to me. I punched in the telephone number for John Cramer, the elderly gentleman I spoke to about his lawsuit against Cutler. He picked up right away.

"Mr. Cramer, it's Tracey Marks. I hope I'm not disturbing you?"

"No, I was just on my way out for my two mile walk. What can I do for you young lady?"

"I was wondering if you had any papers with Ben Cutler's signature on it?"

"After the lawsuit turned out to be a bust I threw everything out. I was so disgusted. Why do you ask?"

"Without going into any details, I found a note and thought maybe it was from Ben. If you do happen to find anything with his signature can you give me a call?"

"Sure. Good luck. I hope you find out who killed Laura."

Well that was disappointing. I picked up the phone and dialed Jack.

"Hi Tracey. I didn't think I would be hearing from you so soon. What's going on?"

"I need a huge favor. What's the possibility of getting a sample of Cutler's handwriting. I know it's a big ask, Jack but I can't wait till the trial. I think Ben killed Laura and I need to prove it." There was silence on the other end of the phone.

"Well if you are hell bent on pursuing this, I'll try and help you out."

"Do you think your boss will be mad?"

"As long as I don't do anything illegal, it's fine with him. Just don't ask any questions."

"Thank you, Jack. I owe you. How long before you can get it?"

"You know you're one pushy broad."

"I'll take that as a compliment."

After hanging up, I felt invigorated. I wasn't going to sit around while Sam got convicted for a murder I was pretty sure he didn't commit. I know I had my doubts about Sam since the beginning but I believe he didn't know about the baby, therefore there was no motive to kill Laura.

The next day Jack called. "Good news. I got something that can be used to compare the note with his handwriting. I have a handwriting expert that we hire for our cases. Why don't I have him do it?"

"How long will it take?"

"If he's not busy, it'll be just a day or two."

"Did you get a chance to look over everything I sent your boss?"

"I'll do it today and we'll talk about it when I get the results of the handwriting analysis."

"Thanks Jack."

I decided to wait before I told Sam about the note in case it wasn't Ben's handwriting.

"My phone beeped. "Tracey, it's Patty, how are you?"

"Good. Is everything okay?" thinking about the baby.

"Yes, I'm taking a personal day and I wanted to know if you would like to meet for lunch. My treat."

"Perfect timing. I'll explain later."

I spent the morning at home doing some administrative stuff that I've neglected since working on Sam's case.

I met Patty at Caffe Dei Fiori on Lexington Avenue between 70th and 71st Street at 1:00. The restaurant was really pretty inside and looked very expensive, a place I could not afford. It had wide wood floors, high back upholstered chairs and flowers on each table. They also have a garden area set up with tables and heat lamps if it gets chilly. We sat in their main dining area.

The hostess seated us. "Can I get you a glass of wine or a cocktail?"

"I would love to have a glass of wine but there is a baby in the oven so I'll have to decline, but my friend here will have something."

"Maybe I'll skip the wine.

"While you two ladies are deciding, I'll leave you menus and congratulations."

"Don't be silly, Alan drinks in front of me, though every drink is costing him more diaper duty."

"I'm trying to picture Alan changing a diaper. I can't even picture myself. I wonder if women are inherently born with a maternal instinct."

"Are you worried there is something wrong with you because you think the maternal gene passed you by? I never had any desire to have children and there are lots of women who choose not to."

"I guess you're right. How are you feeling?"

"Since I'm past the morning sickness, I'm feeling really good."

"Well ladies, have you decided?"

"Yes, I'll have the Insalata Caprese and the Risotto with Asparagus and Ricotta."

"And I'll have the same salad, the Branzino and a glass of Sauvignon Blanc," I said.

When the waitress left, Patty said, "There's something Alan and I want to ask you."

I waited for Patty to continue while holding my breath.

"We would like you to be our child's godmother."

"Why would you do that to an innocent child?"

Patty laughed. "I'm not asking you to raise the kid, I just want you to be a part of our child's life. If anything happens to me and Alan, my sister Jennifer and her husband will raise our child."

"Then of course, I will be honored to be the godmother."

"Good, now that's cleared up tell me about the

case."

In between the salad and my fish, I filled Patty in on what had transpired so far including finding the note, but excluding my roll in the hay with Jack.

"I have to say you have really done an amazing amount of groundwork in such a short period of time."

"Yet I am at my wit's end. Unless I can prove who did it I'm stuck."

"Tracey, what you see on TV is not how it is in real life. Yes, the police follow the leads but it doesn't take them an hour or a day or even weeks before they solve a murder, and in some cases, they may never find the killer. And they have advantages that you don't have, one, being able to obtain search warrants."

"I know. It's just frustrating."

"If you think it's this guy Cutler you should probably keep the pressure on him."

"That's good advice, thanks."

"Are you dating the guy you met at the shooting range?"

"Yes. His name is Danny. We've been going out for a couple of weeks."

"Can you elaborate please?"

"I really like him, but you know me."

"Without sounding too preachy, if Danny is the right guy, you'll know."

"I'm just afraid if he's the right guy, I might mess it up."

"You won't. I promise you."

By the time we both had dessert and coffee, it was almost 4:00. I went straight home. I was too full and too lazy to go for a run. As I picked up my Michael Connolly book, my phone beeped, "Jack, any news?"

"Hi Tracey. It turns out it's Cutler's handwriting on the note. And hello to you to."

"That's great; I was hoping it was his."

"Just because he wrote the note doesn't mean he killed her."

"I know but I plan to do my best to find out"

"I went through the reports. He certainly seemed fixated on her."

"I hear a 'but' coming. Look I know you can't get involved unless your boss says it's okay but I need to do something. I've been thinking about this and the only way is to put a lot of pressure on Cutler. I thought I would come up there for a day or two, talk to neighbors, maybe follow him, let him know I'm there."

"That could be dangerous, and from the few minutes I spent with the guy, he definitely has a temper."

"Well if you have any other suggestions, I'm all ears."

"I'll tell Morgan what you're up to and see what advice he has. Maybe I can talk him into letting me assist you."

"I'm going to check out some motels in your area. If you have any recommendations, text me."

My phone beeped. It was Sam. "I'm glad you called. I have some news. I found a note written to Laura threatening her, well actually Jack, Mr. Morgan's investigator found it. He was able to get a sample of Ben Cutler's handwriting and he had it analyzed, and we know that Ben wrote it."

"So that's good, right?"

"It is, but the DA's office isn't going to help us since they've already arrested you, and we don't know for sure he killed Laura. So what I'm going to do is come up there and try to put pressure on him. See what happens."

The next call was to Susie. "Good news. The handwriting is Ben's. I'm going up there to see what I can find out."

"Just don't do anything stupid."

"Well you would have to define stupid, but you know I'm by nature a coward so not to worry."

"Text me where you're staying."

As I was hanging up, Danny called. "You must have been reading my mind. I was just about to call you," I said.

"Oh yeah! I hope it was to tell me you miss me madly and are dying to see me."

"Something like that. Actually I need to go up to Stockbridge for a few days. I got a possible break in the case."

"Can you tell me what it is?"

"I'd rather wait to see if it pans out. The thing is I might not be back by Saturday for our date. Let's play it by ear, and if I have to stay, I'll make it up to you."

"I have an idea. We were talking about a possible sleepover. Why don't I come up late Sunday afternoon and I'll leave on Monday. I think it'll be fun, a little mini-vacation."

"Let me think about it and I'll call you on Sunday morning when I have a better idea of how things are going."

Danny sounded disappointed but right now work was my first priority and I didn't want any distractions.

I googled hotels in the Stockbridge area. I decided not to go back to the motel I had stayed at before. I was thinking of something along the lines of a small hotel that has a lobby where I might feel safer. I found a Courtyard Marriott in Lenox which is only a few miles from Stockbridge. I packed an overnight bag and went to bed early.

In the morning I stopped for coffee and a banana nut muffin for my ride up. I went straight to the hotel and checked in. My room was on the second floor. As far as rooms go, it looked pretty standard. I dropped off my overnight bag, used the bathroom and went downstairs to the lobby. I noticed there was a sitting area where they had coffee and breakfast foods. It seemed to be a popular place, people sitting with their laptops oblivious to their surroundings.

I called Jack from my car. "I'm all checked in. I thought I would try and talk with some neighbors first and then talk to Cutler's wife."

"I just want to caution you that if Cutler gets wind of what you're doing, he may complain to the police."

"From what I hear, Cutler and the police are not exactly on good terms."

"I'm going to be busy on a case till around 3:00, why don't we try to meet up then," Jack said.

I drove passed Cutler's house hoping he wouldn't be around. His pickup truck was nowhere in sight nor was his BMW.

CHAPTER 41

From the little I know about different styles of homes, his house looked like a cape cod. It had a wood frame with gray shingle siding and a moderately steep pitched roof. All the houses in the area looked pretty much the same. I parked my car down the street and knocked on my first door. A woman who was probably in her late 50's with silver blond hair in a very stylish short haircut, wearing a red sweater and khaki slacks answered.

"Hi, I'm sorry to bother you. My name is Tracey Marks and I'm investigating the death of a woman named Laura Tyler Matthews. I was wondering if I could speak with you for a few moments."

"Yes. Would you like to come in. I'm Veronica Bloom."

"Veronica led me into a small, but very neat living room with furniture that was at one time in style but was now outdated. We sat down on a brown and yellow plaid couch. Opposite the couch were two orange club chairs with velvet upholstery. A square glass table sat in between the couch and the chairs.

"Yes I heard about Laura's death. It's simply horrible and in our town. Can I get you some tea? I was just going to make myself a cup."

I didn't want to insult her so I agreed. It was a few minutes before she came back.

"Did you know Laura?"

"I'm so sorry I didn't ask whether you wanted any cookies with your tea."

"No I'm fine," wanting her to sit down so I could continue with my questions.

"What did you ask me?"

"Did you know Laura?"

"Of course! I used to babysit for her when she was a little girl. She was certainly a very precocious young lady, full of spirit."

"Do you know anyone who would want to harm her?"

"No. I can't imagine. Laura was such a wonderful person. I know she had her share of problems. There were rumors that her father was an alcoholic and then the accident, poor Laura."

"Did you have any contact with her recently?"

"No I can't say I have."

"I was told that Ben Cutler had a crush on Laura. Do you know if they ever dated?"

"Not that I'm aware of. Why are you asking about him?"

"At this point I'm just gathering information on anyone who was close to her. Ben was the caretaker at Laura's house."

"I'm sorry I don't know anything about Ben's involvement with Laura. I can tell you that he is known to have a temper."

"Have you ever seen Ben lose his temper?"

"Once when I was taking out the garbage, I saw Ben coming out of his house slamming the door really hard and kicking the tire on his truck muttering to himself."

"Was there anything else?"

"There were also rumors that Ben was physically

abusive to his first wife."

"Mrs. Bloom you don't strike me as someone who gets involved in her neighbor's affairs, but maybe you happened to have seen something that might have troubled you but didn't say anything to anyone."

"I once bumped into Mrs. Cutler, his present wife, and I noticed she had a black eye though she was trying to cover it up with makeup. When I asked her about it, she kind of shrugged and made light of it and said it was nothing. Why, do you think Ben had anything to do with Laura's death?"

"I don't know. As I mentioned, I'm talking to people who knew Laura."

I left Veronica my card. I thought I would knock on one or two more doors and then try my luck talking to his wife, though I don't know how welcome my presence would be.

The next few houses I went to there was either no one home or they weren't answering the door. On my fourth try, I was greeted by an elderly man who looked like Father Time. As I was in the middle of introducing myself, he slammed the door in my face. Well that was plain rude.

I thought I would try one more house and then call it quits for now. A small boy opened the door looking up at me and a woman's voice yelling from a distance 'Tommy, don't answer the door' with rushing footsteps. A young woman, not more than twenty-five wearing sweats, her red curly hair in a ponytail and her hands holding a little baby was staring at me.

"It looks like you have your hands full," I said.

"Just a typical day. What can I do for you?"

"I'm looking into the death of Laura Tyler Matthews. My name is Tracey Marks and I was wondering if I can ask you a few questions?"

"I didn't know her but I heard about what happened. How can I help you? As you can see, I don't have much time for anything else except these darlings."

"Actually I wanted to ask you about a neighbor of yours. This is a little awkward so I was wondering if I could come in for a second."

At that moment a tiny white poodle came running up to me. I stooped down to pat the dog.

"Okay but just for a moment. What did you say your name was?"

"Tracey Marks, and yours?"

"Jackie Henderson."

I was led into the kitchen that looked like a hurricane had just passed through.

"I'm going to put the baby in her crib; I'll be right back."

That must have been the baby's cue to start crying. As Jackie left the room, the little boy kept looking at me. This little kid was making me uncomfortable. "How old are you Tommy?" not knowing what else to say to him. He stuck three fingers in the air. Thankfully his mother came back into the kitchen.

"Sorry the place is such a mess. Tommy, would you please go into the living room and watch television. So what is this all about?" she asked, sitting down next to me.

"A neighbor of yours, Ben Cutler knew Laura, and I have been making inquiries into people who had any connection to her. Do you know Mr. Cutler?"

"Except for the time he made a pass at me, I don't know him at all."

"What do you mean made a pass?"

"I didn't think anything of it at the time. I mean look at me, though on that particular day I was kid free, so there was no food sticking to my hair and my clothes were relatively clean."

"What did he say?"

"He walked over to me and introduced himself. Though we've been neighbors for a while we never talked. He said I looked nice. Stupid me was actually flattered. I guess it had been a long time since I got a compliment from a man, including my own husband."

"Did he say or do anything else?"

"He asked if I'd like to go for a drink sometime. At that point I was feeling uncomfortable and told him I was in a hurry and got into my car."

"Did he bother you again?"

"No, that was it. We rarely cross paths."

"Have you ever spoken to his wife?"

"Not really. Just to say hello and wave."

"Do you know if she works?"

"I believe she's a decorator, but I don't know if she works for someone or has her own business."

"Well I won't take up any more of your time. Thank you."

I went back to my car, took out my laptop and typed up my two interviews while they were still fresh in my mind. My phone beeped.

"Tracey, it's Jack. I just finished. How's it going at your end?"

"Ready to eat lunch."

"I'll meet you in fifteen minutes at Once Upon A Table. Do you know the place?"

"Yes, I'm on my way." When I arrived, Jack was already seated at a table. We didn't kiss or hug.

"We kind of missed the lunch hour since it ends at

three, but they made an exception."

"You must have charmed the waitress."

"Well at least we know I have one attribute."

The waitress came over and we ordered right away. I had the New England Clam Chowder and the pan seared crab cakes and Jack had the same. I was tempted to also order the Mac and Cheese, but I didn't think my stomach would appreciate it. I ordered a glass of Chardonnay and Jack had a beer.

"I spoke with two neighbors. No one else was home, though one man slammed a door in my face. One neighbor told me that she babysat for Laura when Laura was about ten. She doesn't know Ben all that well but he is known to have a temper and once saw his wife with a black eye. The other neighbor I spoke with said Ben made a pass at her, but she never acted on it, and he never bothered her again."

"It sounds like you had a productive few hours. I think being a woman might have some advantages."

I just looked at him. "I was thinking tomorrow I would stake out Ben's place and hopefully get his wife alone. What do you think?"

"If she tells him, you might get to see his temper first hand."

"I believe it's worth the risk. I don't think he'll physically harm me."

"I think you're right, she needs to be interviewed, but I'll go with you."

"It's better if I go alone. She'll be more open to talking with me if you're not there."

Our food came and I didn't speak for the next ten minutes. "So can you tell me about the case you're working on," I said.

"It's a sexual assault case. Our client swears he's

being set up so I've been interviewing anyone who will talk to me who knows the alleged victim. Most of my work is interviewing people and digging into people's past."

"Are you going to dig into Ben's past?" I asked.

"Along with other people. Thanks to you, we have a head start."

As we were leaving the dinner crowd was coming in. It was after 5:00.

"Would you like to go for a drink somewhere," Jack asked me.

I didn't know what to do. The sexual attraction I had for Jack was electric. If I went for a drink, I know I would sleep with him again. I wasn't sure why I was having a hard time with this. Danny was someone I thought could be more than a casual relationship but that doesn't mean I can't enjoy myself with Jack. We skipped the drink and went back to his place. By 10:00 I was back in my hotel room.

In the morning I went downstairs and joined the breakfast crowd. Everyone had their nose in their computer. I made a beeline to the coffee. I got myself a yogurt and a corn muffin and sat down. I planned on spending today trying to interview Stephanie Cutler and possibly surveilling Ben since I wasn't sure what else to do.

It was 10:30 by the time I left the hotel. I parked down the block from the Cutlers. First I did a drive by and noticed that both cars were there. After about forty-five minutes without any movement, I decided to park my car on the other end of the block not wanting any attention drawn to my presence.

At 12:15 Ben's pickup truck left his driveway. I waited about twenty minutes before approaching the house. I had about thirty seconds to talk my way into Stephanie's good graces. I knocked on the door, my hand trembling slightly.

When the door opened I looked into the big blue eyes of the woman standing in front of me. Stephanie was very pretty even without makeup, with long blonde straight hair that came down past her shoulders. Her jeans and a white cotton pullover sweater looked great on her tall willowy figure.

"Can I help you?"

"My name is Tracey Marks and I'm looking into the death of Laura Tyler Matthews, and I am interviewing everyone who knew her. Is your husband home?" I was holding my breath hoping Ben never mentioned me to his wife.

CHAPTER 42

"I'm sorry you just missed him. He went into the office."

"Would you mind if I come in to speak with you for a minute. I just have a few questions."

I walked into a house that looked like it came straight out of a decorator's showcase. It was very modern. The living room was decorated in shades of brown with a long modular couch and a huge glass coffee table with lots of books placed strategically on the table and two upholstered straight back chairs opposite the couch. We both sat on the couch.

"You have a beautiful home," trying to make small talk, hoping to relax her. "Has Ben said anything to you about Laura?"

"I'm not sure I know what you mean. He takes care of Laura's house, but as far as I know, he didn't have contact with her."

"Has he ever talked to you about Laura's past?"

"Not that I recall though I do know about her parents dying in a car crash."

Now it was going to get a little dicey. "Did you know that Laura and Ben knew each other since they were teenagers?"

"I really don't know anything about their prior relationship," she said, fidgeting with her hands and averting my eyes.

"I was told that Ben had a crush on Laura."

"Like I said I have no idea what went on when my husband was a teenager, and what has that got to do with Laura's death?" She said, raising her voice.

"Probably nothing. I'm just trying to find out as much as I can about Laura."

"Well I think you are barking up the wrong tree. Whether he had a crush on her years ago has nothing to do with the present. I think you should leave now."

"I'm sorry if I have offended you, that was not my intention," I said as I was walking toward the door.

Well that didn't go well, but what did I expect, that she was going to turn on her husband. It appeared she had no clue that Ben had a twisted longing for Laura. I wondered how long it would take before she told him I was there.

I went back to the car and called Susie. "What are you up to?"

"Mark and I are going to the Museum of Modern Art soon. How is it going there?"

"Well let's just say I would rather be there with you and Mark than be here. I tried to interview Cutler's wife, but she was having none of it."

"What did you imagine? She would break down crying, confessing that her husband killed Laura."

"Well that would be nice. At least two of the neighbors had some helpful information about Ben."

"Did you see Jack?"

"Don't ask. I'll most likely be back Monday. Talk to you then."

My next call was to Jack. Before I had a chance to say anything, he asked, "how did the interview go?"

"Not so good." I explained to him what transpired.

"Don't be so hard on yourself. Unless she hated him there was no way you were going to get any dirt on him. What's the plan for the rest of the day?"

"Not sure. From what his wife said he should be at his office. I might go over there and see what he's up to for the rest of the day."

"Do you want some company?"

"I'll pick you up in ten minutes." I thought it would make the time go faster if Jack went along.

When I picked him up, we switched cars and left mine at his place. He had a non- descriptive car with tinted windows. My bug was an eyesore. When we arrived at Ben's office his car was parked in front of his building. We parked in an area where we could keep an eye on his pickup truck but where he couldn't see us. We sat and waited.

"So do you have a girlfriend Jack?"

"No, not at the moment. Are you going to interrogate me?" he said laughing.

"Very funny. I was just curious."

"I'm not a confirmed bachelor, but right now I'm not interested in getting married though that may change down the road."

"There, he's getting into his truck," I said. "Here we go."

We followed leaving plenty of space between the cars. It was much easier to follow on these roads than in the city, mostly because there are less lights and cars to can give you problems. His first stop was at a mini-market.

"Maybe his wife asked him to pick up some groceries," I said.

Fifteen minutes later Ben came out of the store carrying a shopping bag that looked pretty full. We followed thinking he was headed home but after about twenty minutes, he stopped at a garden apartment complex. He pulled into a spot and took out the bag of groceries and knocked on one of the doors. A brunette opened the door. He gave her a quick kiss and went inside.

"Well, well, that is interesting," Jack said. "So he has a girlfriend."

"Why do you think it's a girlfriend and not someone he's just screwing?"

"I don't think most men would bring groceries to someone they're having a roll in the hay with."

"You're probably right. So what does this mean as far as the case goes?"

"It doesn't mean anything. It could help us down the road since we could use this information to our benefit either against him, or possibly to get his wife to talk. Did you get a good photo of them as the door opened?"

"Yeah. Can we find out her name?"

"Give me one minute," Jack said.

Jack did a computer search with the address and apartment number. It was listed to a Rachel Parks, age thirty-two. No apparent husband.

"I think we should stay for a while, see if you're right about her being more than a roll in the hay," I said.

"I agree. We'll give it some time and then leave."

We waited two more hours and decided to call it a day. When we got back to his place I said to Jack, "I'll send over my notes from my interviews from yesterday and the photos I took today. Thanks for all your help." I didn't want to linger too long giving myself an opportunity to change my mind and stay. My brief fling with Jack was just that, brief.

It was after 4:00 when I got back to the hotel. I

took a nap before going out again. When I woke up it was after 6:00. I showered and went over to the restaurant where Leo worked and sat at the bar. Since it was still early for a Saturday night, the place was pretty empty.

"I need a drink badly," I said to Leo.

"What's your pleasure?"

"I think I'll have a cosmopolitan, and can I see a menu."

He raised his eyes, "rough day?"

"You can say."

Leo brought me my drink and I ordered a burger and sweet potato fries. I was proud of myself for having the sweet potato fries instead of regular fries, though I couldn't resist the burger.

"Are you going to be in Stockbridge tomorrow night?" Leo asked.

"I am, why?"

"There's a place called the Lion's Den where they have live music. Tomorrow night Lisa Martin is playing there. She's a Country/American Artist. They also have a pretty good menu."

My burger and fries came and I immediately started devouring my food. After I came up for air, I said to Leo, "Do you think you would recognize the guy that came in with Laura if you saw him again?"

"I can't say for sure, but it's possible. Would I have to be a witness at some point?"

"To tell you the truth, I have no idea. It's my first murder case, so your guess is as good as mine."

After I had a piece of Key Lime Pie and coffee, I said goodnight to Leo. I was looking forward to getting back to the room and watching some TV.

I pulled my car into the Marriott parking lot and

as I was walking to my door I felt a hand grab my shoulder. I quickly turned around, staring into the face of Ben Cutler.

CHAPTER 43

"What the hell," I said as I pushed his arm off my shoulder backing away from him.

"You think you can come into my home, interrogate my wife and try to get dirt on me. Who the hell do you think you are? If you come near me or my wife again, you'll regret it."

"Does that include your girlfriend?"

He was seething, trying to contain his temper. His hands balled into fists at his sides.

"You better watch your back while you're here because you won't see me coming." He turned and left.

My heart was thumping. I can't believe I said that to him. Maybe I did go too far when I mentioned the girlfriend. Too bad. Let him know I wasn't going to back down. Replaying the incident in my head, I realized he could have easily killed me in the parking lot. He was on me without me even realizing it. Maybe I wasn't cut out for this kind of work. I keep getting myself into situations that could get me in serious trouble or worse.

I took a hot shower and watched Saturday Night Live until I fell asleep.

Sunday morning I slept until 9:00. I haven't slept that late in ages and it felt great. Danny was coming around 3:00 so I had some time to myself. I went downstairs with my laptop and joined the breakfast crowd. I spotted an empty seat and staked claim to it by putting my sweater on the chair. As I was filling my plate with some fresh fruit, Sam called.

"Hi Sam. Is everything okay?"

He ignored my question and asked me if I had any news for him.

I told him what I found out about Cutler, hoping it would cheer him up a little. No such luck. At this point unless I found out for sure who killed Laura he wasn't going to be satisfied. Who could blame him?

I took my fruit to the table and went back to get a yogurt and a cranberry muffin. Once I got settled in, I sent Jack and Mr. Morgan copies of my interviews with the two neighbors and the photo I took yesterday of Ben and Rachel Parks along with photos of her apartment complex.

Next I called Jack and told him about my encounter with Ben. He told me to write it up and send it to him, plus he had a few choice words for me confronting Cutler about the girlfriend.

About an hour later I went back upstairs, dropped off my laptop and went into the town of Lenox in search of a clothing store to buy something a little sexier than my jeans and cotton turtleneck.

Lenox is a beautiful old New England town with a charming but small downtown area. I parked and leisurely walked around enjoying being by myself exploring such a lovely area. I found a place called Catwalk Boutique on Church Street, an upscale women's resale shop benefitting the Berkshire Humane Society. I found a silk button down blouse with a leopard design that I could wear with my black jeans. Two blocks away I found a lingerie store and bought new silk underwear. Afterward I stopped for a cappuccino at a cute coffee bar. By the time I finished it was after 2:00. I realized I didn't have much time before Danny arrived.

When I got back to my hotel room, I changed into my new Leopard blouse and silk underwear. Danny texted me he would be arriving in fifteen minutes. When I opened the door and saw him standing there, I was really happy to see him. The next hour or so, we got reacquainted with each other.

"So did you miss me?" Danny asked.

"Couldn't you tell?"

"Just checking. You've been spending so much time here; I'm a little jealous. I know it's what you have to do but hopefully you'll solve the case soon and I can get to see more of you."

"You know that I want to take things slow and that has nothing to do with the case."

"I do, but I keep expecting my charm, good looks and fabulous personality will win you over."

"Well it's working so far, just don't push it, mister. By the way I made a dinner reservation at a restaurant I passed in Lenox. Since we have some time I thought I could show you the area, the little I've seen of it."

"I'm in."

I drove Danny through some of the towns in the Stockbridge area. In Lenox we passed a place called Tanglewood where I was informed that the Boston Symphony Orchestra features performances by well renowned conductors and musicians. In Stockbridge we passed the Norman Rockwell Museum and the Stockbridge Botanical Gardens.

"Bash Bush Falls should be near here," Danny said.

"Oh, have you ever been there?"

"No, a friend of mine told me about it. It was such an unusual name, it stuck with me."

The Alta Restaurant and Wine Bar was very busy when we arrived for our 7:00 reservation, but we were able to be seated fairly quickly. A young man came over with our menus and an extensive wine list.

"This menu is great. I wish I could have one of everything," I said.

"Whoa there Nellie. I wouldn't want to be the one to carry you out of here. Why don't we see how you do after one entrée?"

"Are you willing to put any money on this?"

"Absolutely not. With your appetite, I would probably lose."

"Hello, my name is Greg and I'll be taking care of you this evening. Have you had a chance to look over our wine list?"

"Yes," Danny said. "We'll have two glasses of your Cabernet Sauvignon."

Greg looked like a college student. He was tall and slender with a thick crop of very dark brown hair with wire rimmed glasses.

"Isn't it nice that we have our own personal waiter. I'm impressed."

"You do impress easily."

"That's true. I thought after dinner we could go over to a place called The Lion's Den. They're having a female country singer I heard was really good. What do you think?"

"I'm game for anything."

When Greg came back with our drinks we ordered dinner. First we shared curried wild Maine mussels. We each had a salad with mixed greens, beets with toasted pumpkin seeds. My main course was a seared maple leaf duck breast with mash potatoes and broccoli and Danny had their pistachio crusted salmon.

"So how is the case going?"

"Not as well as I hoped for. Nobody has confessed yet. Maybe my expectations are too high. But on the bright side, I've been focusing on one person who is definitely connected to Laura and is not a nice guy."

"Well that sounds promising."

"Now I just have to prove that he killed her. That being the hard part. And what have you been up to?"

"I brought in two new clients so I've been pretty busy designing their computer systems."

"That's great. I was thinking that I really need to update my website. I never bother with it since most of my clients are from referrals. I basically have it because people think you're more legitimate if they see you have a website."

"There are many businesses that spend thousands of dollars each year so their company will pop up on the top of the list when someone googles the type of business they're looking for. I could take a look at yours and see if I would make any changes."

"That would be great. Right now my business would be at the bottom of the totem pole," I said.

"How is your client doing?"

"I guess as well as can be expected. Though when I last saw him he looked thinner and I thought he seemed depressed."

"I can't blame him. I would be a basket case if I were in jail, let alone facing a murder charge," Danny said.

"I think we should change the subject. I'm getting

depressed."

"Sorry about that. How is your Duck?"

"I love it. Everything is wonderful. Why don't we save dessert for later and have it at the Lion's Den?"

"That sounds like a good idea. I could use a break after such a great dinner."

We got to the Lion's Den around 9:15. We walked down five steps and opened a heavy red door. The room was very interesting. On the back of the wall above the bar was a mural with three lions, one with a red tip on its tail. The tin ceiling was painted a cream color. On the left hand corner of the room was a fireplace and a nook with red high cushioned backs. The stage area was situated on the right hand corner of the room with a piano. There were wooden tables and chairs throughout the room. We were able to snag a table not too far from the stage.

Lisa Martin was just coming on, a guitar strapped around her shoulder. She reminded me of a hippie from the sixties wearing a long flowing skirt and an embroidered peasant blouse, her curly light brown hair resting on her shoulders. Lisa had a beautiful voice. Her first song was by John Denver, Leaving on a Jet Plane. The waitress came over and I ordered a glass of their house red and Danny had a beer.

"This place is so cool," I said.

"It's probably what Greenwich Village was like back in the sixties, though there are still some places in the Village that have folk music. I actually have a Joan Baez album, believe it or not. I'll have to play it for you. Her voice is so pure."

"Wow, I didn't know you had such eclectic taste in music."

Our drinks came. From a distance I heard my

name. I turned around and it was Leo with a guy who I presumed was his boyfriend.

"You came. Tracey, this is Michael."

"Danny, meet Leo," I said.

With all the introductions made, I asked Leo and Michael if they wanted to squeeze in with us. The waitress came over and they both ordered beers. When Lisa's first set concluded we were able to talk.

Leo said to Danny, "You look familiar. Have you ever been here before?"

"No, I've never had the pleasure."

"I usually don't forget a face but then again I see so many faces."

"Leo is a bartender at Elizabeth's in Pittsfield."

For one quick moment I thought I saw a weird look cross Danny's face.

"Michael what do you do?" I asked.

"I just finished college where I studied Photography. Right now I'm working at a studio that photographs weddings and other events. It pays the bills but eventually Leo and I plan to live in New York City where I would like to work for a newspaper, hooking up with a journalist taking photos."

"That sounds exciting but I guess it could be dangerous if you're sent to a war zone," I said. "Danny's brother and his family are in the military stationed in Belgium."

"Was he ever in combat?" Michael asked Danny.

"No, he never was."

"So you're a private investigator, Tracey. That must be interesting."

"It is, but I think people have different perceptions of a private investigator from what they see on TV. They make it look more glamorous then it really is."

Lisa Martin came back on stage. For the next twenty minutes we listened to a variety of folk, rock country and blues songs which included songs that Lisa had written herself.

After the second set, I ordered dessert. It was hard to choose but I went with a brown sugar cake with vanilla ice cream, espresso beans and chocolate sauce. Danny skipped dessert.

"Danny, what business are you in?" Leo asked.

"I design computer systems."

I was gorging on my dessert with one ear on the conversation.

"Do you have to travel at all?"

"No, most of my clients are local or in the surrounding areas."

I was contemplating if anything was bothering Danny since he wasn't very talkative, which was unusual for him.

"Leo thanks for telling me about this place. It's great, not to mention the dessert," I said.

"You're welcome. So are you planning to come back soon?"

"Your guess is as good as mine. If I don't find the killer before my client goes on trial, I'll be here spending time with my client."

Danny signaled to me that he wanted to leave. I didn't really want to go but apparently something was up with him.

"Well guys I think we are going to say goodnight. It's been a long day and I'm ready to hit the sack."

On the drive back to the hotel, I said to Danny, "You were awfully quiet tonight. Is something wrong?"

"No, I guess I'm just tired."

We rode the rest of the way in silence.

When we got back to my hotel room Danny said, "I'm sorry I was such a drag before. I got a text from a client that his computer system crashed today and he wants me to come in first thing tomorrow morning to fix it. I texted him that I wouldn't be back until sometime in the afternoon."

"Why didn't you say anything back at the Lion's Den?"

"You were having such a good time I didn't want to ruin it but I guess I did anyway. I'm sorry."

"Look, if you need to get back first thing in the morning, I understand. If I was in your shoes I might do the same. Think about it, in the meantime why don't you see if there's any wine in the minibar while I slip into something more comfortable."

CHAPTER 44

I put on my new sexy thong and camisole.

"Wow you look hot," Danny said as he looked up. "Red or white?"

"White, thank you."

"Come here you," as he enveloped his arms around me and kissed me hard on the lips.

We pulled back the covers and with wine in hand, we got comfortable on the bed.

"Now I'm kind of glad you couldn't come back Saturday night," he said. Danny's phone started buzzing. "I'm sorry I have to answer it. It could be work related."

While Danny was talking on the phone he got up from the bed and grabbed a pen from his overnight bag jotting something down. He put the pen on the night table and continued talking. I glanced over and saw the pen was from the Lenox Inn. I was confused for a moment. I wondered why Danny would have a pen from a hotel around here when he told me he's never been to this area. I signaled to Danny that I was going into the bathroom.

A pen doesn't mean anything. Maybe someone gave it to him. But something didn't feel quite right and I wasn't sure what it was. I slid down on the bathroom floor trying to remain calm though I felt cold inside. I tried to recall the day I first met Danny. Was it just coincidence that he happened to be at the shooting range at the same time I was there. I remember loading my gun but I don't remember seeing him in the next stall. It wasn't until I started shooting at the target that I noticed he was trying to get my attention.

"Hey what's taking so long?" Danny asked, knocking on the door.

"I'll be right out." It was the look on Danny's face when Leo said he looked familiar that bothered me. I need to be sure one way or the other what's going on and I need to be careful. I took some deep breaths and opened the door.

"So where were we," Danny said as he pulled me down on the bed kissing me all over.

I feigned the right noises hoping my acting was good enough so he wouldn't notice my lack of enthusiasm. The voices in my head were frightening me.

When we finished, I said to Danny, "Do you mind if I turn on the TV? The noise lulls me to sleep, one of my many vices of living alone."

"Sure, I can sleep through anything. Do you want any more wine?"

"No I'm good." I turned on the TV and surfed through the channels. "Are you a Law and Order fan?" I said trying to stay calm.

"Yeah, I like the episodes with Lennie."

"Me too."

About a half hour later with the TV still going, Danny was sound asleep. I slowly tiptoed over to his side of the bed and took his cell phone from the night table and went quietly into the bathroom. My hands were shaking as I was looking through his texts. There were none from the client who allegedly wanted him to come back to New York. So he lied to me making up an excuse why he suddenly had to leave the Lion's Den. Did he want to leave in case Leo remembered where he knew Danny from? I wasn't sure what to do. Should I sneak out now or wait. Just because he lied wasn't proof that he had anything to do with Laura's death. I splashed some water on my face. My palms sweating as I opened the door.

CHAPTER 45

"Danny, Oh my god you scared me," as I jumped back.

"What the hell are you doing with my cell phone?"

No words came out of my mouth.

"Do you think I'm stupid? I know you saw the pen." Danny grabbed me and threw me down on the bed, pinning my arms in back of my head.

"If you scream, I will kill you right here."

"Okay, but please calm down," I said trying to diffuse the situation. My heart was beating in my throat and I was shaking all over. I was trying to focus, but my brain was shutting down.

"You know Tracey for someone who has no experience with murder cases, you were doing really well."

"I don't understand. Did you know Laura?"

"Yes Tracey, I knew Laura. She was a bitch but a great lay."

Danny's face was contorted with rage. It was hard to look at.

"You killed her, but why?"

"Because she didn't give a damn about me. In the beginning it was great, but then she changed. Laura thought I was being too possessive and didn't want to see me anymore. That was a big mistake on her part. Unfortunately, we had a fight at the restaurant in Lenox and it was just my luck that Leo must have been watching."

My mind was going a mile a minute. This man I have been with is crazy. I had to keep him talking since I didn't know what else to do. My head was spinning.

"You could have just walked away. You didn't have to kill her." I tried pulling away but Danny's grip was too tight

"She wouldn't listen to reason. I was just somebody to toy with and then on to the next. I couldn't let her get away with that."

"Why get involved with me?"

"Why not. I was curious so I followed Sam one day and guess where he went. After he left your office, I looked you up. I thought this could be fun so I started following you. Being pretty was an added bonus. When you went to the shooting range, that was my opportunity. Fortunately, my charm worked on you."

"You were right about that. You were really good." I was starting to sweat and feel nauseous. I had to try and get away. It was just a matter of time before he killed me. "Was there anything you told me that was true?" I needed to distract him for a moment.

"Well I do have a brother but he's not in the service and he doesn't live in Belgium."

"So you never went to Belgium? Oh my god. You're the one who tried to kill me at the motel."

"Don't be so dramatic, I wasn't trying to kill you, you just happened to get back to the motel too soon, and I needed to get out without being seen."

"And the threats, that was you also? Of course it was. You were manipulating me. I can't believe any of this." He's a psycho and I was just part of his little game, and now I am going to die here. I couldn't let that happen.

There was a loud commotion in the hallway. It must have spooked Danny since for one second his weight shifted. I twisted my body, his hands loosening their grip on me. I pushed him as hard as I could and he rolled off of me. I ran to the door screaming as he grabbed my arm so hard I heard a pop.

"You bitch, you think you're going to get away from me. I'm going to bash your head in just like I did to Laura."

I kicked him in the shin and I heard a loud howl. He grabbed me by the throat, his hands choking me. One hand useless, I tried desperately to reach the phone on the desk. I got hold of it and swung as hard as I could. He slumped to the floor, not moving.

There was loud knocking at the door. "Security, open up."

"Help," I screamed.

The next thing I knew two guys barged into the room.

"Ma'am, are you all right?"

"Is he dead?" I asked in a panic.

I heard someone calling for an ambulance.

"Is he dead?" I heard myself ask again.

"Please stay calm. An ambulance is on the way."

I couldn't stop shaking. I overheard one of the men say, 'she could be going into shock.'

The next thing I knew I was in an ambulance. "Is he dead?" I asked the ambulance person.

"Don't worry about that now."

"No one knows where I am. Please, I need to call someone."

"We'll be at the hospital in two minutes."

When we arrived at the hospital, I was wheeled

into a private area where someone I assumed was a doctor was leaning over me.

"Young lady, your shoulder has popped out. I have to put it back but it is going to hurt for a second."

"Holy shit!"

"It's done. I'm going to prescribe something if you need to take it for the pain. It's best if you ice and heat it for a day or two. Also I'm going to give you a shoulder harness to wear for a few days. How is your throat?"

"A little sore."

"That will gradually go away."

"Wait, did someone bring my bag in? I need to make a phone call."

"The nurse brought it in. It's right here. But first I need you to fill out some papers for the hospital. Also here is a prescription for the pain if you need it. Now you have my blessing to leave."

At that moment Detective Graham walked in. I wasn't happy to see him.

"Hello Ms. Marks. How are you feeling?"

"Okay. What happened to Danny? He admitted to me he killed Laura."

"Why don't you tell me what happened from the beginning?"

I explained everything that transpired. "What I don't understand is why he said he bashed Laura in the head when you said she was strangled." A strange look passed over his face.

"Oh, now I understand, you never released that information so only the killer would know she was bashed in the head."

Detective Graham ignored my remark.

"Are you going to arrest him?"

"I can only tell you that we're looking into him."

"Is Danny all right?"

"Yes. He has a slight concussion but nothing serious."

Detective Graham left. I picked up my cell phone, "Jack, I'm at the Berkshire Medical Center. Please come and get me."

CHAPTER 46

It was unseasonably warm on Thanksgiving Day. It's been a few days since my confrontation with Danny. Before spending the day at Cousin Alan's, I was meeting Susie for an early breakfast to update her on what has happened with the case since Danny attacked me.

"Hi," giving Susie a hug.

"Glad to see your arm is better. It must feel good to have the harness off."

"It does. I almost feel human again."

"Happy Thanksgiving ladies, what can I get you?" the waitress asked.

"Same to you. I'll have eggs, a toasted whole wheat bagel and coffee," I said.

"And I'll have the same, thank you."

"So what's going on with Danny and Sam?"

"Great news, Sam is being released tomorrow."

"Hallelujah. Did they charge Danny?"

"They did. Besides the bash on the head, which only the killer would have known about, they found strands of Laura's hair in the trunk of his car. They think after he killed her he drove to the inlet where he dumped her body. They still haven't found her pocketbook or laptop. They're probably somewhere at the bottom of the lake but they don't know for sure. He could have dumped them anywhere."

"I don't assume he has admitted killing her."

"No, he pled not guilty. Susie, how could I've been such a fool?"

"Don't be so hard on yourself. Danny was playing a part and he was good at it. Anyone would have been conned by him."

"I guess."

"Did they find out who the baby's father was?"

"It turns out it was Glen McIntyre, though he claimed Laura never told him. We'll never know."

"What was the story with Seth Green and Ben Cutler?"

"Seth was in love with Laura, but unfortunately for Seth, she didn't love him back. As for Ben, he threatened Laura because she rebuffed him. Regrettably, there's nothing illegal about his actions.

"And Laura?"

"Laura was just a lost soul who was desperately seeking approval, but could never get it from the two people she wanted it most from."

"I think we should have a celebration in honor of your first missing persons case. You did a hell of a job."

"Cheers," we both said as we clicked our coffee cups together.

SIX MONTHS LATER

"Carolyn, where is the file on the Power case? Isn't Mrs. Power coming in tomorrow morning?"

"Yes, bright and early. Here it is."

"Great. I'm going to need your assistance on this tomorrow. Mrs. Power thought her husband was having an affair, but then two days ago, he never came home. I'm having his cell phone records pulled. After we obtain the records, I'd like you to begin checking the numbers and finding out whom they belong to."

"Thanks Tracey. I'm really glad you're giving me more responsibility. I know I can handle the work."

"It's getting late. Why don't you head out."

"Okay. I'll see you in the morning. Have a nice evening."

I was fortunate to have Carolyn. Business was thriving. At first I was resistant to the idea of hiring someone since I wasn't too keen having another person underfoot all the time or having to supervise her, but lucky for me Carolyn is a take-charge person and needs very little supervision.

As I was getting ready to leave there was a knock at the door. I opened it and was greeted with a deep, hard kiss on the mouth.

I turned off the lights and locked the door behind me. Jack and I went outside, headed nowhere in particular. Maybe we'll stop for a New York pizza.

ACKNOWLEDGMENTS

To all my friends for their encouragement and support.

To my teachers at the Sarah Lawrence Writing Institute, Eileen Moskowitz-Palma and Ines Rodrigues – they made me a better writer.

To Jennie Rosenblum, my editor, who held my hand every step of the way.

To Barnes and Noble for allowing me the comfort of their leather chair to write my book

About the Author

Ellen Shapiro is a private investigator and the author of Looking for Laura, a Tracey Marks Mystery. Acting on her passion for writing, she enrolled in the Sarah Lawrence Writing Institute where she took courses in creative writing. Her professional expertise in locating people led her to create the storyline and develop  the characters for her novel. She has written articles related to her field for both local and nationwide newspapers. She is a member of Mystery Writers of America. When she is not writing or working, you can find her on the golf course yelling at her golf ball. Ellen resides in Scarsdale, New York.